To TRA

ENJOY.

Allan

Solstice Publishing ⬚⬚2010

# STONE

BY

ALLAN O'KEEFE

# CHAPTER ONE

Alec stood looking out to sea, clad only in his sun-faded shorts and Jesus sandals. The North Sea was like a glass pond; its blue-gray color went on until the sky and sea merged in a haze. His eyes flickered at the occasional white splash that broke the stillness.

He marveled as he remembered pictures on the television of mountainous, near-breaking waves over the oil rigs in the North Sea. *Is this the same sea*, he questioned himself.

In his 45 years, he'd seen this sea more than a few times from many vantage points down the east coast. It never failed to impress upon him the pent up power in its rolling grayness. It did not scare him exactly, although Alec would be the first to admit it was one sea he hadn't or wouldn't sail on. It was more a respect, like a man will cross a field containing a bull knowing what the bull is capable. *Would I cross a field containing a buffalo?* Alec shook his head at the silent question.

He turned and faced the sun, shielding his eyes with his hand in the classic *I see no ships only hardships* stance. The sun was low, and there would be a nip in the air in another half-hour. *Funny. No seagulls. Not one*, he thought to himself. With the amount of small splashes he'd seen out there, it must be a seabird's paradise.

He turned again with his back now to the sea and the seventy or eighty-foot almost perpendicular drop to the granite boulder strewn, miniature beach. His gazed softened as he looked at the two tents pitched some thirty yards away. The bright yellow of the larger and the deep blue of the smaller stood out in sharp contrast to the myriad shades of green surrounding them.

The short grass, a deep, rich green wouldn't have been out of place in front of a suburban semi. Alec had seen it before. The neatness of the grass was down to sheep. It's grazing sheep, but they hadn't seen a sheep, or anyone for that matter, in three days.

His eyes focused beyond the promontory on which the tents were pitched to an incredible backdrop of pine and fir trees. They varied in color from near greens to grays to distant blacks. It was breathtaking. It was silent. It was peaceful.

It was Alec's first real taste of Scotland. Up to now, Scotland had been viewed from the dirty windows of an actors' rehearsal room based over a seedy theatre in the center of Glasgow or on a few minutes' walkabout break from location filming in some back street ghetto. It was definitely not one's idea of an introduction to a wonderful country.

He looked again at the backdrop and silently thanked that perverse streak in him that made him come to Scotland. He could, just as easy but not cheaper, gone with a well-to-do actor friend who owned a pad in Marbella.

A movement from behind one of the tents caught his eye, bringing a gentle, expectant smile upon his face. The figure of a girl emerged from around the back of the tent. She'd been washing. Alec looked at the lithe, sun-bronzed figure, clad in minute khaki shorts and a T-shirt cut off just underneath her breasts.

Her back was towards him as she hung her washing up to dry. Her legs were parted, balancing on the uneven turf, as she shook each item before pegging it out on the line stretched between the two tents.

Alec stood silently watching. His eyes were playing over the wonderfully lithe figure, from the tiny feet up those delicately carved legs to the firm, muscled buttocks that threatened to escape from the surarounding denim. His eyes continued up to the naturally slim waist that spread out to a pair of shoulders. Her body cried out the discipline of a dancer. The whole was topped with a face; though not beautiful, it was exceedingly handsome and stamped with character.

The tight blonde hair bobbed again as she shook the last drops of water out of the tiniest pair of briefs Alec had ever seen or removed. Her unfettered breasts bounced in the tightness of her T-shirt, and Alec felt a familiar sensation beating in his shorts.

"My God, girl. I hope that I have the same effect on you. I just can't get enough of you," he murmured to himself.

# CHAPTER TWO

He met her at Granada Studios in a series he'd been doing. Alex, that was her name, had been cast to do the last two episodes. Alec saw her before, though she didn't know it.

Alec had gone to Birmingham TV Studios to see a producer about a play he wrote and hoped would get taken up. Killing two birds with one stone, he looked up some old friends.

Alex was working with Sir John Mills on a situation comedy. Alec spent half an hour or so watching her make a three-course meal out of an oxo cube without going over the top. She was good and could be brilliant given the opportunity.

In rehearsals at Granada, Alex kept to herself. She talked when spoken to but kept very much to herself. It was this cross between Garbo and little girl lost that reached across the green room and finally touched Alec. He moved in.

With 30 years experience of chatting up girls and women, he thought he couldn't fail. However, he failed miserably! His ego wasn't hurt though. His chatting up was an automatic reaction to seeing an untethered female. Somewhat like a Grand National winner, who passed the winning post, being shown another fence to jump. It shrugs its shoulders, clicks its fetlocks, and automatically jumps.

They became good friends. They shared lunch breaks, an occasional movie, talked, and even held hands (*God that was good*). He found out a lot about her over a glass of wine and some gentle probing. He found it quite amazing that once sex had been put on one side how open she became.

She came from Yorkshire and was married to some prick that used her for a meal ticket. Her husband was a man who would think nothing of beating the shit out of her, if he even so much thought she'd been talking to a man.

Alec had visions of a hulking miner type with one arm around this lovely girl and the other, complete with coal-stained fingernails and blue coal scars, wrapped around a pint of Newcastle Brown. *Wrong Again!*

The husband came into rehearsals on the last episode. Alec was right that he was a prick, albeit a weedy one. He was a good looking, well-dressed prick. Knowing what he was like, forewarned is forearmed, Alec kept well away from her during rehearsals. He talked to her only on set and in the dialogue of the play.

She came in the next day with her left cheekbone all puffed up and swollen. She laughed it off with the walked-into-a-door routine, but nobody was fooled. Alec was filled with murderous hate. He wondered why it came to that. Apart from the dialogue in the script, all he said to her was hello and goodbye.

He spoke to the director, an old friend, who told him that his feelings for Alex stuck out like a sore thumb. It hadn't harmed rehearsals or the characters that Alec and Alex were playing, so of course it was nothing to do with him. However, when one of his cast comes into rehearsals punchy then that affects them all.

The director banned the prick from the studios, telling him that he didn't believe Alex's story. If the prick didn't like it, Alex would be replaced with another actress. The prick didn't like it, but he realized he wouldn't be able to pick up the new suit he'd ordered if Alex wasn't working. Prick lumped it.

Alex was soon back to her old self, and Alec, still scheming how to get into those lovely briefs of hers, enjoyed a basically platonic friendship with her.

One evening they were walking through dismal Manchester holding hands. Their steps took them towards the railway station. Alec looked at her profile and noticed her face slightly sad. He realized with each stride, he also had been feeling down. Each stride brought the railway station nearer, and hence each stride was a stride nearer to their parting.

He suddenly felt elated; she felt the same. He stopped in mid stride, and she turned to look at him. He thought he was going to drown in those eyes. His hands gently lifted to cup her face, and he kissed her warm, moist lips.

He didn't enjoy leaving her at the station, but he pulled himself together with the thought that it was only for twelve hours.

During the course of the next few days, he found out that Alex had married the prick when she was quite young. He, being Jack the Lad, carried on whoring around.

In their second year of marriage, to mark their anniversary, he presented her with a wonderful present. It was small, but then again, good things come in small doses (dose being the operative word). From that day on, they slept in separate beds.

Alec gained an insight into Alex's thinking the more they talked. He found it intolerable that a woman should put up with beatings and distasteful visits to the hospital. Alex's family believed that once you married, however, you stayed married. Oh, she thought many times about leaving, but to go where? Where would she stay?

It wasn't as though she had the certainty

of a steady income. The only thing certain about the acting profession is the uncertainty. Alec agreed with her. Mind you, if she said she'd seen the Pope's arse, he would have believed her. Alex's fingers sought out and caressed the trigger points of his soul.

There was two weeks to go until the end of the series, and Alec knew he was making inroads on Alex's standoffishness to men. He was still more than anxious to make love to this lovely creature, but it was love, not lust. Like a homespun psychologist, he started sewing the seeds of the possible and dousing them with the waters of the probable.

One evening over coffee in Granada's canteen, he knew he made a break through. They'd been sitting there for maybe twenty minutes or so. Now and then, Alec raised his hand and nodded acknowledgement to a variety of actors and technicians who were miming greetings across the tables. He looked at Alex, and she winked at him. He just smiled back. One of the drawbacks to being in the business a long time is they know you and expect the worst.

Suddenly, Alex reached across the table and slipped her hand in his. She looked seriously into his face, and he felt himself slipping into those deep, hazel eyes.

"Alec, what would happen if I ...?"

She didn't finish the sentence, for Alec's finger came up and pressed against her warm, moist lips. Her eyes widened slightly, and Alec whispered, "You'd marry me."

They became inseparable. He even walked her to the loo, pacing up and down outside like a caged bear. He experienced this feeling before when he was about fourteen or fifteen. Like a rutting stag after his first sexual encounter, he kept close herd on his young female partner, knowing he'd got his and to hell with the rest.

Only this time was different. Sex didn't happen but not for his want of trying. He was still quite content with the deep bond that was growing. There was also the thrill of that exciting throb deep in his stomach, stretching way down to his groin at the prospect of bedding Alex. It was a feeling that was becoming more and more regular, being fed on Alex's innuendos, touches, and that peculiar inviting smile. She affected that smile when he or someone touched on the theme of love making.

It was the last week at the studios, and Alec realized time was getting short. He couldn't let Alex go back to Yorkshire, not even to tell prick it was all over. She was leaving him. He might turn nasty. *Might? You bloody fool, it's a racing certainty.*

They'd been given their dressing room

numbers. The PA gave them adjoining rooms, seeing how things were between them. *God bless her.* They signed for their respective keys at reception, and Albert, the commissionaire-cum-security man, laughed and joked with Alec. They reminisced over old times and remembered that Albert had started as commissionaire the very same week Alec got his first job at Granada.

They left Albert chuckling over memories past as they made their way down the stairs leading to the studios and the dressing rooms. Alec opened Alex's door for her and suggested she check her wardrobe before going into make up. He was gently being business-like, knowing the job they got paid for was just about to start.

Alex reached up and pecked him on the mouth, cutting him short. He realized he was mothering her, like an old hand mothering a young actor on his first job. He threw an apologetic smile and went to his dressing room.

He inspected his costume as it hung neatly pressed. *Yeah, everything is fine.* Granada's wardrobe department was excellent, unlike some companies who had a tendency to ask actors to bring in their own wardrobe.

He looked around the tiny room with its mirrored wall, sink, one easy chair, and one metal chair. God, the times without number he'd been in rooms like this one. He picked up his *Daily Telegraph* and folded it neatly to the outline of the crossword on the back page. He sat in the metal chair and put the paper on the dressing table.

He checked his watch. *Half an hour to makeup.* The thought of makeup made him look in the mirror. His hand reached up to flick the switch that turned on the mirror lights. The lights flickered and threw their white glare over his face.

An actor, by very nature, lives in a world of make believe and other people's dialogue, ideas and characters – all nurtured by his own imagination and ability. The perverse nature of the person who put six eighty-watt, neon lights in the makeup mirror put a stop to all the illusions.

Alec looked at himself. *Christ Almighty! It won't be pancake … more like Polyfilla!* His eyes took in the face confronting him. The hair he was just about hanging on to was cut short with no parting. The eyes, though evenly set, were small.

"How the bloody hell can you have small eyes?" he murmured. *All eyeballs are near enough the same size. It's obviously the flesh and skin surrounding them, encroaching that makes them look smaller.* He widened his eyes.

*Yep, it's the skin around sagging with age ... Another one down to Isaac and his Law of Gravity.*

He took in the long, fairly sharp nose and the reasonably square chin. *No, not you're all-American, voted most likely face, but it's still a reasonable face.* Nothing to write home about, as his father would say. Alec smiled to himself at the memory of his father, his image smiling back to compliment the fleeting memory.

Alec's mind wandered into Alex's dressing room where she was changing. A fertile imagination is a wonderful thing, but the reflected face in the mirror brought him back to reality as he saw the ripple of doubt pass over it. *You're forty-five for Christ's sake and nothing to look at. She's barely twenty-six and a Michelangelo.* He wondered if he'd been applying too much pressure. His mind went quickly over the last few weeks.

Yes, at the first encounter that was out and out sexual pressure which he quickly rebuffed. *No pressure after that ... no ... definitely no.* She liked him. She liked being with him, and it was more than mutual.

"You are into middle age, and you have been blessed, Alec. Don't spoil it. Don't blow it," he murmured to the mirror image.

There was a knock on the door. He turned

quickly. The door opened, and Leito, Granada's press officer, was standing there. She was a small, dark-haired lady who controlled all press releases. She was a very efficient lady, allied with a wonderful air of diplomacy which was put to constant use. Her job was not the easiest of jobs, as Alec had more than once pointed out. She dealt with a bunch of middle-aged children, hiding their excesses in girls, boys, booze, and not to mention chemicals.

She smiled at Alec and reminded him of a photo call for the press people. Alec warmly returned the smile and nodded assent. She was just about to leave when Alec, thinking quickly, suggested that Alex should be in the call.

Leito smiled. *Christ, she knows.* "Why not?" Leito said, "Will you tell her?" Without waiting for a reply, she left the dressing room.

Spell broken, Alec turned to the crossword and thoughtfully looked at the first clue. Thinking, his eyes rose to the mirror again, and he caught the reflection of his frock in the wardrobe. A familiar sensation took hold of his stomach as the adrenalin started to pump. *Nerves. Good*, he thought, *I'm starting to bubble.*

He reached across for his dog-eared script. He commenced to do what every actor does before a performance and will continue to do as long as actors work; he went through his lines.

# CHAPTER THREE

It was 1585 when Philip II of Spain, the head of one of the greatest Catholic nations, first thought about launching the *Great Armada*. The recipient of Spain's largesse was, of course, England. This singular bastard and shameless harlot, as the King of France, Henry III, was wont to call England's Queen.

Mind you, anyone who wasn't a Catholic in those days was wont to be a singular bastard. Religion being all-powerful and all-pervading was the very reason that Henry VIII cut through the Catholic Church with a sword stroke. Self-interest apart, it brought a conflict of interests in his advisors, commanders, and subjects. Unforgivable, whilst he was King. The answer was creating your own church with yourself as head.

The Catholic Church disappeared almost overnight, and all that lovely wealth from the Church and monasteries filled Henry's most welcome coffers. The Catholic countries around France, and especially Spain, were outraged but bit the bullet, biding their time.

Philip said the time had come. Henry VIII

had died and had been succeeded in turn by Edward VI and six years later by Mary, Elizabeth's half-sister. She quite ably mismanaged England for five, long years.

Catholicism crept back strongly into England and especially Scotland by the time Elizabeth came to the throne. She, like her father, had a subtlety that hurt more than the sword. She pushed out the Catholics and the scheming couple, Philip of Spain and Henry of France, both of whom wished to rule this sceptered isle.

Henry of France bestrode the country like a colossus with deep roots in Scotland, courtesy of Mary Queen of Scots. Her family ties and fervent Catholicism fuelled his ambitions.

Philip, meanwhile, obtained a secret brief declaring that Mary Queen of Scots' succession to the English throne had been willed to him in the event of her death. Philip was offered the key to the front door.

An armada of ships and troops of such magnitude the world had never before seen began to be assembled. It would take three long years of careful planning and building before it set sail.

Huge sums of money were obtained to add to the huge sums already spent. Just as much stress was laid on the good of religion, and the soon to be, subsequent conversion of England back to the true church. Even the Pope promised payment of one million ducats to the armada fund.

The subsequent religious conversion of England was placed in the odious hands of the chief inquisitor, who had been pressing Philip for a ship. Philip quickly realized the fear of a religious inquisition on the scale outlined would quickly bring England to its knees, so he agreed. The frightening, cowled figure duly set sail on the *San Domingo* alongside the ill-fated armada.

# CHAPTER FOUR

It was evening, and they were unwinding over a glass of wine at *The Stables*, the club behind Granada.

Alex had been very good in front of camera. Her part didn't call for much, but she played it with a simplicity that was sheer brilliance. Alec fervently hoped how good would be realized by the unseen viewing audience, especially the battery of casting directors and producer/directors scattered throughout the country.

By the end of the second glass, the nerves and the bubble had receded and a flash of inspiration hit Alec. He put his arm around Alex, pulled her gently towards him, and whispered in her ear, "Why don't you and I go camping in Scotland straight after we've finished the last episode?"

Alex turned her face towards him and said, "I'd like that."

Alec's mind was blown. He shot to the bar for more wine. At the bar, he suddenly realized the implications of what he said.

*Camping? Scotland? God, what the hell*

*made me say that? I've already arranged to go to Marbella?* Taking Alex there would have been no problem. His mind worked furiously as Joan, the bartender, went for his wine.

Christ, he was twelve years old the last time he put up a tent. Where the hell would he even get a tent?

Joan arrived with the wine. He paid and tipped her with a big smile.

*Hang about ... hang about. Tom's son goes camping. He's got all the gear and then some. A quick phone call, a few bob, and we're fixed up.*

He composed himself and turned away from the bar with a broad grin on his face. Alex laughed back at him.

"You look as though you've just solved all your problems," she said.

He bent down and kissed her lips. "I have darling. I have."

The last few days passed quickly. True to his thoughts, a quick phone call paid off handsome dividends. Tom's son had everything - the full Monty, as he put it.

Alec called his brother's pub to pick up the camping gear. He was amazed by the amount, luxury, and ingenuity that now made up the modern camper's equipment.

Young Paul leeringly showed him, with

dexterous fingers and the manner of a Sergeant Major, how to cope with what appeared to be the worst of the equipment. Then, with an ease that widened Alec's eyes, he packed everything up into two large but manageable rucksacks. With a few notes rustled into a sweaty palm, a last knowing, leering look, and Alec was driving back to Manchester.

*Thank Christ for randy nephews*, thought Alec, harking back to what young Paul had said,

"You can't whack a tent for a quick legover, Uncle Al."

Alex committed herself by bringing a few items of clothing and various other things with her each day. On the last morning, she was able to leave Yorkshire and the prick without a giveaway suitcase in her hand. She had just a small makeup case, which she always carried with her. Instead of containing makeup, it contained her lingerie. By the time the series party came, her rucksack was well prepared.

The last scene had been in the can some twenty minutes, when Alec started to remove his makeup in the dressing room mirror. Flowing through him was the wonderful feeling that always filled him at the end of a performance. It had been a long schlep, but he was well satisfied with his work. He'd find out at the party whether the director and the producer were satisfied.

He gave a final look around the dressing room, checked his pockets, and closed the door. He walked the two paces to Alex's door, knocked, and entered.

Alex was without her skirt. Her long, tapering legs disappeared into the tiniest of white, lacy briefs. She was hanging something up in the wardrobe. She was frozen in the exact pose Alec had created in his mind that first day in his dressing room a week or so ago.

Her face relaxed into a smile when she saw Alec. He apologized with a dazed look on his face. He started to leave, but Alex quickly stopped him, deftly sliding into a pair of jeans.

*Sacrilege*, Alec thought, *hiding those legs.*

She gave a quick shimmy of the buttocks, zipped up, and clapped her hands together. Putting one foot forward in the manner of an old music hall routine, she said, "Doh, doh," accompanied by the most beautiful smile he'd ever seen.

The party was held in the backroom of *The Stables* and was in full swing when they arrived. All in attendance: the technicians, sound, camera, casting, makeup girls, PA, the little call girl, the Man himself, producer, and of course, director. The actors from the six episodes had been invited, and the room was humming. Wine flowed, curly sandwiches and sausage rolls were downed as though they were caviar and oysters. Music was played by a young DJ. All indulgences were courtesy of Granada and a generous producer.

Janet, the PA, already the worse for wear, saw them and near shrieked across the room, "The two Alexes!"

Alec turned to Alex and said with a smile, "Now either I look gay, or you look butch, depending on which interpretation you put on Alec's and Alex."

Janet gathered them, one in each arm, and took them to the bar. They enjoyed themselves, talking and joking side by side. Only once during the evening did they separate, and that was when the producer took Alex on one side. Her eyes never seemed to leave Alec even though she was talking to the Man.

The party would carry on until the early hours, but Alec and Alex said their goodbyes after a respectable stay. Pecks on the cheek and keep in touches were ringing in their ears.

They went back to reception, where Albert was still on duty. Alec organized a taxi to take them to the railway station and asked Albert to look after his car in the car park, slipping him some notes and his car keys.

"No trouble, Alec," he said and thanked

him for the money. "Enjoy your break."

# CHAPTER FIVE

Rabbie Stewart argued his point until he was blue in the face. For three years now, and years were not on Rabbie's side, he sat at this table in the Sub Aqua Club's small office based above the Co-op in Gourock and talked total sense. It seemed sense was out of the question with this lot. They were adamant, pig-headed, or just plain Scottish!

The facts were on Rabbie's side right enough but for weekend searching. They figured his location was too far. Fair enough, that he could understand. He couldn't understand the holiday period of three weeks that they all took together. They took it together, so they could work as a team, and once more, they outvoted Rabbie's choice in order to search the bloody Lochs again! Rabbie had it up to his eyeballs with bloody monsters.

He snapped, and rose to his feet. "It's as plain as the whisky in yer glass mon," he yelled at them. "The bloody English routed them. They ran from Howard, Drake, and Hawkins hoping to reach Ireland and safety by going around Scotland. The English chased them as far north as the Forth and then pulled back. They knew the weather and the sea would take over and by hell it did. They dropped into our back garden like flies."

Rabbie paused in mid flow to look at the members faces. "It's like an underwater paper chase out there, but instead of paper, it's Spanish Galleons. Men O' War. They're littering the ocean bed from the Forth right around to Dublin Bay."

He cut short, looking at the blank faces around the table. There was none of the excitement he felt showing, not a gleam in the eyes. He felt nothing.

He gathered up his research that was scattered on the table in front of him. He paused to look at the silent group. "Yer know," he said quietly, "I might as well blow air through the hole in my arse as talk to you lot."

With that, he left the club and walked the hundred yards to *The Thistle*. Two hours and almost a full bottle of Glenmorangie later found Rabbie 100 percent determined to go it alone.

# CHAPTER SIX

The captain looked back and crossed himself in relief. It was Devil takes the hindmost, and his ship was next in line.

He had seen the smaller, English ships, brilliantly captained and sailed, one by one picking off the stragglers. He cursed and grudgingly admired their brilliant strategy.

They broadsided the straggler with their accurate cannon and then immediately left the stricken ship to their compatriots, as they raced on towards their next victim. They did it all without losing one knot of pace.

Now, the captain could see the English ships hove about. Why?

A few more dreadful minutes and he would have been in range of their heavier cannon. He crossed himself again and busied himself with keeping what was left of his vessel afloat.

That first skirmish with the English, for it was merely a skirmish for wind position, had been unbelievably damaging to his vessel. It left his ship badly limping. His ship and crew were decimated.

He looked over his shoulder at the remains of his helmsman. He was standing by the helmsman issuing orders, when he saw the flash then the puff of smoke issue from the tiny English ship. He smiled. *A range finder…much too far*, he thought to himself.

He was watching the smoke form a large ring when the whistling sound came at them and passed them with a *whoosh*. He turned to question his helmsman, a squat, sturdy, twenty-year sailor, but the words died in his throat. Still obeying the last command, his brawny arms pulled at the huge wheel, and his legs were splayed out to counteract the roll of the ship. The helmsman was headless.

The captain was rooted to the spot, staring at the obscene sight of blood pumping and spewing out from a gristly white and red stump that formerly carried the helmsman's head. For a full five seconds, the lifeblood flushed out. The earthly command to go to starboard ten degrees was completed in the Nether world.

The huge wheel came to a rest under the brawny arms. The legs collapsed, knees hitting the deck in unison with a thud that broke into the dazed mind of the captain. He reached forward to take the wheel from the death grip of the helmsman.

\*\*\*

Hours later, the captain was still trying to convince himself that he hadn't fled, that he just followed the other ships. He'd been outgunned at range and outmaneuvered. The most galling part was he hadn't fired one return shot.

Why couldn't he stop shaking? He gripped the wheel tightly to stop the trembling in his hands, but he couldn't stop it in his body and legs. He looked down the length of his once proud ship. It now was an open grave to soldiers in cuirasses and sailors. A mast sails cut away, laid full length. It's majestic, oak thickness was doing as much damage on deck as the English cannon.

The armada, after several hours of dog fighting off the Netherlands coast, flagged up the fleet *cut and run for home* signal. With an unknown number of ships lost, the captains were only too eager to oblige, even in spite of the fact that not one English ship had been lost, or even touched, by a cannonball.

Obviously, they couldn't return via the English Channel. It had to be the long way up and around Scotland, then down through the Irish Sea. Perhaps, he could provision and doctor what was left of his crew at Dublin.

It'd be a good three to four weeks at sea, if he

could keep afloat that long. He would have to follow his colleagues or the coastline, since his cabin which held his charts was nonexistent.

He reached out a shaking hand for the leather wine gourd and took a long pull. He could feel the thin, harsh, sailors issue hit his empty stomach and start coursing through his veins. It gave him strength to look at the cowled, brown-cloaked figure that was standing forward.

There was something unnatural in the way the figure stood there on deck as they left the warm shores of Spain. The figure was unmoved by the clamor of sailors and soldiers as they embarked. Even more unnatural now, the figure was surrounded by the carnage of battle but untouched.

He shivered as he looked at the still figure and then concentrated on keeping the overweight vessel on some semblance of a navigated course. The tattered sails flapped violently as the wind suddenly changed direction. From the northeast, an immense sea was coming in, and dark, heavy clouds spattered rain in his face.

He looked desperately to port for the coastline of Scotland, praying that he could turn and perhaps survive the rapidly descending squall. If he could gain the leeward side, there was a chance. If he gained broadside on, then nothing would survive.

The rain lashed his face with terrifying force. The ship shuddered and was thrust to port. At that moment, the captain had a split-second glimpse of coastline ending and sea beyond.

He heeled hard to port; the action sent debris, corpses, and even wounded men sliding overboard. It was a mistake.

The captain had made a few in his short career. Some mistakes were rectified, some weren't. He wouldn't rectify this one. It would be the last one he made.

Without a chart to guide him, the captain unwittingly turned his vessel towards the Moray Firth and had not circumnavigated Scotland as he thought. It was a simple error but fatal in that squall.

As if to acknowledge the mistake, the cowled, silent figure turned slowly to look upon the captain. Wind tugged and skirled around the robe. Spray lashed across the figure. The captain looked briefly as he wrestled with the wheel.

An unexplained anger overtook him as he searched the darkened interior of the cowl for the face that was obviously staring at him. "Damn you!" he screamed at the figure. The words went no further than his lips as the squall hit again with tremendous force. It would have been impossible for the cowled figure to have heard the words. The captain knew this, but his anger was suddenly replaced by a bowel-moving fear. The figure commenced to slowly raise its right arm towards the captain. The arm was fully extended, palm outwards, and fingers splayed. Caught mid breath, the captain gasped as the pain gripped his chest in what felt like a band of iron.

The hand moved upwards, and the Captain's feet left the deck. He rose and was stuck there under the awesome power of the extended arm. He was suspended some twelve feet above the deck, immobile in the powerful wind of the squall.

His eyes, unable to leave the dark cowl, flooded with tears of pain as his ribs creaked under the great pressure. The deck beneath him bucked and jerked in the violent storm. Whilst he hung immobile and unmoving in the cold, lashing wind, tons of water gushed onto the deck.

The wind was whipping at the robed figure and for a second, flicked away the darkening cowl. That second melted into an eternity for the captain as he was able to look upon the face.

The face was of undefined age, neither young nor old. It was deeply tanned from years in the sun, though conversely, the cowl always hid it.

A hawk nose set the contours of the cheekbones and above lie unblinking, deep, deep black eyes. Above the eyes and across the forehead lie what appeared to be a stone pendant.

The arm moved again as the cowl whipped back into position under the lashing spray, and the captain rose another two feet. Mockingly, a sound boomed forth from within the depths of the cowl, cutting through the roaring storm and above the creaking timbers of the dying ship. It was laughter.

The captain tried to cross himself, but his arms wouldn't move. He felt his bowel and bladder empty as he saw the arm flick contemptuously to one side.

Suspended and immobile in the rushing storm, the captain suddenly moved forward with what appeared to be the speed of light. He smashed against and impaled upon the immense broken end of the oak mast. He could scream at last.

# CHAPTER SEVEN

It was about four o'clock in the afternoon of
the next day that the two of them jumped down
from a friendly lorry drivers' cab. He dropped
them in what seemed to be the middle of
nowhere; however, it was a beautiful scenic
nowhere. He'd picked them up just outside
Inverness barely half an hour after they
detrained.

He was a talkative soul. He needed to be on
that lonely road, and he soon found the kind of
site for which they were looking. His
recommendation was quickly seized upon by
Alec. Alec bowed to his superior knowledge in
all things camping, and they set off walking.

"It's beautiful," Alex said to Alec, "but
where the hell are we?"

*Christ knows*, he thought. He didn't care
though as his eyes riveted on Alex's buttocks.

Since the lorry driver dropped them off, they
had been walking northwards for a couple of
hours. It was very warm. Alex disappeared
behind a bush. Alec thought it was for a pee,
until Alex emerged in the tightest pair of khaki
shorts Alec had ever seen. To make things
worse, she spent the last twenty minutes in front

of him. Alec just couldn't take his eyes off her. His mind was working on the various positions he'd soon have that lovely arse in.

He raised his eyes at Alex's voice and looked around him. "My God, she's right. It's the perfect spot," he murmured.

The grass was short and spongy. Behind them, a mass of fir trees paraded into the distance. In front, barely some fifty yards ahead, was the open sea.

Alex walked forward some ten yards. She spun out of her rucksack and collapsed star-shaped on her back heaving a sigh of relief. It was then Alec realized that she had carried that rucksack all the time without a murmur.

He slipped out of his straps and sank to the ground next to her. The blood pumping afresh through derestricted veins provided a delicious agony.

They lay there for ten minutes or more in silence, simply soaking up the atmosphere of this delightful spot. Then Alec rummaged through his rucksack and came up with two tin mugs and a bottle of wine.

The smell of the wine, pungent in the crisp, Scottish air, opened Alex's eyes. She smiled as she took the mug, "You think of everything. Cheers."

"It's to recharge my batteries," Alec said,

"I've got to get the damn tents up yet."

***

Alec stood back, hand on hips, surveying his handiwork. The two tents he erected were taut and well-positioned about five yards apart, but in line with each other.

*That has got to be some kind of bloody record*, he thought, as he mentally patted himself on the back. He looked at the smaller of the two tents and harkened back to what young Paul said when Alec queried taking two tents.

*If it doesn't work out, Uncle Al, she's always got somewhere to sleep, whilst you get out your Playboy magazines and play with yourself.* Paul ducked Alec's swinging arm with ease, grinning all over his youthful face.

Alex was unloading the tins of food and other supplies they brought, stacking them neatly. The fresh food, bought at a little village shop, had been put into insulated bags. Alec watched her for a few moments and then in a copy of Alex's musical hall routine, sang loudly, "Ta da." He spread arms wide and towards the tents.

She turned her head, saw the tents, and clapped her hands while laughing.

"Well Madam, which room would you

like?"

She looked at him mischievously, "Why Sir, the bridal room, of course."

His heart jumped into his throat. Looking at her, it slowly dawned on him that she had deliberately changed into those shorts and deliberately walked in front of him. *Why the little… so it's not going to be one way traffic after all*, he thought.

They sat back cross-legged around the fire that Alec coaxed into being. A gentle tiredness encompassed them as they looked in the flames. Alex competently whipped up a meal from various tins and cooked on the Calor gas double burner. Now, with cups of wine in their hands and the aromatic smell of coffee brewing in the air, it seemed they were relaxing in a way never before experienced.

Alec leaned back into the springy turf, eyes closed and head thrown back. He breathed deeply of the evening air. The light faded, and there was just the suggestion of a nip in the air.

He opened his eyes and looked across the flickering fire at Alex. She was watching him. He looked into her eyes for a full minute, totally at peace with the world. Then something gleamed deep within her eyes.

He smiled gently and held out his hand. They arose in silence as Alex took his hand, and they walked to the tents. His arms wrapped around her waist as the fire's flickering flames threw dancing shards of light on their backs.

Alex slipped out of her shorts with the simplicity born of women. The whiteness of her lacy briefs was highlighted by the campfire's flames. Dropping to her knees, she raised her arms above her head, and suddenly her proud breasts were revealed as she took off her T-shirt. She knelt there, knees parted and shoulders back, looking up at Alec's rapture-filled face.

He started to undress like a sixteen-year-old on a first date. He calmed his fingers down and in the same movement, removed his jeans and sandals. He dropped to his knees in front of Alex, and her slender fingers reached out to unbutton his sports shirt, allowing it to fall to the ground. Her fingers caressed his chest, and she leaned forward and kissed his nipple. She proceeded to play with it gently between her teeth.

He felt his penis rise and throb with lust. He bit into her neck, and his hands played down her back to rest on her thrusting buttocks. Alex gave a gentle moan.

Hooking his fingers into the delicate fabric of her briefs, he eased them down. Her hands slid to his French shorts and lowered them, releasing Alec's throbbing organ. He rocked forward and with a backward movement of his left hand, unhooked them over his feet.

Alex lay back on the quilted floor of the tent as Alec finished the wonderful act of removing her tiny briefs. He knelt between her parted knees and caught the rapid intake of breath as she caught sight of his oversized, throbbing extension. She moaned and closed her eyes.

The flames, through the open tent flaps, threw weird, but beautiful dancing shadows across their bodies. Alec looked down at her. His eyes ingested her jutting breasts and neat waist dropping down to a flat stomach. Her small mound of pubic hair started to part in excitement.

He lowered his head and kissed her breasts, nibbling them with his teeth. She moaned again in anticipation of what was to come. He moved lower and kissed the smooth skin of her stomach. His tongue played among the fine, peach like hairs covering it. He moved lower. The muscles of her stomach tensed, and her breathing almost stopped. His tongue worked its way through the fierce briar of pubic hair and gained an easy entrance.

"Oh ... my… God," Alex whispered, finally daring to breathe. Her stomach was panting in unison with Alec's flickering tongue.

Her head was rolling from side to side, and

her pelvis was reaching upwards to take in more of the moist tongue caressing her soul. Her back was arched as taut as a marksman's bow, when Alec heard a sound that started deep within her.

It seemed to start under his tongue and well up through her stomach and breast. The sound increased in volume until, under a final caress, it ripped from her throat in an orgiastic scream.

She collapsed back onto the quilt as Alec rose from between her legs. "Oh, Alec," she whispered and looked at his swollen organ.

Alec placed his hands under her knees and lifted them up. He placed the massive, swollen head of his penis between her hirsute lips, where seconds before his tongue was playing. He looked down on her face, while he thrust partway into the moist opening. Her eyes widened, and she stopped breathing again and moaned.

He slid out and thrust again a little deeper. She moaned again. He pulled out again and thrust deeper still.

"All of it, Alec. Oh my God … all of it," she whispered.

He took her legs and eased them onto his shoulders. Leaning forward, he gave a vicious thrust, and the enormous, swollen organ was completely buried in her. She stifled a scream and with arms outstretched for leverage, smashed herself in unison against his thrusting.

The sound started again, as before, somewhere deep inside her. It bubbled on a parallel course with Alec's and ripped from her lips to entwine his hoarse, triumphant shout.

Six years of celibacy burst in a maelstrom of thrutching, damp thighs, and an orgasm that put Halley's Comet to shame.

# CHAPTER EIGHT

Rabbie, true to his convictions, went at it alone. It was against all his diving principles, being a great believer in what the Americans call buddy diving. The sea was a fickle and oft times, a dangerous mistress. He took his holiday early out of a question of having to. Late April to early May wasn't the ideal time to be diving alone in the North Sea.

Through a diving club magazine, he'd managed to pick up a portable compressor for his air tanks. *Cheap at half the price*, he thought. *Damned if I go cap in hand to the club and borrow, even though my fees helped buy the equipment there. No bloody way!*

He set off, after packing his equipment in the back of his van. Destination, though not unknown, wasn't exactly pinpointed either. He'd know it when he was there. He'd feel it!

\*\*\*

He lay propped up in the back of his van with the duvet from his bed back home wrapped around him. Wet scuba gear and air cylinders were drying off at the lower end; whilst immediately around him lay his maps and daily diving notes in what appeared to be organized chaos.

Rabbie took a pull from the ubiquitous whisky bottle and laid back again with his arms behind his head, deep in thought. He was tired, and his thoughts didn't come easy. It had been another hard day. He went over everything that he saw that day: analyzing, criticizing, and collating.

He reached across and retrieved his daily dive notes from the mess. He looked through them carefully by the yellow light of the battery lantern, and a thought struck him.

He turned hurriedly to the words he'd scribbled down three days before. He stared at the scrawled words until the pages of his memory started to turn over and coincide with the written page.

Yes, he could see it clearly now. He'd been swimming at about fifty feet to give himself maximum airtime from his single tank. He had passed over the deep, sandy depression. The fine sand reflecting the light around made it unusually clear for vision.

The hollow lay a good eighty to ninety feet beneath him, making it a possible 150 feet. He cruised slowly over it. There was no debris visible, and as airtime was at a premium, he carried on.

So what was unusual? Why did his mind keep going back to that spot? He lay there wondering, and suddenly, Rabbie had a gut feeling. His brain picked something out, but his memory couldn't recall or place what it was.

He weighed up the chances of inspecting the site a little closer. He'd feel a lot happier if he had another diver with him, but he hadn't.

*150 feet ... Jesus, that's a lot ... especially alone. No stop-time would have to be about seven minutes. It must not be a second more to allow for decompression, and those figures are based on an assumption of 150 feet.*

He took another pull from the bottle and immediately regretted it. The last thing he needed was alcohol in his blood stream. As he weighed the pros and cons, a feeling of excitement and apprehension gripped him. He lay back waiting for the dawn.

\*\*\*

At first light, Rabbie loaded the boat he hired from the fishing village further down the coast. He checked all his equipment twice. He, yet again, checked his compass and the grid marks on his charts. He checked that he had enough fuel for the boat and the compressor. He suddenly stopped himself as he realized he was repeating what he had just done.

"Bloody old fool," he muttered to himself, "get on with it."

An hour later, after some searching, he was in the grid area where he first seen the depression. He secured the boat from drifting and threw over the longest decompression line he had. All was ready.

He looked back at the shore a good half mile away. Nothing stirred. All was still, apart from a little smoke rising from an odd, peat-fire chimney in the white-washed fishing village down the coast.

He strapped the tank on his back, checked his wrist depth gauge and watch, and then cleared his mask in the water. It was cold. He was glad he'd put on two sets of thermals under his wetsuit, which should offset the cold. There was also a bottle of whisky lying in the stern of the boat waiting for his return.

He was ready and once again felt the excitement and apprehension grip him. He looked at the whisky bottle. *No ... no way.* He had to drop to 150 feet.

He quickly dropped into the water and went down to about fifty feet. He leveled off, checked his gauge, and set his timer. He looked upwards at the bottom of his hired boat and noted his compass heading on his underwater pad. He set off on his search.

Rabbie was, if nothing else, a patient man. He knew it was a million to one chance of him finding anything on his first dive. Three dives later, he still had no feelings of déjà vu. He swam on.

Ahead of him was an outcrop of granite stretching up from the seabed some 100 feet. It was covered with waving fronds, crustaceans, and tiny fish weaving in and out of its small, dark openings. It lost all semblances to hard rock and looked, for the entire world, like a soft, moss covered hill. Rabbie smiled to himself at the simple, quiet beauty of the underwater world.

The similarity of underwater diving to flying never ceased to amaze him. Two totally different mediums yet bring the same sensations.

He'd been in a pub in Glasgow one night and heard this young man describing something. Rabbie pricked up his ears as he recognized a familiar pattern of phrases the lad was using.

"The quietness … air rushing passed the goggles. The looking down …" Two whiskies later, Rabbie found out the lad's hobby was gliding, not diving. Rabbie duly got himself invited for a flight on an exchange basis. You take me upstairs, and I'll take you downstairs. It was a total success for them both. Yes, both sports did have a great deal in common.

He could be gliding now as he looked down at the approaching pinnacle of the outcrop. *It would be a good hundred feet from tip to ... Ah, there it is - the sandy depression.*

He hovered over the center and looked around, bubbles from his mask flowing sporadically upwards. He trod water gently to conserve energy and air, his eyes narrowing to check every detail of this underwater hollow.

The depression was shaped like a soup bowl. One side of the smooth-faced granite hill reached down to the sandy ocean bed. At a depth of fifty feet, he swam above the circumference of the large, natural hollow.

A small vortex on the other side was naturally created by centuries of swirling currents coming in from the northeast and hitting the outcrop. In turn, it shaped the edge of the soup bowl, which protected and lowered the center. Rabbie saw the effect before on dives around oil rigs, sand dishing around the rigs' massive legs.

He looked for debris in the protected zone, but saw none. Puzzled, he looked again. There was nothing, but why did he have this gut feeling? "There's something not right," he muttered in his mask.

He swam to the outcrop and hovered some ten feet above it. To his left, the outcrop's misshapen green boulders fell away to the rock strewn ocean floor. To his right, the smooth, in comparison, face of the outcrop fell down to the basin.

Rabbie's eyes flicked from one side of the Col to the other. No, nothing was visible. He checked his watch. Christ, he'd almost overstayed his time. Looking at his compass, he set off for the boat at the surface.

Hours later, Rabbie was standing forward in his boat peeing over the side, his wet suit flapping from his waist. He'd broken surface to find the sun broke through quite strongly. Instead of continuing the dive, he took advantage of the sun.

He broke into the bread and cheese he'd brought with him. He laced his flask of coffee with a slug of whisky. The *putt, putt* of the tiny compressor was filling the air tank he'd taken off, even though his spare tank was full.

He lay back in the bobbing boat, relaxing under the warming rays of the sun. All was well in the world with his stomach full and the whisky-laced coffee easing through his veins.

"Shit!" The word ripped across the quiet

ocean. Rabbie sat bolt upright with eyes gleaming and face excited. It hit him like a thunderbolt. *Why should one side of a mountain be as rough as a bear's arse and the other as smooth as a stripper's pussy? It's not natural. It should be the other way around. The side facing the currents would be worn smoother.*

He leapt to the back of the boat, scattering equipment. He turned off the compressor, pulled in the securing line, and started up the boat's engine. He set off to position the boat closer to the depression.

"If I have to go down to 150 feet, every bloody yard will count," he muttered.

He hovered underwater just above the peak of the outcrop and looked. He nodded to himself and floated down to the basin side of the outcrop looking carefully. He took his knife out and chipped at the flat, mollusk-covered rock. After several blows, a large, thin, dinner plate size piece came away in his hand. Beneath it was a cavity.

Rabbie looked at the lace-like plate in his hand and then at the cavity. He looked at the large, sickle-shaped, lace wall that sloped down to the basin on the ocean floor. *Nature's camouflage*, he thought, b*ut camouflaging what?* He shone his diver's lamp into the cavity.

The beam splayed on the granite rocks of the

outcrop. He moved the beam slowly across. The yellow rays picked out a cylindrical object resting at an angle against the outcrop. It then disappeared into the shadows towards the ocean floor.

Excitement gripped Rabbie. "That's man made," he muttered to himself.

He paused, cutting through his triumph, his brain working overtime. He was down barely ten minutes, so that left him a good half an hour's air supply at this depth. He checked his gauge, and it read fifty-two feet. He'd have to go down further. Who could resist?

If he went down further, it would mean using more air and therefore, less time. If he went the whole hog to the bottom, there was even less time still. He'd have six maybe seven minutes maximum no stop-time, especially with no decompression chamber handy.

He made his mind up quickly. He chipped away a large section of the coral covering to enable him to slip through and down. He moved effortlessly to the cylindrical object he'd seen. *My God, it's a ship's mast.* The mast was decaying and covered with silt and mollusk but still recognizable. Rabbie followed it down, pulling himself hand over hand, to the tangled mess that had once been the disciplined deck of a proud ship.

"I was right. I was right," he kept saying to himself.

He turned to let his feet touch the deck, and he paused to look above him. A veritable cathedral of lacy coral hung over him and the remains of the ship like a web. Light from his torch and the sands outside reflected ethereally from the white lace, giving it a churchlike atmosphere. Rabbie never saw anything quite so beautiful.

The ship came to rest on its port side. The mast abutting the granite escarpment prevented it from rolling over fully. The current rushed around the escarpment and by some freak of nature, tightened and filled what was left of the torn sails. This action gave the impression that the dead ship was still in full flight.

The sails quickly became the home and resting place for millions of tiny sea creatures. Their calcifying bodies formed a fragile framework that became increasingly thicker and stronger through the centuries, long, long after the canvas had rotted away.

Rabbie shrugged off the sense of awe. He just didn't have the time for sightseeing. He turned, and a gruesome sight met his eyes.

Immediately in front of him, the skeleton of a sailor appeared to be riding a thick, broken spar.

The skull and upper body were lying

alongside the spar. The corpse's mouth was wide open in a hideous grin. Its arms hung down, gently flailing in the currents. Remnants of cloth hung around the body. Tatters of a once fine uniform clung here and there to the body.

The apparition startled Rabbie so much that he dropped his torch, but he continued staring at the skeleton and its position. "Christ Almighty," he breathed, ignoring the loss of his torch for the moment. "That must've hurt."

He moved forward, for under the skeleton and lying amongst the algae-strewn deck timbers, he could see the remains of what was once a leather pouch. Scattered nearby were several stonelike discs.

Rabbie's heart jumped, "Silver, by Christ, silver coins. The leather pouch must have been a purse." He collected them without inspecting, but he knew they were silver. He'd seen the chemical reaction of sea on silver before.

He carefully placed them in his booty bag hanging from his belt. Tiny particles, disturbed by his hand, floated and hung like dust in the rays of the sun. He checked his watch, and he had three minutes no stay left. He turned to look for his torch, easily noticing the beam spraying its yellow light around.

He reached it quickly, only to find another corpse at the end of its beam. This skeleton was shrouded. The skull was hidden in what was left of a hooded cassock. The skeleton was lying on its back with the white bones of its legs protruding from leather knee jerkins. Sandals were still thronged on the fleshless bones of its feet.

From around the neck, a leather thong attached to a dark pendant rested on the deck timbers. The right hand of the skeleton was clutched tight around the thong, as though in an attempt to pick it up.

In its aged and tattered clothing, the body moved and stirred gently in Rabbie's backwash. The bare bones lifted horizontally off the listing deck held only by the weight of the dark pendant. Rabbie stared at the scene for a few moments and then moved in.

The finger bones were tight around the thong. *Panic tight*, Rabbie thought, *Mind you, I'd have panicked too, if I'd been on this ship.*

The body picked up Rabbie's backwash again and started its obscene flailing. The thong was almost free from the bony grasp. "Come on … for Christ's sake," Rabbie muttered and took a quick look at his watch. He had one minute.

He freed the last of the fingers when he felt the arm circle his shoulders. "Jesus!" He turned his head; the left arm of the skeleton had come around and held him in a grisly embrace.

Rabbie's eyes locked on the cowl. He watched it slip back to reveal the skull, which rolled as though to look at him. He stared into the sightless sockets, his blood turning to ice water. If that wasn't enough, the skull's clenched teeth parted in a horrifying grin.

*Jesus. Jesus. Jesus.* For the first time in his life, Rabbie panicked. He used his arm to propel him backwards out of that deadly embrace. His feet and legs were jackknifing against the deck in an almighty push for the surface.

He shot through the gap he'd made in the coral. The sharp coral sliced through his wetsuit, thermals, and latissimus dorsi muscle as though they were tissue paper. Rabbie never felt a thing.

It wasn't until he reached fifty feet that discipline overtook the panic. He made for the weighted line hanging from the boat and hung onto it. He felt comforted by it and the nearness of the boat. God, he felt weak. He shivered violently and looked up to see the sun shining on the surface. The warm sun, God, it was inviting.

He wrapped the line around his wrist and gritted his teeth. Neither looking up nor down, he hung there decompressing until his tank almost ran dry. Too weak to swim, he hauled himself up to the surface via the line. With great effort, he pulled himself into the boat and immediately passed out.

It was some fours hours later that a fishing smack from the village passed close enough to realize that something was wrong. The fishing boat captain looked down at the squat, red-haired man from Gourock, lying prone and helpless at the bottom of the boat he'd helped him hire. This was the very same man he'd had a dram or two with and who had filled the smoky bar with his laughter.

Well, he wouldn't be laughing for some time to come; he lost a lot of blood. When they finally got his wetsuit off, his hair was as white as snow.

# CHAPTER NINE

Rabbie's extremely rapid exit from the 400-year-old, underwater time capsule created a backwash. It was the likes of which it hadn't experienced in all its centuries at the bottom of the ocean.

For a full ten seconds, after Rabbie's pumping flippers had disappeared, stillness reigned. The water rushing in to replace Rabbie's body space started the movement. Slow, at first, but building up to reach almost violent proportions as Newton's Third Law of Motion took hold.

The skeleton on the mast jerked and flailed as though urging on his wooden steed in some frantic ride to Hell. Pieces of timber and rigging, rotten and sea-sodden, parted and fell around in a slow-motion ballet. The once hooded skeleton floated above the dark pendant. It was held by the thong around what was once its neck, now just a whitened, knobby spinal column. In some weird, dance macabre, the two rocked backwards and forwards. Their bony arms and legs moved to a soundless tune the Devil whistled.

The pendant moved a millimeter along the deck planking. Its owner was pulling it as he reached the limits of the leather thong in his hideous floating dance. Each movement of the pendant brought it closer to the edge of the angled deck. The peak of turbulence passed and movement all around was subsiding. Still, the pendant moved with each gentle pull of its dead master.

It was a full ten minutes before everything was finally as still as Rabbie had discovered it. The only differences being a little more debris and the hooded corpse moved. It moved by the pull of the pendant that was now balancing delicately on the edge of the deck above a drop of some twenty feet down to the sandy basin.

# CHAPTER TEN

They had five days of sheer bliss. The weather was superb, the location incredibly beautiful, and it cocooned them in its peacefulness. Across the length and breadth of the small plateau on which they were encamped, they could hear their voices, never raised above a loud whisper.

After that first awe-inspiring evening together, they just couldn't leave each other alone. They had that lovely way young or old lovers have of reaching out their fingers to touch their partner, but somehow the touch lingers and gently becomes a caress.

By the second day, they were virtually Adam and Eve in their Eden. They disdained to wear shorts. Their skin started to bronze, and the whiteness of their buttocks started to fade. They abandoned, along with their clothes, all rational, bourgeois attempts at confining their lovemaking to the interior of the tent. For Alec, it was impossible. He just couldn't take his eyes or his hands off Alex.

He would look at her whilst she was doing the simplest of chores. She'd strike some everyday pose, and then she would turn and look at him. Her look would drop to his groin and his quite obvious growing excitement. Her eyes would flicker, and she'd laugh out loud. In a split second, she would mount him.

Their orgasms were crescendos. Sometimes, to Alec, they were frightening in their intensity. He wondered if he could last the pace at almost 46 years old. It seemed his mind had doubts, but his body certainly didn't. *What the hell*, he thought, *at my age, grab it while you can.*

It was after one particularly heart-stopping, earthy, lovemaking session he heard Alex call to him. He was on his back with his eyes closed. The grass was cool on his back. He was trying to make his heart come down to a more normal seventy-two beats.

He opened his eyes and rolled over looking for Alex. He could see her waving by the stream she had found on the first morning. It was where she would go to bathe after making love. He rose, and his heart rate shot up again.

*This girl's going to fuck me to death*, he thought and then smiled. *What a way to go, Al.* He loved it.

He looked down at his body and was reasonably pleased at what he saw. He definitely had no surplus fat, not the body beautiful either. He was not in too bad of shape for a middle-aged actor known for his wild excesses.

She called again, and he tried not to stagger as he took a few steps forward. Strength, returning to his legs, took over from the momentum of the first few strides. He was with Alex in less than a minute.

She was standing in the small stream, ankle deep in the crystal clear water. Although the water was icy cold, she splashed herself all over. Watermarks were drying on her pouting breasts under the hot sun. Her nipples were once pink little moles, but now turned a deep brown to almost black with the sun. They had diamondlike drops of water hanging from them. A random line from Shakespeare shot through Alec's memory banks ... *like a jewel in an Ethiop's ear.*

He marveled at the sight. Water chased lines across her flat stomach and somehow her navel retained its full capacity of water, defying gravity and refusing to be ousted from its gentle prison.

Alec lowered his eyes to the thick hair that grew at the top of Alex's parted legs. His face was immobile, but his mind turned somersaults. The thick, dark hair was strewn with a million, crystal clear droplets of spring water that caught the sun reflected from the stream like a jeweled garland.

*Michelangelo couldn't do justice to that*, he thought, *she is sheer beauty.*

Alex broke the spell by putting one hand on her hip, tilting her head to one side, and saying, "Well?"

Alec laughed and entered the stream. God, it was cold! She took his hand and like a knowing child with a secret she wants to share, led him splashing down the stream towards the sea. As they neared the cliff's edge, she turned to him and made him stand whilst she went a few yards further on. Then, standing on a large, flat granite slab from whence she could see both Alec and her secret, she beckoned him on.

Alec felt more and more like the father whose daughter has found a bird's nest complete with little feathered chicks. He smiled at her. He liked her joy for life. It touched forgotten, dusty corners in Alec's life.

He stood facing her on the rock with a smile upon his face. She reached up and kissed his mouth lightly, and then she turned his head with her hand whilst pointing down with the other.

Alec looked as his arm slipped around her warm-skinned waist. She had found where the stream finished. It dropped, in a miniature Niagara to the boulder-strewn beach below.

She laughed like a little girl and looked at him. "Isn't it pretty, Alec?" she said to him.

He agreed; it was indeed. She leaned over the edge, looking down.

"Not only pretty Alec, but practical. I think we've found a shower."

Ten minutes later proved her right. They climbed down with reasonable ease to a point halfway down the drop. The waterfall hitting an outstanding ledge had, through the centuries, formed an oversized shower tray. The granite underfoot was smooth as velvet.

In a trice, Alex was under the falling water, gasping as the cold water hit her sun-warmed body. Alec joined her. The shock of the cool water forced him to reach out and hold Alex's body close to him. Her arms wrapped around him, and under the rush of water, he could feel the heat of her breasts pressed against his chest.

She looked up at him, blinking as water slipped through her partially closed eyelids and into her eyes. He bent his head forward and kissed her lips. Her mouth opened and her tongue darted over his.

Underneath his hands, he felt her buttocks tighten, and an all too familiar sensation started throbbing between his legs. Alex could feel the penis rising against her thigh, and her hand slid down to hold it. She marveled at its size as it grew in her hand. She slipped to her knees, and water cascaded down her back, splayed out in a million directions. She caressed Alec's penis with her tongue. His moans were lost in the sounds of rushing water. She opened her mouth to take in the head, but the throbbing, swollen size was against her.

She turned on her hands and knees, lowering her head, so it was resting on her folded arms. She deeply arched her back so it thrust her buttocks high in the air, enabling her to take every millimeter of Alec's swollen member.

 Alec dropped to his knees in front of that most wonderful sight. He paused to watch water rivulets playing between her buttocks. He took his penis and placed the enormous head against the entrance of her warm cavity.

He looked at her. Her eyes were closed, but even under the rush of water, he could hear her expectant moans. He reached forward and with his fingers, spread the thick hair and lips of her moist, warm canyon. He gently inserted the swollen head of his penis. Alex's mouth opened, and her tongue flickered over her white teeth. She gave a long expectant "Ahhhhhh."

He thrust in further, and half of his organ disappeared. Alex stopped breathing. He thrust again to bury his swollen length deep inside her. Her eyelids parted slightly and seemed to roll over showing only the white. Her moaning increased in intensity with each thrust of Alec's penis.

He could feel his orgasm start as he could hers. He withdrew his penis to the very tip and slammed it in, giving her the full, love-moistened length. She screamed in ecstasy as she felt his love shoot into her.

*** 

"Dinners ready," came the shout. It startled him back to reality. He must have been daydreaming for twenty minutes or more.

*Who the hell wants to think about dusty rehearsal rooms and absent husbands on a day like today?* he thought.

Alex finished her washing and readied a meal. The tangy smell of smoked bacon thickly hung in the air. It amazed him that he hadn't picked up on the mouth-watering odor before now.

Alex sat on her haunches making the khaki shorts tight against her. She beamed as he approached. "Light the fire darling," she said to him.

He smiled to himself. They were like an old married couple. They instinctively took up the menial jobs that generally sorted male from female. She cooked the meal on the gas rings, and then they ate and relaxed by the fire he set.

The flames were bursting through the twigs and pinecones he had laid that morning. The fire filled the air with a wild scent, when Alex approached him with plates in hand. They plates were laden with steaming hot bacon and tinned beans.

Alec was ravenous; his appetite, almost nonexistent before the holiday, was now voracious. They ate in pure silence that was only broken at their giggles, as they laughed at each other's greasy mouths.

Alec finished and put down his plate. "Heart attack on a plate," he said. Alex exploded into laughter.

They settled back into what had become their favorite position at this time of early evening. They were propped up with the sleeping quilts and their arms around each other. They kept warm by the fire as a gentle nip crept into the air.

They faced the gray-blue sea and the massive expanse of darkening blue sky. The sun behind them was gradually changing color as it approached the horizon. The shadows from the pine trees lengthened and began to slowly cover the plateau and the two lovers.

# CHAPTER ELEVEN

Alec and Alex were laid back under the sun, when the explosion occurred. They were totally unaware of the explosion. Not many people were aware of it, for that matter. Only poor sods in the immediate vicinity of Murmansk and the trail of geological survey stations dotting oceans and countries around the world were aware. The Richter scale reading wasn't high. The center of the minor, so-called earthquake was pinpointed, as information came in from the various stations. The intelligence agencies of the western world raised their eyebrows and nodded knowingly.

It didn't take a great deal of intelligence to put two and two together and realize a near empty Russian nuclear arms dump had gone up. They had the location, and they knew exactly what was going on at the location. The Richter reading was much lower than a full blow out, ergo, near empty.

Near empty or not, it wiped out hundreds of people in the short time it takes to say *Bang* and no time to say *you're dead.* The ensuing shockwave continued mostly underground and dropped buildings like playing cards.

Ships in Murmansk harbor, unloading Cuban sugar, tobacco, oil container vessels, wheat, and grain from America, all listed violently, breaking moorings and spewing crude. Dock cranes smashed down on a ship unloading grain from America. A spark ignited the volatile grain dust, and the secondary explosion and tremendous heat set off the crude and sugar ships.

Murmansk Harbor was a mess, to put it mildly. The shockwave set up in the harbor and raced out to sea. A spy trawler just outside the harbor turned turtle. An hour later, life was difficult for the captains of returning fishing vessels.

It was early evening that the shockwaves' Tsunami, cushioned by thousands of miles of ocean and almost spent, finally gasped its life out on the outcrop of granite in the Moray Firth that Rabbie Stewart had found.

The little extra energy added to the natural current swept around each end of the scythe shaped outcrop, swirling the fine sand at the edge of the basin. Sand moved upwards in a vortex like sand devils in the desert.

The ship, cocooned in its cathedral of lace coral, moved slightly upright and away from the outcrop with a silent creaking of its 400-year-old timbers. It held the position for several seconds and then fell back. Its broken masts were abutting once again against the granite.

The pendant, teetering on the edge of the deck, slipped off and plummeted the twenty feet to the sandy ocean bottom. Its weight pulled the hooded skeleton down with it. The body floated behind like some gruesome vulture about to land.

The pendant landed with a small explosion of sand, followed in quick succession by the body. The shock of the landing snapped the upper spinal column and the thong floated free.

All movement slowly ceased. Grains of fine sand gently floated back to their age-old position on the seabed. Timbers ceased their silent creaking, and the hideous horseman rested on his wooden steed. The sand devils disappeared, and all was still again.

Several minutes passed, and then something moved. The pendant crept some inches through the fine sand and stopped. Nothing stirred. It moved again as though being pulled by a ghostly hand and then stopped again.

It inched forward, yet again, to draw level with the skull and paused in its movement. The skull rotated as though to watch through sightless eye sockets. Under the approving, sightless gaze of the skull, the pendant moved again. It was slow at first, then faster as it scattered sand and created a furrow.

The skull's jaw opened in a frighteningly, ghastly grin as the pendant's speed increased and headed for the surface at a tremendous rate. It smashed through the coral dome and exploded through the skin separating ocean from air like a miniature Polaris missile. It arced through the clear evening air.

# CHAPTER TWELVE

Alex saw the object at almost the same time Alec felt her hand squeeze his arm. The object arced through the evening sky in a huge parabola trailing a thin wisp of vapor. It was moving fast, yet in contradiction, seemed to hang in the crystal clear air as it neared the top of its flight path. Then gravity took over, plunging it earthwards on its downward journey.

"What the he-?" Alec was cut short as the object smacked into the earth with such force that shook the plateau.

They stared in disbelief at the small crater barely six feet from their outstretched legs. Their feeling of bliss was shattered by the arrival.

"What on earth is it?" whispered Alex.

"Well it wasn't bird shit, that's for sure," Alec grimly replied. He released himself from Alex's grip and crawled around the fire to the small crater.

"Don't go to near it Alec. You don't know what it is."

He knelt looking at the crater for a second,

then rose to his feet and ran the fifty yards to the cliff edge. The sea was a flat, blue-gray mirror with not even a ripple or a white fish breaker. He quickly looked beneath him at the tine, boulder-strewn beach. There was nothing, not a sound. The sea wasn't even lapping the shore.

He turned to look back at the campsite. Alex was approaching him. His eyes touched on the small hole made by the impact. He rose to follow back the object's trajectory. Head rotating, his eyes ended up on a section of sea possibly half a mile off shore.

"Flat as last year's pay check," he mused, "nothing."

Alex arrived shivering. "Where did it come from Alec?"

His arm reached out and pulled her into him.

"Somewhere out there, girl."

Her eyes followed his pointing finger. After a silence, she turned and said, "But that's impossible." Her eyes were wide, searching his face for an answer.

"Right," he said with a tinge of grimness in his voice.

"But it came down like a cannon ball, and the whole ground shook."

Alec said nothing as his mind was working and then said, "It most certainly wasn't a cannon ball. The hole is too small, and we would have heard a bang. Take it easy, Alex. Look on the bright side; the damn thing didn't hit us."

He took a final look at the horizon. "C'mon. Let's go see what it is," he said cheerfully.

They walked back to the campfire. The flames were still flickering and lighting up the campsite as the evening sky rapidly soaked up the last of the daylight. They paused just short of the small crater and looked at it.

The hole was small and appeared fairly deep in the gloom. It was approximately the size of a demitasse cup, although rectangular in shape.

Alec circumnavigated the wound in the rich turf and salvaged a burning brand from the campfire. Holding the brand high, he dropped to his knees by the hole and peered closely.

It was fairly deep, possibly eighteen inches, and something shiny glinted at the bottom through the covering of soil. He thought it didn't look to be metal shiny, but more like rock.

He looked at the hole. It could have been a bloody cannon ball. He'd seen that dull glint a dozen times in museums and stately homes, where they neatly stacked old cannon balls. Only something tremendously heavy could have reached so far into the earth and given rise to the shockwave they had felt. On the other hand, they no explosion was heard, and the hole it made wasn't around.

He looked back at Alex, who was standing several feet back with questioning eyes. He shrugged his shoulders and pulled her towards him with a beckoning movement of his head. "I can see it, but I can't tell what it is."

Alex dropped to her knees next to him staring into the hole. "Where did it come from?" she asked again.

Alec shook his head. "Christ knows, and he isn't telling. It wasn't fired, because there was no bang. It wasn't thrown; we haven't seen a soul all the time we've been here. The angle of trajectory tells me it came from out there."

He looked towards the now darkened area that was the sea, "and it didn't come from out there." His eyes looked up to the dark, velvet sky that was rapidly filling with stars.

Alex followed his look and said suddenly, "Why not? It could be a small meteorite. Don't meteorites skip like stones on a pond when they hit our ozone layers? That could count for the low trajectory."

With his hand resting palm down on the earth near the hole, Alec said, "No. Feel."

Alex reached down to feel the turf. Its cool, damp tendrils encased her fingers.

"It's cold, Alex. If that was a meteorite, then this immediate area would be very warm. No, girl. It definitely came from out there." He sat back on his haunches pondering like an Arab in the Souq.

Alex, her confidence back, looked into the hole with her nose barely six inches above it. Alec couldn't resist the smile creeping across his face as he looked at her. *Typical nosey, bloody female looking to find the ins and outs of the cat's arsehole*, he thought to himself.

"Whatever it is, there's something tied to it, Alec."

His smile faded as he watched Alex's fingers enter the hole and take hold of something. He rocked forward on his haunches, and sure enough, Alex's finger was looped through a thick string.

"Hang about, girl. Let's have some more light on the subject." He rose and crossed to the fire, throwing on the burnt brand he was holding. He quickly built up the fire.

As it hissed and spat with the sap from the wood, he went to the tent and picked up the small gas lantern.

He knelt beside Alex and lit the lantern. The powerful white glare of the wire mantle imprinted itself on the irises of their eyes for several seconds. Shielding his eyes, Alec held the lamp above his head. He paused to let his eyes become accustomed, and then he touched the thong, for that's what it was. The leather thong was so wet that Alec could squeeze out drops of ice cold moisture. Almost blackened through age or tanning, it looped over Alex's finger where it finished in an unusual knot. As he pulled on the thong, he met great resistance. They assumed the other end of the thong went through or around the object that was buried.

Alec gave the lamp to Alex and put both hands onto the thong. He applied the strength of both hands in an effort to raise the object. It didn't budge. He tried again, but all he got for his efforts were some deep wheals across his fingers. He sat back panting.

He regained his breath and looked at Alex. She was shivering, and for the first time, he noticed that it was indeed quite cold. "Sod it," he said, "it's not going to run away. We can dig it out tomorrow. C'mon. Let's get near the fire. You've gone goosey."

He sat Alex near the fire with a quilt wrapped around her, whilst he salvaged what was left of the coffee. They spoke very little as they warmed by the fire. Occasionally, their eyes would wander over the far side of the fire to the crater.

The question in their eyes remained

unanswered and would continue to be so for
weeks to come.

# CHAPTER THIRTEEN

"Well, are you ever going to get out of bed?" Alex's voice from outside the tent bored into his subconscious.

He didn't answer; he was busy mentally pulling the strings attached to his nerve endings. He was trying desperately to make sense out of the kaleidoscope of images imprinted on his memory cells.

*Christ, it was just like wakening up after a piss-up.* The only thing Alec didn't say was *where am I?*

He forced his eyes open. The sun beating down and through the open tent flaps raised the temperature in the tent by several degrees. Alec rolled over onto his hands and knees and crawled to the entrance.

He took in deep breaths of the clean, salty air. The light was bright to his eyes as he raised his head. He blinked to clear his vision. Alex was standing on the far side of what remained of last evening's fire.

Clad only in her shorts, she struck the classical whore's pose. Her weight was over one leg and the other pointing out at an angle. Her left hand was on her hip as she swayed from side to side, and her right hand was twirling her necklace.

Alec realized she hadn't been wearing a necklace. His vision honed in on the object. It was that damned leather thong being twirled by Alex.

He groaned and looked down at the sweet smelling turf. He breathed deeply. *How dare she look like that when he was still trying to emerge from that black hole called sleep?*

It wasn't sleep. It was a short course of death with all the silent nightmares that made up a private viewing of that nonliving state. Intangible, subliminal pictures were thrown up so quickly in succession that it was impossible for his memory cells to thread two of them together. He could not make any kind of sense out of it. He felt exhausted and drained.

He raised his eyes a few inches and saw Alex's pretty, little bare feet in the grass in front of him. A towel was dropped around his neck, and her hand grasped and pulled his hair gently upwards. He followed the motion with his body until he was standing upright.

She grasped him by the shoulders to turn him in the direction of the stream. Laughingly, she whispered in his ear, "Shower." She pushed him forward, and Alec staggered naked towards the ice cold water.

He returned almost an hour later. The smell of coffee hit his nostrils and made his mouth water. He couldn't remember climbing down to the waterfall. In fact, he literally awoke with the first impact of the ice cold water. It was cold enough to wake a 3000-year-old Egyptian mummy.

The journey to the shower was a somnambulistic fog. The action of the water beating on his body made him gasp for breath. The memories, facts, understandings, and senses were misplaced and whirling around in his brain. They smacked into place with an accuracy that was eye-opening.

He left the shower and laid on a nearby flat rock to dry off. He'd been so dopey that he'd walked under the downpour with the towel still around his neck. He laid the towel out next to him to dry in the hot sun.

With arms behind his neck and hands cupping his head, he lay looking and not looking at the cliff face. *The missile ... who threw it? What threw it? What in the hell is it? Why was the bloody thing so heavy?* he questioned.

The hole it made was as wide as the object itself, so it allowed for a little outspills. It should have left the hole quite easily. It had a thong around it or through it, so it couldn't be that big. Unless, it was a fuse of some kind, like one of those 18th century hand grenades the cartoon characters throw around with *Bomb* written on the side.

*No, not a fuse. Fuses weren't made of leather, and that was definitely leather I was pulling on like the leather thong that Alex was twirling.*

The vision of Alex in a whore's pose and twirling her necklace shot into his mind. *Jesus Christ. She's dug the bugger out. That's what she was so pleased about.*

He reached out and felt the towel. It was bone dry. He stood up and wrapped the towel around his loins like a kilt, then started to climb up the cliff.

Alex didn't say anything when he arrived back. He didn't bother asking and played along. The smile on her face and the all-knowing look told him everything. He furiously held on to his curiosity until halfway through his second cup of coffee.

"I'll have to go and dig that thing out this afternoon," he said, looking at Alex.

"Why this afternoon, Alec? Why not now?"

He smiled at her over the coffee mug. "Because, lover, if I leave it till this afternoon, it will give you time … Time to put it back, so when I laboriously dig it up, breaking fingernails and temper into the bargain, I'll 'ave somefin to show for me hefforts."

He delivered the last line standing up in the manner of a drill sergeant. Alex laughed at him and walked towards him to stand close. "So?"

"Where is it, girl?"

"That's for me to know … and for you to find out."

Alec looked at the smiling face. He knew it was hidden by the way she was smiling. It couldn't be far, in fact, it had to be on her.

She was barefoot and wearing only her shorts. Her lovely breasts were bare and pouting. He looked at her face again. She loved the game. His eyes fell to her breasts, then down to her navel. He saw the tip of the leather thong peeping above the top of her khaki shorts.

Alec's eyes glinted. He crooked his finger in a slow, beckoning manner, and she moved slowly closer to him. He reached out his fingers and hooked them into the thong as she sexily pulled her stomach in to make room for his exploring fingers. Her breathing became shallow, and her nipples puckered and hardened.

Alec started to pull gently and evenly at the thong. His eyes were fixed on her face as he kept up the slow pulling action. Alex's eyes, laughing to begin with, started to glaze under the erotic pulling pressure. It was then, Alec realized exactly where she hid the mysterious object, and he marveled at her devious sexuality.

He felt himself harden under the towel he was still wearing. Alex reached out for his shoulders as her knees began trembling under the inexorable, pleasuring pull. Her head fell into his neck and started to bite. His fingers, wrapped around the warm, damp thong, kept up the pressure.

Millimeter by millimeter he withdrew the thong, enjoying the pleasure he was bringing her. His towel dropped to the ground after losing the battle to stay in place against the pressure of his erection. Following the towel, they both dropped to their knees on the spongy turf.

Alex's hand caressed the pulsing head of his penis, and he continued to pull the thong from between Alex's, now widespread, legs. The object was nearing the end of its wonderful journey. He could tell so by the amount of warm, damp thong wrapped around his fingers.

Still keeping up the pressure, he heard the sound start deep within her. It rose, muffled in his neck, to a crescendo that coincided with his sperm ejecting in a warm, creamy fountain to spray Alex's breasts.

She collapsed on her back panting. She was the fleeting owner of a most welcome, but unplanned orgasm. Alec looked down at her with his face a picture of love and wonderment. He looked to the object dangling from his fingers that had brought about this erotic moment.

His chest rose and fell as he looked at the object swinging like a pendulum from his finger. The thong was tied to a dark, highly polished, triangular-shaped stone through a hole pierced at the apex. It was moist from Alex's body. The moisture added sheen to the stone, and it glinted in the bright sunlight. It was maybe two inches across at the base and slightly more in height. The base was about a half an inch thick and shaving down to almost wafer thinness at the apex where the thong was threaded. The weight was about three or four ounces.

He turned to look at Alex. He could tell by the look in her eyes that she was hanging on to the memory of her climax. *She doesn't know whether she's on this earth or Fuller's earth*, he thought. "You've been well and truly fucked, girl," he said to her, "and you've still got your shorts on."

"Oh, Alec. You were wonderful."

"Wonderful? I didn't do a thing."

"You are joking," she said and rolled over

on to her stomach.

*Christ*, he thought, *I've been cuckolded by a bloody rock.* He looked at the stone swinging from his fingers and laughed out loud.

Alex gave a pleasurable, remembering moan and ground her hips into the turf.

"Shower, young Lady."

She turned to look at Alec. He was pointing down her body. She looked at herself and then looked up at him. "After?" she said, cheekily.

"SHOWER."

Alec crossed to the small crater after Alex had gone and stood looking at the hole. There was no sign of Alex having dug the stone out.

He looked up to the edge of the plateau and the sea stretching away in the distance. All was peaceful. The sea was very calm.

He walked forward towards the edge of the plateau and looked down over the beach and sea. He stood there as naked as the day he was born, his body soaking up the warm sun and his lungs filling with the rich, tangy, salt air.

Alec was puzzled. Here dangling from his fingers was an object, possibly a piece of jewelry of some kind, that was propelled from out there. It was not from land, but out there from that vast, calm sea. He tried to solve this mystery in his mind.

*Aerodynamically, the stone would be about right for flight. It was similar to a raindrop in shape, the bulbous front end tailing off to nothing at the rear. The thong would surely create drag; unlike a javelin used in athletics, which was about as aerodynamically perfect as one could get for a projectile.*

*What was the World Record for the javelin? 300 to 350 meters? Let's say we have a superman type throwing the bloody thing ... 400 meters? Allowing for the shore would bring it to about 300 meters out. Oh, no way, Jose. This thing came from damn near half a mile out.*

*Besides that, it made more impact than someone putting the shot. It went down ten to twelve inches. To make that kind of impact, it would have had to come from where?*

*Dropped down an airplane loo maybe? It was flushed into the stratosphere and fell at thirty-two feet per second. Was the gravity multiplied by weight then? Was weight involved? Jesus, do I remember anything from school?*

*But dropping from that height would certainly give it the impact. No, I seem to recall it going upwards in a curve; therefore going backwards down the curve means it came from out there and not from an airplane.*

Alec palmed the stone; it felt cool and

smooth. It had an unusual smoothness. He thought it was a near perfect smoothness until his fingers touched a blemish. He held the stone up to his eyes and inspected the blemish his fingers found.

It appeared to be an indentation. It seemed to be the last remaining evidence of something once inscribed on the stone. The rest had been worn away. Yes, it was, in all probability, the corner of a letter. It was a piece of jewelry and tremendously old for the inscription to be worn away.

He looked at the thong. A white rime formed on it as it dried in the morning sun. He scraped the whiteness with his fingernail and tasted salt. The stone had been in seawater. Alec's eyes went to the sea again. "I just don't get it."

# CHAPTER FOURTEEN

It was midafternoon, and the sun was blazing down on them as they lay naked in the grass. They were making the most of the hot sun, and Alex was dozing. Today was their last day.

She was utterly at peace with the solitude, the sun, and her lover beside her. She was alarmed when Alec imparted his thoughts to her. Their site was so peaceful that days just drifted by. Memories of an outside world, not to mention a cuckolded husband, faded away. The very idea that the other, mercenary world even existed was an intrusion, nay, an invasion of their Eden.

Alec saw the various reactions to her flashing thoughts written clearly on her face. *She'd be easy to play poker with*, he thought.

He spent a good ten minutes in calm reassurance. He especially covered what her husband would do or might attempt to do. She gained strength from his calm, even, matter-of-fact tones and relaxed once more in the heat of the day. Alec gave a look to the stone thrown on the grass between them and then rolled on his back and promptly fell asleep.

They awoke, within seconds of each other, as that familiar coolness edged into the Scottish air with the sun sliding down in the west. Pangs of hunger hit them both, and they busied themselves.

Alec, after slipping on shorts and a thin sweater, put the stone into his pocket and prepared the campfire. He had saved about half of the wine box, so they could have a celebratory dinner. Unbeknown to him, Alex had done the same with the food, having the same thought in mind.

Alec told her to use everything up, so they didn't have to yomp it back to civilization. She took him at his word.

The resultant potpourri of beans, crumbled tinned burgers, remnants of smoky bacon, tiny tinned carrots, and God knows what else gave off a wonderful aroma. The aroma and hunger made Alec impatient. He kept looking across and finally asking, "Ready yet, girl?"

"In a minute," she replied, laughing and stirring the pot slowly, "Why don't you go and get the wine?"

Alec watched her stirring the stew as he rose to get the wine he had in the stream to cool. He made a detour and passed deliberately close to her in order to fill his lungs with the aroma of her cooking.

"You look and sound like a Bisto Kid," she said.

"And you, my lovely," he said, sniffing deeply, "remind me of a line from a sonnet."

"And which one would that be, kind Sir?"

Alec started walking towards the stream putting some distance between himself and Alex. He recited in a loud Shakespearean voice, "When icicles hang by the wall, and greasy Joan doth keel the pot."

The distance wasn't great enough. The hot, stock-covered spoon thwacked against his right shoulder with a force and accuracy that would have made an Apache Indian proud. He broke immediately into a run, staggering with laughter towards the stream. Alex stood looking at him with her arms on her hips and a pseudo *just you wait* look on her face.

The meal was an astounding success. They both had two huge helpings with plenty more left in the stew pot. They were at that moment when the food, wine, heat from the fire, and the general peaceful ambience were all at once combining to cocoon them.

The fire was larger than normal and flamed strongly in combat with the deepening night.

Alec refilled the tin mugs with the wine. He sat back with a sigh and sipped his wine. He slipped the stone from his pocket and looked at Alex. "Tell me. How did you get the stone out of the ground?"

"Believe it or not, Alec, I just lifted it out."

"Just like that?"

"Just like that."

"What? No digging, no levering?"

"No. Just one little finger through the thong."

"That's bloody strange. I couldn't pull it up with two hands last night."

"I know."

He held the stone up to the light from the fire. "You know it had an inscription on it at one time?"

"No, I didn't," she said as she leaned forward to look more closely.

"Yeah. It's mostly worn away from age, I reckon."

"So what was it, Alec? Some kind of pendant?"

"Possibly."

"So where in Hades …?"

"Did it come from? I think I'm more interested in that, than what it is."

They both stared at the stone swinging from Alec's fingers. The flames of the fire were flickering between the movements of the leather thong. An almost hypnotic quality entered the simple movement that held their gaze. Alec's eyes grew tired.

The too-ing and fro-ing stone went from hard to soft focus, highlighting the flames beyond. They, too, soon lost their sharpness, and the brown towel some ten yards further on, no doubt put out to dry by Alex, seemed to move. Light and shade from the fire played over the towel giving the illusion of movement. Light from the flames would rest for a millisecond to be replaced immediately by a variety of dark, moving shades.

The thin towel took on a depth in the deceiving, wavering light. It seemed to be rising in the center almost tent-like, floating, and forming upwards. Alec's stupefied mind was working at freeze frame speed.

"We - don't - have – a - brown - towel." The words formed letter by letter in the congealing mess in his head. He tried to bring his mind back to reality, but like a rat mesmerized by a cobra, he could not tear his gaze from the rising brown towel. It rose some five or six feet off the ground, floating and undulating in the weird half light.

"We - don't - have – a - brown - towel." He forced himself to repeat the words as the towel now hovered vertical. The fire rippled light and shade over it, giving depth where there was no depth.

Alec's mouth was dry. He tried to break his tongue away from the roof of his mouth, but to no avail. His limbs were ice cold, and he started to shake. Beads of icy perspiration dripped from his face, underarms, and back. The arm holding the stone was locked in its position as though carved from marble.

The stone was still swinging slowly from side to side. Two bright objects appeared at the top of the towel and became part of a pale, oval shape. His slow-moving brain formed a scream that refused to escape his tight-lipped mouth.

The fire suddenly stopped flickering as if it was damped down, but deep in the embers, a fir cone gave a half-hearted crack. It wasn't loud, but it was sufficient enough to snap Alec back to reality.

The stone was still swinging like a pendulum. He stopped the motion and stuffed the stone into his pocket. He looked quickly at Alex. Her eyes were closed as though asleep with tin mug in hand. He shook her gently and her eyes opened. Her eyes were glazed at first and then slowly focused beyond the fire. Alec looked intently at her as her face changed.

Her eyes were widening and her mouth contorting into a grimace. Her head started to move slowly from side to side with a look of sheer terror and disbelief gradually gripping her face.

As a feeling of cold dread overtook him, Alec slowly swiveled his head to follow her gaze. The fire, seemingly, thrown off its ghostly dampness and suddenly flickered bright tongues of light upwards and outwards. Caught on the edge of this ever-moving circumference of light was the figure of a brown-cloaked man.

The figure, under the frightened, spellbound gaze of Alec and Alex, shuffled a weak, tentative step forward towards the heat and light of the fire. Alec stood up with legs like jelly and Alex hanging on to his left arm for dear life.

She was shivering. He could feel her spasmodic shaking as she tried to control it. His stomach turned over, and he could taste Alex's ragout again. It was better the first time.

As light played on the figure, Alec could see the thick, brown woven hassock hanging heavy from the thin stooped shoulders. It was torn and threadbare in places. A hood on the hassock was displaced to the back of the head, revealing a thin, lined face.

The face was brown in color from either birth or sun-topped with long, lank hair disappearing from either side of the head into the recesses of the hood.

On either side of the hawkish nose were deep set eyes of a color somewhere between dark brown and black. Deep in those eyes was a red glow. *Probably the flames from the fire*, thought Alec.

His cloak hung below the knees, showing brown, thin legs finished in sandals. They were simple sandals that conformed to the sole of the foot with a simple leather strip over the big toe to keep the sandal in place.

Alex relaxed her grip on Alec's arm and moved. Alec looked at her.

"I'll have to go to the tent," she whispered, embarrassingly. Alec nodded.

*I don't blame you girl*, he thought as she disappeared towards the tent. *I almost had an accident myself.*

The figure moved again with another shuffling step. Alec looked, and the man was looking him straight in the eyes. His arm came upwards from his side with his palm outwards as though asking or even begging.

Alec moved quickly around the fire to the figure as it tottered on obviously weak legs. He grabbed the man around the shoulders to support and lead him closer to the fire.

He could see the man's cloak and hair were completely wet as he seated him by the fire. He could see the brown skin puckered and wizen, as though from long immersion in water. A rich, salty smell mixed with an odor Alec just couldn't put his finger on emanated from the old man.

Alec quickly wrapped the duvet quilt around the emaciated shoulders and thrust the tin cup of wine into the brown, gnarled hands. He helped him to drink. All the time, the deep, black eyes were looking at Alec.

After several sips, the old man seemed to be regaining his strength and could handle the cup on his own. Alec refilled it.

Over the old man's shoulder, he could see Alex returning in her jeans, having changed out of her soiled underwear. He called to her to bring over the stew.

She did so, and Alec took the wine mug from the old man's fingers. He placed the hot food on the man's lap. They could see his nostrils flare as they caught the aroma. Immediately and ravenously, he started eating with his fingers to the amazement of Alex, who was still holding the spoon she'd brought.

The two looked at each other. Alex's eyes widened with yet unanswered questions, and Alec gently and silently shook his head at her. "Alex, bring me a pair of my jeans and an anorak. Oh, and a towel as well." Alex looked at him. "He's wringing wet through," he added in reply to her questioning look.

The man finished eating as Alex departed to the tent. His eyes rose to fix Alec's face with the deep black orbs. Alec knew what he wanted. A word, gesture, or expression hadn't passed, but Alec knew.

He refilled the plate with stew on one side of the plate and a thick hunk of near stale bread on the other. The man's expressionless face thanked him, and he attacked the food again. Alec watched as the old man tapped the bread on the side of his plate, sniffed it, and then broke the bread and dunked it in the stew.

# CHAPTER FIFTEEN

Steam from the boiling kettle filled the kitchen as Alec finished wiping the cups. He turned the kettle off and slowly prepared the tea. His mind was elsewhere. He automatically filled the cups and took them into the smallish room he called his lounge. He paused to turn off the kitchen light with his elbow.

The old lady sat in her usual place by the unused television. She was staring out of the window and not moving. Alec placed the tea at her elbow and looked down at the whitening, thinning hair and the wrinkled nape of her neck.

He bent down to kiss her gently on her forehead. The skin was cold. She didn't move or acknowledge the kiss.

He pulled the wooly cardigan she wore a little tighter around her shoulders. He knew she wouldn't touch the tea, and still he replaced it an hour later with another one. She wouldn't touch that one either. He squeezed her shoulder affectionately and silently left the room with his tea.

He went up the cottage stairs to the spare bedroom he'd converted to a study and sat by the window. He lit a cigarette, pulled the smoke deep into his lungs, and slowly exhaled. The smoke buffeted against the rain-spotted window.

It was dark outside, but he could see the tall evergreens swaying majestically in the inclement weather, highlighted against the evening sky. They swayed and sang to nature's tune with leaves rustling and wood creaking under the force of the gusting wind.

Alec wondered which one would fall this year. Every year, one of the tall pines succumbed to the pressure of the weather. It seemed a contradiction to Alec. *Surely, the taller a tree, the stronger the tree.*

Yet, it was always the tallest that fell as though outgrowing the strength of its roots. Not that Alec gave a damn, large or small they provided enough logs to get through a winter. He couldn't remember when he last had to buy logs. He must get the chain saw out and give it a service.

The wind gusted in another direction, and the room grew quiet. Alec was still and apart from the occasional movement to draw on his cigarette, motionless. His eyes turned to the distant hills where sheep, appearing as tiny white dots, meandered over the fields grazing.

The clattering sounds broke irreverently into Alec's reverie. His old golf ball typewriter came to life from the makeshift desk in the corner. Alec's only movement was dragging on his cigarette.

The typewriter clattered on. A full minute passed before Alec turned his head to look. In the gloom, he could see the golf ball whizzing and imprinting its usual gibberish on the paper he had left.

He leaned forward and lit another cigarette from the end of the last one. He leaned back to drink his tea and reverted, once more, to the hills. He ignored the clattering typewriter. *I really must get a mechanic to look at the damn thing or better still, buy a word processor*, he thought.

Minutes passed as Alec sat there listening to the wind and the noise of the typewriter. He put his cup down, stood up, and switched on an old brass oil lamp that he'd converted. Its warm glow flooded the room. The typewriter paused its frenetic pounding for a moment, as if disturbed by the light, then renewed its efforts frenziedly.

Alec reached down and calmly pulled the plug from the back of the machine. It stopped. He looked at the paper disgorged by the machine and shook his head at the gibberish. He checked the platen for wear, before winding in a fresh sheet.

Then he returned to his chair by the window,

waiting. He was waiting to see the lights of a car bringing someone to his door. He lit yet another cigarette. As he leaned forward to put out the old cigarette in the ashtray, his eyes fell on a slim, cardboard box. It was the type of box used by watch repairers to return watches.

A feeling of outraged horror crept through him as he looked at the box sitting on the window sill. His horror was slowly replaced with a quiet, smoldering anger. He took his eyes away from the box to search the lonely, country lane again. As he did so, his mind slipped back to that last, eventful night in Scotland three weeks ago. The night the old man appeared.

# CHAPTER SIXTEEN

Having somewhat recovered from their initial fright and shock at the old man's sudden appearance, they gave him food and drink and provided dry clothes. The old man ignored the fresh clothing. He preferred to sit by the fire with steam rising from his wet robe. Alec tried to converse with him, but he remained silent and immobile by the fire.

Alec built the fire up with the old man's deep, dark eyes watching his face. Whilst Alec was squatting to build up the fire, the stone pendant slipped from his pocket to lie gleaming on the grass beside him. Unknowing, Alec turned to warn the old man to be careful not to burn his robe. The words never left his throat. The old man's eyes were staring at the stone. He had an expression of intensity on his face, similar to an addict staring at his next overdue fix. Alec looked at the stone in wondering amazement.

The old man leaned forward with a slight movement that was almost imperceptible. It was brought to an immediate halt as Alex's arm shot down to retrieve the stone. Looking at the old man through slightly narrowed eyes, he slipped it over her head for the stone to settle on the breast of her sweater. Alec saw the old man's expression relax, but deep in his eyes came a reddish glow.

Unable to converse or do any more for the old man, they went to bed. The old man stayed by the fire. They didn't talk much, and they didn't make love.

Alec was still awake when Alex's breathing became shallow and rhythmic. She was finally asleep. He lay there for an hour after that thinking. He thought about the man, the stone, the unusual appearance of both, and the effect the stone had on the man. He was wondering if the two were connected when he slipped into a troubled sleep.

They awoke the next morning to find the fire dead and the man gone. Alec's spare clothes were left untouched, where he had placed them near the old man. Alec looked at Alex and shrugged his shoulders.

They soon forgot about him as they busied themselves with breakfasting and breaking camp. They laughed and joked as they did so, but somehow not with the same spontaneity as before.

The events of the previous two days were provoking thoughts that took the fine edge off the wonderful time they both had. Alec caught

Alex looking around her several times as though she was reacting to someone softly calling her name. All was quiet, but he knew what she was feeling. He had that same feeling all morning; the feeling that they were no longer alone and that someone or something was watching them.

The campsite was left as clean as a whistle, apart from the circle of black and gray ash left over from the fire. They took one last look, and Alec took a few snaps with his cheap camera. Then they departed back to reality and the modern world.

It seemed to Alec that the journey to Inverness took no time at all. One minute, they were leaving the campsite, and the next, they were at the railway station. In reality, almost four hours passed. They walked and hitched in absorbing silence.

Their arrival at the station was opportune with just twenty minutes to wait for a train. Not quite true, the train was already at the platform with a twenty-minute wait for departure. They took their seats and stowed their rucksacks.

Alec wandered back down the platform to the buffet bar. He bought sandwiches, teas, some newspapers, and a couple of magazines for Alex. He was trying to navigate the swing doors of the bar without having an accident, when through the upper glass window he thought he saw a familiar figure.

The figure was clad in a hooded brown robe standing on the platform and looking into the train windows at about the area where Alex sat.

The inward door of the bar swung inwards as a fat mother with two scampering kids came charging through. Alec was forced to do his impression of a circus balancing act, swaying out of their way and sliding through the open door. He stood still amongst the moving people, and between the bodies, he glimpsed again the immobile, brown-cloaked figure.

A tinge of something a kin to fear flushed through him. He started forward and was immediately engulfed by a noisy gaggle of school kids off on a school outing. It was back to the balancing act again as the tidal wave of blue-blazed imps attempted, and almost succeeded, in washing him back through the doors.

He surfaced with his right hand wet with tea from one of the plastic cups. He brought his hand up in an attempt to lick away the hot, thin tea and the pain. In doing so, he looked down the platform. The figure had gone.

*This is crazy*, he thought, *I'm bloody seeing things now.* Nevertheless, he strode down the platform to the spot where he estimated the figure had stood and looked around.

He saw nothing. He turned and looked down the train. In the window seat opposite him, Alex was engrossed in a Woman's Weekly. He stared at her as she read. He looked up and down the platform. It was a long train with many windows. He knew he had seen the old man. The coincidence was too great. He boarded the train thoughtfully.

The train journey, as usual for Alec, was boring. He attempted to solve a crossword, but his mind kept slipping away. He just couldn't concentrate. He found his gaze constantly wandering across to sleeping Alex. Her head was leaning against the window, and the stone suspended from her neck was swaying to and fro with the motion of the train.

They arrived in Manchester hours later and stiffly disembarked onto the platform. How can you do nothing for several hours and arrive at your destination tired? It was always a thought-provoking contradiction to Alec.

They headed through the very busy station towards the taxi rank. The smell of diesel fumes was thick in the air, and the peculiar taste electric engines brought about in the mouth played havoc with their senses.

They were in luck; there were plenty of cabs. They threw the rucksacks on the floor as they entered a taxi. Alec told the driver to head to

Granada TV, and he spun the wheel and set off.

Alec looked through the window at the disappearing railway station. He looked past the throngs of people at the passenger section to the freight area where crates of vegetables and fruit were haphazardly stacked. Porters on silent electric cars were pulling mounds of bananas and constantly tooting high-pitched horns as they navigated hurrying commuters.

A subliminal picture of a brown hooded figure appeared, only to be immediately hidden by the taxi's rear door pillar. Alec hurriedly turned to look back through the dark, smoke-glass rear window of the cab. The figure was there right enough.

Alec saw it for about three seconds, before it was obscured by a porter pulling a huge trailer of tomato boxes. Alec turned to the front and gave a little unconcerned half smile to the unknowing Alex. Alec started to become a little worried.

# CHAPTER SEVENTEEN

They reached Alec's home about an hour later. Alex was excited and cuddling close to Alec, talking incessantly as he drove. She made him laugh with her frankness in all things, especially sexual.

He realized weeks before that she would make a wonderful partner for him; they really did have so much in common. A feeling of contentment seeped through his bones as he took a quick glance down at her head leaning against his shoulder.

They passed the *The Ship*, crossed the bridge, and swung into Alec's driveway outside his cottage.

Wincle was a lovely, old village. Actually, it was more a hamlet with its possibly twenty cottages, a dozen farms, and of course, *The Ship*.

*The Ship* was a village pub of distinction. They were purveyors of a good English pint in a remarkably spotless, copper and brass atmosphere under the aegis of a larger than life landlord and landlady.

Many times, Alec found it a relaxing place, unwinding over a pint and a chat with the regulars. It was about as far away from the false world of spotlights and makeup as you could get. In fact, the only brut the locals knew was Fred's huge white bull that sired most of the cattle around. Occasionally, the bull took it into its head to go walk about around the country lanes. It was not a nice sight to see when exiting the pub after a skin full on a dark and lonely lane; the huge form of that bull blocking your unsteady path.

One night, to end all nights, the bull went to walk about heading for *The Ship*. Mine host was entertaining the regulars somewhat later than usual. He was in full flow of a pep talk to the local tug o' war team who were doing battle the next day.

Their opponents were from a village about six miles away; a lot of needle and not so friendly a rivalry existed between the two. Honor was at stake, hence the flowing pints. Frank nipped down to the cellar to change the bitter when an almighty bellow ripped through the pub. Eighteen-inch biceps holding pints of Frank's best froze.

Mary, playing the one-armed bandit, turned at the noise to see the huge bull had tried to enter the pub. It got stuck in the open doorway. Mary was in very close proximity to the enormous head and promptly fainted. Her hand hit the play button as she fell. Her recumbent body was receiving, in due course, the full force of the coins from the jackpot to the accompaniment of the snorting bull.

"Christ … the buggars stuck," shouted Joe, a seventy-year-old, red, weather-beaten faced regular.

And stuck it was. The huge mass was wedged firmly in the old oak doorframe with mucus dripping from flaring nostrils. The noise brought Frank quickly up from the cellar. The trapdoor entrance ripped off the back buttons of his trousers to which his braces were attached. He shot up through the trap like some overweight, miscast, pantomime fairy with his braces flying over his head. He scrambled around the bar, with one hand holding his trousers up, to view the errant bull.

"Holy ... Mother Mary of God," he whispered, staring at the ton and a half of prime sirloin on the hoof. "Is it stuck," he asked fearful of the damage to his lovely pub.

"It's stuck," came back the calm reply in unison.

Several seconds passed in quiet thought and calm drinking; the bull was almost ignored.

"Right," said Frank to the tug o' war team, "all a yers, troo de bar, get yer rope. Go around the pub, and pull the bloody thing out by its tail."

The big farm lads looked at each other. They loved the idea, and after all, the man who buys the drinks names the tune. They shot through the bar, and that's where chaos commenced.

Frank, in his rapid exit from the cellar left the trap open. The first three didn't have a chance. Like a ton of bricks, they fell to the cellar floor. Numbers two and three weren't too bad. It was number one, the overzealous anchorman of the team, who felt the full force of the cellar floor.

In rapid succession, the sixteen and seventeen stone, respectively, of his two mates dropped on him. Numbers two and three staggered out bruised and laughing. Frank's best bitter momentarily anaesthetized them to their pain, leaving the anchorman spark out on the cellar floor.

"Where's Larry?" asked the captain securing the rope to the bull's tail.

"Pissed," was the swift reply.

Meanwhile, the regulars opened up all the windows and were leaning out to view the spectacle and to shout advice. They were offering sips of bitter to the ale-less tug o' war team.

Finally, the team stood back and surveyed the task before them. The enormous white rump and hindquarters of the bull projected into the lane with the rope attached to its tail. Inside with eyes rolling and nostrils flaring, the bull gave out an eardrum-bursting bellow. Much to the distress of Mary recovering from her faint, she promptly returned to the peaceful state.

Outside, the lads spat on their hands and grasped the rope. They gently took the strain until the bull's tail was at full extension. They took deep breaths, and in unison shouted, "Heave!"

Their shout was cut short, because the bull decided it was time to evacuate his huge bowels. It shot forth in a green, forceful, evil-smelling fountain.

Numbers one, two, and three just didn't stand a chance. Their mates behind them, spattered to some extent, collapsed along with the onlookers from the windows in total hysterics.

The bull, in disdain, shrugged its mighty shoulders and backed out. Complete with the framework of Frank's oak door embracing its huge body, the bull calmly and ponderously ambled down the lane, towing the rope behind it and disappearing into the night. It was a majestic, awe-inspiring, sight.

Alec dined out on that story many times and others like it. Yes, it was good to be back. Alec somehow felt deeply relieved as he put the key into the lock.

His mother met them with a shouted greeting from the kitchen where she was cooking up some magic concoction. He kissed her and introduced Alex. After a peck on the cheek and a lovely warm hug, Alex sank into one of the kitchen stools. She accepted Mother's offer of a cup of tea.

It was obvious to Alex that Mother was given a thumbnail sketch of Alex's background. The warm welcome was a giveaway, and she could see from whence Alec received his fine attributes.

Within five minutes, the two females were talking away like old friends about everything and nothing as typical females do. Alec almost felt left out. A smile crossed his face as he looked and listened. The kitchen was filled with a happy sound of a Lancashire girl and a Yorkshire girl mixing their two different dialects.

He looked at his mother with a proud, tender look. She never failed him. That one was salt of the earth. Her once immense shock of thick, red hair mellowed over the long years to a gentle auburn. He remembered what she'd said when he pointed out that she had some gray hairs coming through. *They're just as warm as the others, and let's hope that you can keep yours long enough for yours to turn gray.*

She was as sharp as a razor blade. Her deep green eyes had also faded down with the years. *Dad used to call her The Dragon. She must have been one hell of a handsome woman in her youth. It's no wonder Dad married her.*

It was the joining of two proud families from the *Auld Country*. Mam was an O 'Gaunt and damn proud of it. Someone once told Alec that the first King of Ireland was an O'Gaunt. Whether true or not, to Alec, his mam was every inch a Dowager Queen blood, and as they say in equine fraternity, blood will out.

He left the happy domestic scene and went into the small lounge. Mother was busy whilst he was away. The smell of lavender polish filled the air, and there was not a speck of dust to be seen. The brassware and copper lamps shone with warmth and richness against the old oak beams. The beams supported the walls and stone-clad roof for over four hundred years. Yes, it was a lovely room.

"Four hundred years," Alec said to himself as he looked at the beams. "Your average modern semi will be lucky to see forty years without some major fault occurring." He looked proudly around the room. This was standing proof of an art that was second nature to an Englishman.

They knew how to build a good solid home and probably built it in the same time it takes to erect the average suburban home today. He turned and went down the two steps leading to his small dining room. The furniture was glowing with rich wax sheen, and once again, the pervading bouquet of lavender filled his nostrils.

He looked through the windows at the front of the house as he sipped tea from his cup. He looked through the windows and across at the large trees. Pines, elms, and oaks dipped down to the River Dane, the sound of which he could hear even above the girls' chatter from the kitchen. *Must have been raining further inland*, thought Alec.

The running of water against the rocks was a peaceful sound. Most sunny days when he wasn't working, which was often for an actor, he'd sit at the front of the cottage listening to the lapping of the river. Occasionally, a fly-tormented cow would bellow. He'd also hear the sound of Ken and Ada's lambs gamboling and calling out.

When the mood caught him or an idea struck him, he'd put pen to paper and write. One fine day, he'd get around to that novel he promised himself he would write. Meantime, it was bread on the table with scripts for TV.

He had some success, though nothing great. He was ever the optimist. The feeling was there that one day he'd write the big one. It would be the one that took you into respectability and being accepted as a person with something to say.

He looked across the narrow lane and then further down to look at the little Methodist church, known locally as *The Chapel in the Valley. Must have been a lost Welshman who called it that*, thought Alec.

Large sprays of flowers were hung on either side of the open church doors. The massed banks of normally unkempt azaleas and rhododendrons in front of the church were neatly clipped. Obviously, Fred, one of the church elders, had been busy with his shears.

"Now why is that?" he asked himself. "The Flower Festival," he muttered to himself, suddenly remembering it was the chapel's 200th anniversary.

His eyes slipped over the stout, stone building. It was built to stand the test of time, solid as the Rock of Gibraltar. *Amazing really*, he thought, *how we have moved on.*

People were kneeling and praying here in the 1800's. In Oldham, they were hanging an eleven-year-old boy for sheep stealing and no doubt praying too.

In America, settlers were being tortured in that vast, empty land for taking a few acres and raising crops and animals where Indians couldn't. It just doesn't make sense. Mind you, America and Oldham have come on a bit since then. The only thing you get hung for now in Oldham is nicking someone else's ale.

A movement down by the rhododendrons caught his eye and then disappeared. Hidden for a few seconds by the large olive green leaves, a figure appeared and stood motionless by the church door. It paused momentarily under the white spray of flowers, and then it turned to look up at Alec's cottage.

Alec felt the lump in his throat rise up from his stomach. The gourmet smells erupting from the kitchen soured in his nostrils as he stared down into the dark cavity of the hood, belonging to the brown-robed figure. Seconds that felt like an eternity passed before the figure turned and entered the church.

Alec turned away from the window with his hands were shaking. "What the bloody hell is going on?" The question was futile. He put the cup down before he spilled what was left of his t.. He knew there was no answer, but there had to be.

He moved quickly to the side door and closed it softly behind him. He paused before crossing the narrow lane outside his cottage. All was peaceful. The smell of the hawthorn hung heavy. A bunch of swallows wheeled and dived above the trees. The only sounds were country sounds. There were no cars, nor human voices.

He crossed the lane to rest his hands on the dry stonewall. Peering down at the open doorway of the chapel, he saw all was still. Nothing stirred; no sound came from the church. He tried to calm his racing heartbeat and nerves, but the adrenalin was flowing and fear knotted his stomach.

Never taking his eyes off the church entrance, he followed the stone steps of the narrow pathway leading down to the entrance. His feet were leaden. He couldn't feel them, as if they didn't belong to him. Somehow his brain commanded, and they hesitantly understood. He rounded the newly pruned bushes and came upon the doorway. He stopped and groaned under his breath.

He didn't want to enter. What was that line he had heard someone say? *Fear of the unknown. So you lose the fear by knowing what's scaring you half to death? Those are words of a crazy man.* He still didn't want to enter, but he knew he was committed.

The sun ceased being hot on his back after one pace. The coolness of the church enveloped him. Coolness? Jesus, it was cold. His heartbeat was now totally out of control, and his breathing was short and fast. His veins were trying to pump oxygen into his blood cells to keep pace with his heart.

He could see two beautiful bouquets of flowers on either side of the interior doorway that led into the main body of the church. It was a single rectangular room with the pulpit on the left, pews to the right, and a central aisle. The whole building was built for £320 in the 1800's. Back then, it was described as a commodious place of worship; a simple, single, large room where some eighty people could gather and sing the Lord's praises.

Alec knew there was but one entrance and exit, and he was standing in it. It seemed to grow colder as he stood there plucking up courage to enter the room. The damp coldness touched his skin in a way that made one want to rub it briskly away. He shivered and something inside of him told him that no amount of rubbing would warm his skin.

He moved forward from the entrance into the room itself. His teeth clenched hard against the cold and fear. He looked around slowly. His eyes became accustomed to the soft, natural lighting of the church as they fell on the pulpit.

The pulpit was an absolute mass of color

from the huge displays of flowers of all varieties and hues artistically arranged. A credit to the artistry of the churchgoers filled the entire end of the church. Flowers of white and blue in delicate sprays spread down the walls on either side to disappear behind him. He knew without looking that the back of the church would be a similar mass of color. It was indeed a most wonderful sight and at any other time than this, a sight to gladden and uplift.

Alec was riveted to the spot. The cold was unbelievable and breathing became difficult; even his mind seemed to be icing over. He sensed, rather than heard, a movement. The hairs on the back of his neck rose stiffly in an animal instinct that millions of years of evolution couldn't wipe out. He was shaking violently now with no pretence of trying to control his panicking mind.

His head was facing the wooden, carved pulpit unable to look around. He had that feeling again, this time accompanied by a rustling sound. Alec felt like he was under attack. He knew not from what, whom, or for what reason. He was under attack in this place of all places. In God's house?

Alec did the only thing his congealing brain would allow him to do; he silently prayed and took another faltering step forward. His eyes locked on to the simple, carved cross hanging on the pulpit. He gasped for breath fighting the intense cold as the rustling sound grew closer. There were no pauses, just a constant rustling.

Waves of cold and damp pressure thrust against his back and arms, raising the hairs on the back of his hands as stiff as the bristles on a pig's back. Whatever was behind Alec knew what Alec was trying to do. All the time that damned rustling sound was intense and evil.

Alec's teeth clenched so tight he thought they would crumble under the pressure of his jaws. Tears commenced to roll from his eyes and seared his face. He managed another step forward, and his hand outstretched towards the cross. He was inches from it, but the rustling was now like thunder in his ears. He didn't have the strength for another step. He threw his body forward and grasped the base of the wooden cross, knees hitting the hard floor. The pain added to the moisture already in his eyes.

Was he safe from whatever was in the church? He didn't know. He'd done all that was possible.

The presence passed close to him down the aisle and was followed by the intense rustling. It crossed the flower bedecked dais and went along the other wall. Then there was silence.

Minutes passed, and Alec was still kneeling with his fingers touching the cross. He kept repeating a prayer. It was the only prayer he remembered from a childhood long gone. The repeated words came slower now in time with his breathing.

Alec gained the strength to open his eyes as the air warmed around him. He stared at a knothole in the wood on the church floor. Sweat from the fear he felt dripped and stained a dark uneven blotch around it. To Alec, it looked somehow obscene and out of place on the floor of this neat church. A flush of embarrassment shot through him at childhood things remembered.

He released his hold on the cross, reached in his pocket for a hankie, and stood up. He could feel the moisture on his face drying stickily. He slowly opened the crumpled hankie like an old man. He could see his hands and legs were shaking, and he could feel something akin to shock begin to ripple through him. His heartbeat began to increase its rate again, and he breathed deep and slow to combat the adrenalin. He buried his face in his hankie.

Seconds passed, and then he took one large deep breath before removing the hankie from his face and looking around the church. He was aghast at what he saw. The wonderful display of flowers - the reds, the blues, the whites, the pinks, the myriad shades - was no longer. The stems were shriveled as though by an intense frost. They gave up their colorful petals and lined the walls and dais with blackened, bent fingers. The church floor at the base of the walls was ankle-deep in withered, brown flower petals. The petals lay like the leaves of trees along a country lane in deep winter.

Alec looked open-mouthed at this scene of desecration. A solitary petal fell in a spiral down to join its comrades. It slipped sideways to the left and right until gently resting on the other petals with a soft, rustling sound. Hypnotically, Alec watched the progress of the petal. The sound of its gentle rustling sent a flash of fear through him.

# CHAPTER EIGHTEEN

The rain stopped momentarily, but the wind kept up its buffeting. Spots of rain on the window reflected tiny points of light from *The Ship* across the valley. Hung in desperation against the wind's force, the drops clung to the window panes. Eventually, they finally succumbed to the inevitable and slid diagonally across to merge and disappear.

Alec could see himself reflected in the window by the glow of the small brass lamp behind him. The reflection distorted as the pressure of the outside wind on the glass bowed the panes.

He lit another cigarette. The glow from the burning tobacco pictured brightly in the mirror image. He reached for his cup, but it was cold and empty. He stiffly rose and went quietly down the stairs to the kitchen.

He hefted the kettle and found it half full, so he switched it on to make himself a coffee. He paused as he poured the steaming water into the cup. He thought for a few moments and then reached into the cupboard for a second cup. He proceeded to make two cups of coffee.

Impassively, he picked up a cup and left the

kitchen. He crossed the tiny hall to the lounge door, opened it, and stood looking at the seated figure in the gloom. Nothing stirred. There was no sound apart from the wind and spattering rain on the window.

He crossed to the figure and retrieved the untouched cup he had put there earlier. He replaced it with the fresh one. Steam from the cup spiraled lazily upwards until it was caught in some minute draught from the window. It hovered, spread, and then disappeared.

Alec looked down at the figure. She sat as still as stone, as though carved from marble. Her breathing was so shallow that her breast hardly moved. Her gnarled fingers, interlaced with each other on her lap, looked to be stumps in the gloom. The obscene thought made Alec cringe as he bent down to gently kiss her.

He left her staring out of the window to retrieve his coffee from the kitchen. He went back upstairs and sat in the chair facing the window. His hands gripped around his cup as it seemed to be the only source of warmth in the cold house.

"It isn't a cold house," he said softly to himself, "it never was a cold house." He reached his hand out to touch the radiator, and it was red hot. "But, by Jesus, it's cold now," he muttered.

He shivered as the thought touched his

mind. This was a familiar coldness he'd experienced before. Before sounded like years ago, but it was only weeks. Was it only weeks since he sought out Phil?

He shook his head as though to loosen and re-assemble the memory banks in his brain.

# CHAPTER NINETEEN

Alec parked the car with difficulty. Have you ever tried to park a car near a university? Every bloody student has a car.

They all plead poverty and scream about their grants. They spend two or three hours every night supping subsidized ale after their studies, putting the world to right. They pick the next England football manager. They decide on their next screw, finding out who has herpes and who is likely to get it.

*How the hell do they pass their exams for whatever it is they're studying?* "Beats the shit out of me," Alec murmured as he looked up at the red stone entrance to Manchester University.

He went up the steps and through the large, high doorway. The hallway was spacious with the Enquiry Office on the left. The wall opposite was transformed into one massive notice board.

The various rules and regulations of the establishment were covered over with hundreds of tiny squares of paper. Each advertisement offered something to someone's advantage. The quality of the writing struck Alec. There was a major lack of spelling and command of the Queen's English.

The wall had a hypnotic quality about it. It certainly did its job. People couldn't resist looking. Students were hovering, fingering, commenting, and moving on all the time.

There was a polite cough from behind him. Alec turned and saw it was the receptionist. She was an old dear with an easy face. Alec smiled and apologized. She instantly smiled back.

"Could you tell me where I could find Dr. Philip Grossman, please?"

# CHAPTER TWENTY

Alec said nothing to the two girls when he came back from the church. They were still rat bagging in the kitchen. He slid past the kitchen door and walked upstairs.

"Is that you, Al?" his mother's voice pealed after him.

"Yes, Ma. I'm just running a bath," he answered. "Shit, she's got ears like bloody Jodrell Bank," he added under his breath.

He didn't hear the rejoinder to Alex, so obviously it was at his expense. He ran the bath as hot as he could stand it. He laid back and allowed the heat to enter his frozen marrow. He closed his eyes and stage by stage, went over what he'd seen and felt.

He knew that no amount of reasoning could ever explain the horror he felt in the church. After twenty minutes or so, the bath was cooling, and Alec was fully relaxed. He opened his eyes.

"No," he muttered, "I'm not going bloody daft. I saw what it did. I felt it, and what's more ... I could damn well taste it."

There was a movement in the open doorway. Alec, still jumpy, turned his head quickly to see no one. "Christ. I'm jumpy", he said softly.

There was a giggle from the doorway and, as Alec looked, he could see a curl of blonde hair sticking out. Quickly he reached out and with a wet hand, pulled the still giggling Alex into the bathroom.

"Oh, Sir," she said in sham embarrassment. "Doing your Peeping Tom act, eh, woman?" he said sternly, hoping against hope that the sudden throb between his legs wouldn't show itself above the level of the bathwater.

Too late, there was the cry. "Ohhh … Sirrr," she repeated with an entirely new emphasis as she gazed down at the bathwater. He suddenly pulled her forward, so she dropped to her knees on the carpeted floor with her face level with his. He continued to pull until she was over the bath. The stone pendant fell from her open-necked blouse and swung from her neck just above the level of the water.

Their faces were almost touching. She reached out her left arm to support her balance as she reached for the water with her right. Her aim was excellent. He groaned and buried his tongue in her mouth. The pendant touched the water.

One second, Alex was returning his passion and lust, and the next; she was literally torn from his grasp. Her face was down under the bathwater and her legs pumping in the air as the edge of the bath acted as a fulcrum.

Split seconds passed as Alec stared in total bewilderment at Alex's threshing figure. Bubbles broke the surface of the water as her hands flailed the air and smashed down on the water. "My God. She's drowning!" he screamed silently. He reached forward to grasp her, only to slip in the slipperiness of the bathwater.

A tidal wave of water whipped down the bath to slap against the far end, sending water up the walls and through the open doorway. It rushed back down and for a millisecond, revealed Alex's head. Her eyes were rolling and her mouth shut tight. Then the wave hit him, making him lose what was left of the balance he had regained.

*The plug, for God's sake! The plug.* Something was shouting in his brain. He reached behind him and felt the steel chain. He yanked on it and in the same movement, threw the chain over the side of the bath. He reached forward and grabbed Alex's hair to lift her face out of the water, but it was immovable.

"Jesus Christ, there's something fucking holding her." He knelt, put both arms under her, and heaved. Panic gave him strength, and the adrenalin raced through the distended veins in his neck. He could have lifted the QE2, but he couldn't budge Alex.

His hand reached down under Alex and brushed against the leather thong around her neck. It was as tight as a bowstring. Realization dawned on Alec, *Jesus ... the fucking stone!*

The gurgle of the exiting bath water broke through his thoughts and realigned them. He twisted Alex's head to one side in an attempt to bring her nose and mouth above the water. They were still a good inch below the surface. Alex's left eye rolled open. Alec's body felt like a mass of gelatin as he stared down at her. His whole world was encompassed in that one staring, pleading, helpless eye.

Alec exploded out of the bath to the bathroom cabinet. There were bottles, jars, and toothpaste scattered under his searching hand. He grabbed a near empty shampoo bottle. Unscrewing the cap, he took the base between his teeth. Under any other circumstance it would have been impossible, but flowing panic and adrenalin allowed him to rip the base off.

He quickly moved back to the bath and rinsed out the bottle. He jammed the screw neck into Alex's mouth, making a crude snorkel.

"Breathe, Alex. Breathe," he shouted. He held the snorkel with one hand, and he pressed down hard on her back with the other.

For a second, nothing happened. Then

Alex's hand came around and grasped the plastic bottle. He could see her body move as air flowed into her lungs. Alec squatted back by the bath and watched the water slowly recede from Alex's face. Slowly but surely, the water receded uncovering her nose and mouth.

The seconds ticked by. Only the gurgling bath water and the labored breathing of the two shocked occupants marred the silence in the bathroom. Alec, for some unknown reason, synchronized his breathing with Alex's. Breathing in as she breathed in and exhaling as she exhaled. It was as though he was helping her to breathe.

His eyes never left her face, and some time passed before they realized that the bath was empty of water. He reached forward to remove the plastic bottle from her mouth, but Alex clung on to it like grim death.

"It's alright, darling. It's alright. The bath's empty," he said, gently easing the make-shift snorkel from her grasp.

He lifted her head up easily. The stone was swinging, glinting blackly like a devil's eye hanging from its leather thong. A deep, red groove, where the thong had lain, encircled the back of her neck. Beads of blood began to show in places it had broken the skin.

Alex opened her eyes and looked up at him.

"I only came to bring you a towel," she said hoarsely. Then her voice strengthened and the familiar banter came bravely through, "I don't normally bathe with my clothes on."

Alec smiled as her face worked hard to hide shock and attempt a grin. He seated her on the loo and retrieved the towel from outside the door where Alex had dropped it. He took another one from the airing cupboard. He removed Alex's wet blouse and dried her carefully.

He stood up. "Now get the rest of your wet things off," he ordered, fetching a short-sleeved shirt that was too small for him. "Here, try this on lover. But do it slowly."

"You lecherous sod," she said with twinkling eyes.

Alec toweled and dried himself off in front of Alex and then sat on the end of the bath. "Well girl, what happened?"

"God knows, Alec. One second I was kissing you … the next, I was being pulled down."

Alec thoughtfully looked at the stone resting between her breasts. "Yeah. I've got a good idea what it was. Don't ask me how," he added quickly in answer to the look in her eyes. "I only know I couldn't pull your head out of the water and besides … look at the mark on your neck."

Alex fingered the painful weal.

"Take the damn thing off."

"I can't."

Alec questioningly looked at her, "What do you mean you can't? Take the bugger off."

"I told you. I can't ... I've tried."

Alec stared at her in disbelief. "You put it on, but you can take it off? Just slip the damn thing over your head."

"Alec, I've told you. I've tried, and it won't come off."

Alec stood up and crossed over to her. He palmed the stone and slid his fingers under the leather thong to lift them over Alex's head. They didn't go over Alex's head. He couldn't get the thong further than Alex's chin.

Mystified, he let the stone drop back to its resting place on Alex's breast. The thong was plenty long enough to go over the largest head. He tried again with two hands on either side of the thong and lifting slowly and gently. By the time the thong reached Alex's chin, somehow the thong lost some six inches of its length.

There was no way it could go over her head. For the next ten minutes, he tried over and over again. Each time he tried, it brought a fit of giggles from Alex. He tried picking the strange knot. The fact that, he too, started giggling made it more difficult. That proved impossible as well. The bathroom scissors made little impact; they

137

couldn't cut or even mark the damp leather.

"Aw… the hell with it," he said between fits of laughter, "You're lumbered with it, girl, and for Christ's sake, don't ever take a bath."

Alex wrinkled her nose, "Uhhhhh," she voiced. It sent them both into a paroxysm of laughter.

# CHAPTER TWENTY-ONE

Alec journeyed to Scotland by train. He left the car with the girls in case they needed it; it was a five-mile journey to post a letter from Wincle, never mind the shopping.

He'd spent a few days with the girls, getting Alex acquainted with the cottage and her new surroundings. He'd filled Mum in with more than a few details about Alex and persuaded her to stay and keep her company. Luckily, they got on like a house on fire. In fact, when he left they were deep in conversation discussing the merits of Yorkshire pudding.

Yorkshire pudding? A world may be falling apart at the seams, and they were discussing Yorkshire pudding. Alec never ceased to be amazed by the female brain and the female logic.

It was good for Alex though. Mum was good company for her. It would help keep her mind off the things that had happened. She looked a bit peaky and tired, although she slept well. Sex hadn't occurred since Scotland.

Alec kept himself busy over the last few days, but thoughts and questions persistently nagged him. In the end, he decided to try to get some of the questions answered. What better place to start than where it all started? Scotland.

He didn't have a clue as to who could help or explain. One thing was for sure though; if anything strange happened it would have been reported. It was news if it had been reported, and for news, you went to the Glasgow News Department. Luckily, he had friends there. His friends were in Drama, not in the News Department. They could put him on to those who could help.

He decamped from the train into the grimy railway station. His knees were slightly aching from hours of sitting. He stuffed *The Telegraph*, with its almost completed crossword, into his anorak pocket. He looked around him at the alighting passengers, judging their mood.

Alec was a seasoned train traveler, and he knew from experience that crowds alighting from a train fell into two categories. They either got off the train nice and easy, ambling to the exits, or they couldn't wait for their feet to hit the platform and started hurrying. Thank Christ they were ambling. He was in no mood for a mad dash for a taxi.

The black cab took him through the side streets of Glasgow avoiding the more obvious route. Alec had time to look at the grimy granite tenement houses towering over them on either side of the narrow streets. They were superbly built a hundred years ago, but had been allowed to lapse into decay by successions of inconsiderate or poor owners.

*How can a council let such beautifully built homes fall by the wayside like this?* Alec thought to himself. The cabby turned a sharp corner onto the answer of the unspoken question. On both sides of the narrow street, council workmen were cleaning, painting, and sandblasting a section of houses. The workmen were doing a magnificent job.

The full glory of the architecture and stonework of the houses had come back to life. It gave Alec an insight of what an incredibly wealthy city Glasgow had been in the 19th century.

Alec caught the cabby looking at him through the rear-view mirror. *The bugger must have guessed what I was thinking*, Alec thought as he smiled and nodded to the mirrored eyes.

"About bloody time," came the rasped response with an accompanying nod of the head in the direction of the renovations.

Having avoided the heavy traffic, the cab joined the main run up to the BBC. He'd made good time. Apart from being an amateur psychologist, he was also a damn good driver.

He dropped Alec off at the main entrance and smiled wryly as Alec tipped him handsomely. Alec checked his watch as he walked through the main doors. He'd made good time himself; arriving at lunchtime was perfect.

He crossed to the Commissionaire and flashed his BBC club card. He needn't have; they recognized him and waved him through. He made a beeline for the club. At lunchtime, that's where he'd find Rod. Let's face it, where else would you find news reporters?

Sure enough, Rod Graeme was there deep in conversation with a glass in hand. He was listening to three conversations at once, and his eyes were flickering about like a shithouse rat.

This man, one of the best producer/directors working under the aegis of the BBC, stood some six feet tall and weighed in at some sixteen stone. He had a rat trap mind, spoke English like the Queen's First Secretary, and buried himself in Glasgow.

Alec could never quite work that one out. From a drama point of view, Glasgow would never be a London. On the other hand, it wouldn't be through lack of trying on Rod's behalf. Against some pretty hefty odds, he turned out some marvelous work whilst at Glasgow. His flickering eyes fell on Alec in the bar doorway and rested for a second.

"Alec," the voice boomed out, immediately silencing the three conversations aimed at him. Fifty pairs of eyes focused onto to the recipient of the greeting. "My wee, little Lancashire lad, come and join us."

Alec smiled at the royal us, crossed to the bar, and took Rod's proffered hand. Rod bellowed over his shoulder to the barman, "Alistair. A gin and tonic, not too small, for this poor Englishman."

Lowering his voice to Alec, "I saw the first episode of your new series. Congratulations. You continue to improve."

"That's kind of you, Rod. Thank you, cheeky sod … Cheers."

"Don't mention it, Alec," and with tongue firmly planted in his cheek, "We all need the best help we can get in this business, Alec." He smiled back at Alec and took a large swig of his drink.

"So what are you doing up here in the Badlands. You on tour with a play?"

"No … Actually, Rod, I came to see you."

The eyes settled on Alec with a querying look. Still looking at Alec, he introduced his PA and director to him. Alec shook hands all around. The conversation took off in the direction of writers' lack of new ideas, quality of student actors from the dozens of polytechnics that sprung up around the country; as opposed to the old actor learning his trade the hard way, the only way … in weekly rep.

Alec joined in with gusto. As usual, he found the level of conversation lively and intelligent. There's something about people in the business; they don't nit-pick. Alec was enjoying himself, so he allowed the next half hour to fly by without buttonholing Rod. He bided his time.

He and Rod had known and worked with each other many years. He knew that Rod would know it was important and, although he was a busy man, would make some time for Alec.

Two more gins followed, and then Rod slipped his bear-like arm around Alec's shoulder. "Have you had lunch yet, Alec?"

"No, as a matter of fact, I haven't."

"Well, look," Rod said, glancing past Alec's face at the watch on his wrist, "you shoot off to the canteen and have some haggis and neeps. I'll see you at …what … 2:45, okay? Room 301."

"Yeah, that's fine with me Rod."

Rod slipped his arm down from Alec's shoulder, gave his upper arm a friendly squeeze, and immediately dropped into the technical conversation they were having prior to Alec's arrival. Alec downed his drink, said his farewells to the PA and director, and left for the canteen.

*Christ*, Alec thought, as he surveyed the fast food trays in the canteen. Rod was right; sure enough haggis and neeps was on the menu. He looked at it and toyed with the idea of trying some. The little fat lady, immaculate in her kitchen whites, smiled up at him.

"Yes dear," the Glaswegian accent as thick as butter on an Irish Navy's bread.

"Ham salad, please, love." He clucked silently to himself as he chickened out.

Alec took his tray to a corner table and unloaded the tray. He sat and commenced eating. The first mouthful told him how hungry he was.

*Funny*, he mused, *how you can go for hours and hours without eating. Possibly age. I certainly wouldn't have missed a mealtime when I was younger. Then again, what did Wally used to say? You can dig your grave with your knife and fork. Sound advice Wally. Sound advice, especially after seeing the haggis and neeps.*

He looked around the canteen. Not many were in at this time. The few that were in shoveled chips and God knows what else down their throats like there was no tomorrow. Some had their little carton of yogurt ready to follow the fat and calorie onslaught. It was a salve for their conscience no doubt.

Alec found himself wondering at the seating arrangement of a nearby party of five, consisting of four males and one very large female. The four men were sat opposite each other, and the woman sat at the head of the table.

*Now, did she arrive first and choose that position? Or did she arrive last and was given that position? Either way, it shows she had the authority. Why that particular table? Well for that matter, why did I choose this table? I always have a corner table. Why maybe it's because I want to do a Garbo? Bullshit. It's because it's the only position where you can see and be seen.*

Alec's eyes slid over the rest of the canteen and then through the window to the street below. The traffic journeyed silently along the broad street shadowed by the dark granite buildings on the opposite side of the road. Its shadings of darkness were impressive, only relieved now and then by blotches of green from the trees planted for that very purpose. *A dark city. Almost a colorless city*, Alec thought. However, its people were something else entirely. They were the very opposite.

"And talking about being seen. Why is it that I haven't seen you? Eh?" he muttered with his mood changing. "You're not with me are you? You're not here. Now why is that, I wonder? You follow us all the way from Scotland to Wincle. No, no. You are definitely not here; I can tell. Now … why … is … that, I wonder?"

Alec's face suddenly altered, and the fork in mid journey to mouth clattered to the plate. Alec felt his chest constrict and his breathing became shallow. "Oh, Jesus, no. Oh, sweet Jesus, no. It wasn't US he was following. It was Alex."

"Why Alex? Why Alex for Go-," Alec closed his eyes and clamped his jaw shut as realization dawned on him. *Shit … shit…shit. The fucking stone.*

Alec could feel the salad lumping in his stomach. Christ, if that thing puts Alex through what it had put him through in the chapel, it would blow her mind. *And what about Ma? Oh, no… For God's sake, it wouldn't … It wouldn't.*

Alec knew it would though. That thing, that old man, wasn't human. It didn't have feelings. Alec experienced the awesome power it commanded at first hand. It had only been playing with him, showing him, telling him. Telling him what though?

Was it not to get involved or to keep out of the way? He was already involved, and what would happen if he didn't keep out of the way? Alec's mind was spinning.

He searched in his pocket for his cigarettes and lit up. He was oblivious to the *No Smoking* sign. The intake of nicotine quieted his mind down.

*To keep out of the way, or else. Yeah, that sounds more like it. Why? It can't be frightened of me, no way. That thing's frightened of nothing. Fright doesn't enter its vocabulary, only to inflict it.*

He sucked on the cigarette again drawing the smoke deep into his lungs. Alec's mind, trained through years of acting, flipped back through the sightings he'd had of the presence with the precision of a seaside *What-the-butler-saw* machine. *Click - campsite. Click - railway station. Click - railway station, again. Click - the chapel. So why show out to me and not Alex? Because it's not sure of me? Which must mean he's sure of Alex.*

Alec put his cigarette out and rubbed his temples, where the beginning of a headache started to throb. The logic of it all escaped him. The whole fucking thing was illogical. Maybe the stone did belong to the old man. He reached for it that night he appeared, but Alex beat him to it. Maybe he wants it back. Who the hell is he? How do you give something back that you can't physically give back? *Would we be doing right by giving it back if we could give it back?*

Alec's head started to throb again. *Too many avenues. Too many maybes.* What he wanted was some facts, and then maybe, he might be able to sort it out.

He looked at his watch. It was time to go see Rod.

*** 

Rod's office door was open. He, his director, and PA were in deep discussion regarding a model that was lying on top of the desk. Beautifully made out of balsa wood and paper, it resembled the three interior, upper walls of a large hall with huge gothic windows.

Alec realized the problem straight away. Rod was obviously producing a play, and its major scenes were set in the room.

Unfortunately, TV studios are a mass of electronic gadgetry: lighting, sound, and cameras. All the gadgets require the necessary power to do their jobs, and all their power cables have to be hidden from viewers.

Television is a fairly close-up medium. What the viewer doesn't see is about four feet above the actors' heads. A million and one struts hold lights and monitor screens across the set. There is so much in such a large room that a long distance master shot is difficult to achieve.

Rod and his director were attempting to find the best position for the camera, thus masking out the ceiling and, no doubt, have his actors walk into shot in the background. Once establishing the effect of a vast, high room with large gothic windows, he could cut to the other cameras and work normally. Time on screen would be possibly ten seconds, but the time making and setting up the model could be possibly three weeks.

Alec smiled to himself. Rod was a bugger for detail. Rod looked up as though reading Alec's mind. "Ah … just in time young Alec. These two have just finished boring the arse off me."

The director and PA smiled knowing full well it had been the opposite. They left the office, and Rod turned to his percolator. He replenished the water and threw fresh grounds into the filter. The wonderful aroma of fresh coffee sang through the office.

Rod took a deep breath. "I just love that smell. Come, Alec … must go to the loo" he growled, squeezing past Alec in the doorway.

Alec smiled to himself and followed the shambling figure down the corridor. "Having problems Rod?" asked Alec as he unzipped his fly.

Rod kicked open a closet door behind

Alec. "No, not really. You know what these things are like. Dimensions have to be spot on, or the whole thing's a cock up."

Alec turned to see Rod drop his trousers and sit on the lavatory. He saw the thick thighs bunch, then overlap the seat like the ears of a cocker spaniel. *He's a big man*, thought Alec.

Rod grunted, changed color, and then farted. The makings of what passed for a smile eased across his face.

"Whatever happened to dignity?" asked Alec smiling.

"It went to the same place I'm going to flush this lot," grunted Rod.

Alec, still smiling, turned to wash his hands and looked at himself in the mirror. He was still washing his hands and looking at his image when Rod joined him some five minutes later.

The big bear arm came around his shoulders and softness crept into Rod's voice. "C'mon son. We'll have a cup of that fresh coffee and a chat."

His softness told Alec that Rod had been watching him in the mirror.

# CHAPTER TWENTY-TWO

Rod sat back in the chair after topping up the two mugs for a second time. The office was quiet and the smoke from Alec's cigarette hung in layers on the still air. Rod watched the smoke with lips pursed. The seconds ticked by. His fingers came up to pyramid his nose, and the gentle eyes flickered to cover Alec.

"Well, old son," came the measured tones, "I've known you some years now, and the very fact we're in this business tells us both that we have imaginations. Not," he said a little heavier to offset Alec's reaction, "that I think what you have just told me is just imagination."

The room seemed to grow quieter, "What to do, and where to start are the main problems," Rod continued.

"Don't try sticking me with some weirdo exorcist priest, Rod," Alec countered with a slight edge in his voice that didn't go unnoticed.

"It just won't bloody work. The cross, holy ground, and holy water ... Do me a favor. This thing or whatever made mincemeat of me ... IN A CHURCH."

Alec stood up in an effort to control

himself.

"Aw, what the hell. Hey, I didn't come here to involve you, Rod. You have enough on your plate. I just wanted help in trying to pinpoint why it happened and why us?"

He paused and looked at Rod. "I thought maybe the News Department could get me started."

The pyramid of fingers slid from either side of Rod's nose as he nodded. "Yes, yes. That's a damn good idea for a start. Here give me a cigarette, Al, for Christ's sake."

Alec proffered his packet to the eager Rod and for the first time in the past hour, started smiling. Rod promised his wife to give up smoking four years earlier. According to Alec, all he had done was giving up buying them. He was able to tell his wife and friends with a clear conscience that he hadn't bought a cigarette in four years; thus giving all the impression he stopped. A man of iron will.

After inhaling the nicotine, Rod continued,

"It might help to solve the problem why, but it won't solve the problem what and how to get rid of it."

"True," said Alec, "any ideas?"

Rod mused for a moment and his eyes gave to their flickering again. "Yeah, as a matter of fact, I do. What you want is someone with specialized knowledge. Not a priest, but someone who has made a life's work out of delving in the past ... say 2,000, 3,000, 5,000 years. Someone who translates Aramaic, Greek, Hebrew, and Latin like you and I reading *The Telegraph*. Because," he paused to look at Alec, "from your description of this thing and the stone, I get the impression of great age. Do you?"

"Yes. No doubt about it."

"Right then," Rod continued, "about seven years ago, I did a program on Massada, Israel. Specifically about some scrolls that were found during the excavations. I don't know if you know it, old son, but you're sitting right on top of one of the best universities in the world – Manchester. Obviously, from the look on your face you didn't know it," Rod grunted and continued.

"Anyway, the scrolls were sent there for reclamation and deciphering. It seems that part of the scrolls had been deciphered in Israel before being sent to Manchester, and news of their contents leaked out from Israel. It was, to put it mildly, earth-shattering, if true. So, I'm there with a crew and two jumps ahead of everybody, having already put two weeks in at Massada. It was the makings of an absolutely wonderful program."

Alec started smiling. If Rod said it was wonderful, you could bet your life it was brilliant.

"Then in walks this bloke, a little fella. He'd been away on a sabbatical whilst all this was going on ... Philip somebody or other. I'll find his name in the files," he said waving his hand behind him at the tin boxes on the floor. He leaned forward and stubbed out the cigarette with a movement that suggested he was really drilling for oil.

"Well, he takes a fragment of the scrolls, no bigger than a large postage stamp, and slots it under a microscope. He peers at it closely for maybe ten minutes, scribbles a few notes, and then quite calmly, in a very husky voice, tells one and all that they're fakes. Yeah ... fakes.

He then walks out of the room, leaving me with my bare arse hanging out. To cut a long story short, it took a further two months of the best brains in the country, if not the world, to concur with his ... well ... snap diagnosis."

Rod paused for a moment and shook his head in remembrance of the whole affair. "Now that's the kind of help you want. If this thing's got a past, he'll know about it."

Alec looked at Rod thoughtfully. "Yes, it sounds as though he could help."

"You can but try, Alec," said Rod, "meantime, why don't you nip down to 205, and ask for Megan. I'll phone her to let her know who you are. Whilst you're down there, I'll root out this fella's name.

If I'm not here when you get back, it's because I'll be in the studio. I'll leave the name on the desk."

Rod moved around the desk, his huge frame slightly dwarfing Alec. The friendly arm once more slipped around Alec's shoulder as they moved towards the office door.

"Thanks, Rod."

"Yeah. Hey, remember, I'm as far away as the nearest phone."

Alec nodded with a weariness starting to show through the smile on his face.

"Good luck, Alec," Rod whispered at the departing back.

# CHAPTER TWENTY-THREE

Alec knocked on 205 and entered. The office was large by BBC standards. It had four desks, four familiar-looking, shirt-sleeved bods, and phones that seemed to be ringing incessantly. It was a chaotic mess.

Alec stood there in silent wonderment as phones were answered, keyboards struck, and instructions and enquiries shouted. All of it was very reminiscent to Alec of Wall Street on a bad shares day. He gently shook his head at the noise and excitement generated by the room and its inmates.

*... and out of this ... comes order*, he thought, *twenty-five minutes of local news to be calmly and clearly enunciated by a news reader ... if the viewers only knew.*

"Alec?" questioned a strong, warmly-accented voice through the noisy room. Alec turned and realized that the office was partitioned off at one end with another smaller office. In the doorway was the owner of the voice. No wonder the men in the main office were familiar; it was the large lady from the canteen.

He returned the smile she gave as he threaded his way through to her. Nobody gave him a second glance. She thrust her hand out and shook his hand strongly. She was a whole lot of woman.

"Sit down Alec, sit down. I'm Megan," she said, closing the door behind her. It was like closing the door on a pressure cooker. "Rod's just phoned me and told me all about you. Told me to help, if I could."

She moved around the desk to sit down "Mind you, I recognized you in the canteen." Her voice was like warm milk and honey.

"I don't recall you looking at me, Megan."

"You wouldn't. We all thought you had swallowed your fork." A smile started across the round face, pleating her incredibly smooth complexion.

"Oh, Christ. That," said Alec, feeling slightly embarrassed. "Mind if I smoke?"

She looked at him with her brown eyes steady as Gibraltar. "No," she said quietly and shook her head as he offered her one.

It wasn't until he lit up and relaxed after the first lungful of smoke, he saw the little placard on her desk. It read *Thank you for not smoking.*

He looked at her, but she was one jump ahead. The smile started again as her hand reached out and tipped the placard face down. "Doesn't apply to you," she said calmly. Her brown eyes never left his face.

*My God, an understanding woman ... a forgiving woman*, he thought. Alec found himself instantly liking her.

She was big; she was just short of six feet, he guessed and around the twelve stone mark. She was very solid, and very, very shapely. The breasts under the pink lamb's wool twin set moved with a weight when she walked that was definitely not with fat.

Her face was round and encompassed with baby's skin. Whilst she was not exactly pretty, she was strikingly handsome and strong. Her hair, as thick as fuse wire, gleamed and fell in a brown cascade. Her eyes, whilst darker in color than her hair, held the same bright gleam.

*Yeah. All around, one helluva woman*, he thought.

"Right, Alec. How can I help?" Her eyes became serious, and the same seriousness tinged her lilting tones.

Alec paused in mid smoke and searchingly looked at her. She read his mind again. "Yes, Rod did tell me something about it. Just an outline, no bones."

Alec nodded and then looked beyond her to a large map of Scotland on the wall. He rose and crossed to the map. Using his finger, he indicated a circle around the Moray Firth where he and Alex had encamped.

"I'd like to know if anything strange … No, I'll rephrase that. I'd like to know if anything at all has happened in that area in the last month or so … newsworthy that is. I'll put the interpretation on it, whether it was strange or not."

Megan must have moved up behind him to look at the map, for the perfume of sandalwood pleasantly assailed his nostrils.

"The Moray Firth? Well thank heaven for that, Alec." The soft voice laughed in his ear.

The hairs on his neck started to lift, and the blood thumped through his veins as he felt the gentle pressure on his shoulder blade. It was like a little boy's finger poking in him.

"Not too much happens around there," she continued.

The full pressure of her breast came against him as she reached across to point at the map. She pointed at Glasgow, Edinburgh, and then at Fass Lane, the nuclear submarine base.

"Now if it was here, here, or here," her fingernail tapped the map, "… mountains of stuff."

Her face was now inches from Alec's as their two angled profiles stared at the map together.

Alec turned his head slowly towards her. Her brown eyes left the map to gaze steadily at Alec. The edges of her mouth lifted in a smile. Alec looked into the eyes, and under the veneer of calmness, he read pure lust.

*Fucking amazing*, he thought bitterly, *I come down here for help … my bare arse hanging out. I'm in the office two minutes and I'm getting propositioned.*

The seriousness of the situation immediately registered with Alec. Knock back Megan. He could well lose the only chance to clear up the Scottish end. *Hell hath no fury* … The only way to help Alex was to be unfaithful.

*Fuck, fuck … fuck. Talk about the devil and the deep blue sea.* He was caught between a rock and, in this case, a soft place.

He started to smile. "I agree," he said to her.

"With what?" came her soft reply.

"With what I see in your eyes … but," he said in quick answer to the gleam that was all too apparent in the brown depths, "later … Now the Moray Firth."

The smile on her face widened. "You're on," she said firmly. The tone of her voice told Alec there was no way out.

Almost immediately she turned back to the map. Her eyes narrowed in thought as her memory banks turned over. She turned to sit at her desk.

"Moray Firth … Moray Firth," she muttered as she mentally flipped through the millions of pieces of information stored there. Alec swore he could hear the whirring of her brain cells as the seconds ticked by.

"There was the Murmansk explosion that affected the fishing. A couple of boats got damaged, and fish moved from their traditional breeding grounds, etc …"

Alec looked at her and quietly reached for another cigarette in order not to disturb her. Her voice took on a monosyllabic flavor in the manner of a school child reciting an uninteresting poem.

"A private plane ditched; though, that was more towards Cromarty Firth … no bodies found, but three kilos of heroin was … estimated country of departure was Holland."

Alec shook his head after quickly weighing up the possibilities of the stone coming from a light aircraft.

"A sub aqua diver was found floating in his boat by a local fishing captain. He'd lost a lot of blood. Possibly a shark or moray eel attack, but no way of finding out. He was in shock … so much so that his hair turned white."

Alec froze. What in hell could turn a man's hair white in seconds? "Hold it Megan … When

162

and where?"

***

Alec sat on the bed with his back against the padded headboard and knees up. The gin and tonic Megan made for him was balancing on one kneecap. He looked steadily through his parted legs at Megan standing at the foot of the bed.

She was unshakeable. She was determined to have her pound of flesh. The way she was standing and slowly undressing, unconsciously tantalizing, it would soon be a pound and a half.

She took him to a lovely, little restaurant. She wined and dined him with no expense spared.

She was damn good company and with an intelligence that Alec thought was vastly superior to most men. Underneath it all, there was shyness that limited her. How the hell she ever picked up the courage to blatantly proposition him was beyond Alec. He must upgrade his ranking. There again, no need since he had the adorable Alex.

When it came to paying the restaurant bill, Alec reached in his pocket. She firmly told him that if his hand didn't come out empty, he'd be making love with a broken arm. He believed her. His first real taste of female emancipation, and he was all for it.

163

Megan kicked off her shoes. The wrap-around skirt slowly came undone and fell to the floor. Alec gave a sharp intake of breath. It was quite audible to Megan and made her smile more confidently.

The falling skirt revealed a superb statuesque figure. Her legs, thighs, and hips were molded in classical Greek form. White nylon stockings encased the legs to the lower thigh. They were held up by a tiny, frilly, white lace suspender belt, overlapping the sheerest of French cami knickers. The knickers clung tightly against her large thighs and buttocks. A dark mass of pubic hair, clearly visible under the skin-tight laciness, spread dark and inviting. She paused in her movements, and

Alec's eyes lifted to her smiling, confident face. "More girl, more." She complied. Her hands crisscrossed to the waistband of her sweater and with one neat, but oh-so-slow movement, removed it.

*Jesus H. Christ*, thought Alec. She didn't wear a bra. Normally, a bra is a must for such a big figure, but Megan had no need whatsoever for such a superfluous garment. Her breasts were proud, twin marble monuments of staggering shape and size. He could feel himself swell up, and the glass balanced on his knee began to shake and slide. He quickly caught the glass and placed it on the bedside table.

Megan moved towards the bed and in doing so, caught full sight of Alec's intumescing organ. Her eyes widened, and Alec swore blind that she visibly paled. Her breasts heaved with an intake of breath, and she didn't need Alec's hand raised in a stopping motion to root her to the spot.

Her eyes never left Alec's penis. He pulled himself forward until he sat at the foot of the bed facing her. He put his hands on her wide hips and pulled her towards him.

The smile on her face set. Alec noticed the playful gleam in her eye was replaced with not a fearful look, but definitely a look of uncertainty.

He smiled at her gently, but inwardly he was shocked to think Megan was as near to a virgin as *damn it* is to swearing.

He unbuttoned her suspenders and slid each stocking down as she obediently raised each knee in turn. He unclipped the belt and allowed it to slip to the floor. He raised his head and looked her full in the face.

"Megs," he whispered, "I swear to you by all the things you hold dearly that you will remember this night for the rest of your life."

With that, he put each thumb up the outer leg of her cami knickers. Holding the silky fabric, he gently slid them down. Millimeter by millimeter, the silky garment slid over her smooth belly until pubic hairs sprung over the lowering waistband.

Megan's breath was labored, and Alec's wasn't far behind. He looked up to her contorted face, and there was pain in her eyes. She was an atom away from an orgasm.

Alec leaned forward, and his lips touched the soft skin. Tiny swan's-down hair brushed his lips as his tongue played around her navel. His tongue went lower to contact the bramble of pubic hair.

Megan sucked in her stomach at the unusual, new pleasure. She groaned out loud and brought her arms around Alec's shoulders to support her buckling knees. Her breasts caressed Alec's face. Lost in swan's-down and sandalwood-perfumed flesh, Alec moved his hands to spread them over the large, firm buttocks. He felt them bunch with muscled power as Megan's orgasm burst through.

She gasped for breath and hung on to Alec's seated figure. She trembled throughout her whole body. Her knees, unable to sustain her weight any longer, folded, and she collapsed onto Alec's protruding knees. Her head came up slowly to look at Alec. Her brown eyes were glowing in wonderment.

"Alec … that was … incredible," she

whispered.

He kissed her on her soft moist lips. "I haven't got started yet, girl," he whispered back, "It's time you had a real orgasm, not a second hand one."

"Ohhhhh, yes please."

Alec supported her as she regained her composure, and stood up. He finished removing her French knickers, and the full spread of her pubic hair came to light. It amazed Alec. The hair, as thick and wiry as the covering on an afro head, spread in profusion up her belly and across her thighs. Alec stood up.

"Don't move," he said, "don't move a muscle." He leaned in and kissed her on the mouth as he slid between her and the bed.

He disappeared into the bathroom and returned holding something behind him. He sat on the bed as before and with his knees between Megan's, began to spread her legs. He smiled at the quizzical, but expectant look on her face.

"I like to see what I'm eating, woman, so stand by for a Vidal Sassoon."

A buzz hummed through the room as he switched on the razor he found in the bathroom. His left hand slipped through her legs and grasped her large, firm buttocks. His center finger caressed the velvety channel lying between them. The muscles tightened under his playing finger and trapped it firmly.

He laughed as he took the trimming edge to the thick bramble. Megan's fingers dug into his shoulders as the vibrating instrument fleetingly rested against her. She leaned her body over Alec's head, and her huge breasts once more surrounded him with their sandalwood scent. She squirmed in delight.

Alec stuck to his task with great delight, stopping occasionally to kiss and tongue her breasts that were lying warmly against him. With the finesse of a farmer collecting silage in a ten-acre field, he neatened the mass of wiry bramble to a vertical, half-inch strip. He looked down between his feet at the scattered pubic debris.

"You've got some carpet sweeping to do tomorrow, Megs," he muttered, just before he caught the tiny pink nipple of her left breast between his teeth. Megan moaned but didn't answer, and her nails dug deeper in his back.

Alec played the body of the vibrating, humming razor over the widening lips of her, now visibly wet, cavity. Her head came down, and her tongue played in his ear. His organ was bursting; it stood immensely proud.

He felt her knees start to buckle. Dropping the razor to the floor, he gently pulled her down to position her over the head of his organ. She gasped in anticipation for what was to come and threw her head back. Unable to sustain her weight any longer, her knees gave way, and she sank. With an exhaling of breath that was almost a scream, she impaled herself on the full massive length.

It was early morning. Alec could see the dirty grayness that tinged the blackness of the night peeking through the panes of Megan's neatly curtained windows. He moved his body carefully, so as not to disturb the exhausted, sleeping Megan.

He looked at his watch and read 3:00 am. He reached his hand out further and picked up the remains of the gin and tonic. It was warmish but cut through the clag in his mouth.

*Where the hell are my cigarettes?* He could murder one. He looked at the bedside table where he retrieved his drink, and the small lamp was still burning. He saw an ashtray. The sight of the *Thank you for not smoking* sign on Megan's desk at the BBC flashed through his mind.

*That's funny. She doesn't smoke. Why have an ashtray by the bed? For men friends ... lovers? No, no. Megan certainly wasn't promiscuous. She acted like a virgin ... almost. Or like a woman with many years between sexual encounters. No. That's not quite right*

*either. She would know what it was all about in
that case.*

Alec looked down at her. She was lying
on her stomach with her left arm across his
lower stomach, her head turned away. His eyes
roamed down the Michelangelo figure, down the
dipping back and the rising mound of her
buttocks.

Memories of the bunching power thrusting at
him brought a pleasurable flame into his groin.
He could feel himself growing. He looked at the
dark brown, shining mass of thick hair curled
across his shoulder. He remembered the scared
look that crept into her eyes. Tenderness flooded
him, and he had an urge to stroke her head as
one would a small child.

His eyes dropped again to the mound her
buttocks made under the thin sheet covering. He
eased the sheet away, and the full glory came to
view. He was fully rampant now. He leaned
over and kissed her silky skin, allowing his
tongue to twist and curl in the valley.

Her breathing altered and slowly, oh so
slowly, her legs parted under his gentle
fingering. A low moan came from her throat.
His fingers became moist, and she was ready to
take him.

Her moans were coming quicker now as he
bestrode her magnificent body and placed the

head of his swollen organ between the lips. He thrust the head into the tight orifice, and she came instantly. He could feel the moisture flood over him as her buttock muscles tightened.

It gave Alec immense pleasure, since he knew she would have another orgasm before he finished. He threw himself forward onto that wonderful body and slowly thrust into her. Her moans started again and drove Alec wild.

\*\*\*

Alec awoke about an hour later. It took some moments to realize exactly where he was and the position he was in. He found himself lying on the back of the statuesque Megan. Further more, he was still buried inside her. He kissed her shoulder and as gently as possible, withdrew himself from her.

"No ... No. Stay in," Megan's voice, still in deep sleep, muttered.

Alec was dying for a cigarette. He looked at the ashtray. *She's a reformed smoker. That must be the reason for the ashtray. Now then, does she keep a pack around in order to make her feel good, or did she throw them all out?*

He slid the tiny drawer open in the bedside cabinet. He found a partly used packet of cigarettes and some matches. He lit up, and

171

the movement and sound disturbed Megan.

She turned her head, still in sleep, to rest her cheek on Alec's chest. He looked down at her; her face was totally unlined in sleep. *How old did she say she was? 29? She looks more like 17 lying there.* A touch of guilt flushed through him as he thought of Alex.

He inhaled deeply on the smoke. "Shit," he muttered more loudly than he thought.

Megan's eyes flickered and opened. "Robert L. Stewart," she mumbled.

Alec looked at her and after a moment, "Robert L. No, don't tell me. The L stands for …"

"Right the first time, Alec. Louis." She sucked in the moisture in her mouth; some of it already seeped onto Alec's chest. Embarrassingly, she rubbed it in with her fingers and rolled over onto her back. Her breasts jutted upwards.

"He lives out at Gourock. He has a small cottage there." She stifled a yawn and looked at Alec apologetically. Alec smiled and nodded. He knew she had every right to be tired. Multiple orgasms can be draining.

"We tried for an interview," she continued, "… on film, of course, but it was a no-go. He wouldn't speak to anyone, let alone be filmed.

172

I caught a glimpse of him through the cottage window ... a squat, craggy type with an incredible shock of white hair. According to the neighbors ... That's a laugh.

The neighbor nearest to him is about a mile or two away. Anyway, according to them, a fortnight before, his hair was as red as a boiled lobster's arse."

She paused and looked at Alec. "So we don't know what happened, but the time and the area are right for you."

Alec listened quietly, pulling gently on what was left of the cigarette.

"Now then," she took his hand and placed it firmly on the thin line of fur between her legs and then crossed them, "are you going to tell me what it's all about, or are they going to find us dead from exhaustion?"

Alec narrowed his eyes and put on his Humphrey Bogart expression. "Exhaustion, kid, exhaustion."

Alec breakfasted in the canteen. He hadn't allowed Megan to fuss over him in her neat flat. He had coffee and that's all. They drove into Glasgow in near silence.

It was not a forced silence, but a silence that both required. The silence was replete. *The cat that's had the cream*, thought Alec as he looked at her profile.

He thanked her for a wonderful evening. Coloring slightly, she insisted the pleasure was all hers.

"Not quite, Megs, but I understand what you're saying." Alec smiled at her. She really was one hell of a girl.

He pecked her on the cheek as he broke for the canteen. He knew full well he'd be seeing her shortly for Robert L. Stewart's address. He'd also go to see Rod. Getting entangled with Megan forced him to miss calling on Rod for the information he had.

After breakfasting light and lingering over his second coffee to pass some time and to allow people to surface, he decided to phone home before going to Megan's office. His mother must have been sitting on the phone. He didn't hear it ring before she answered.

"Just dusting Alec, just dusting," she answered his query.

"Yeah? I know your dusting, Ma. So what have you been doing?"

"What else, but managing."

"Without your favorite fella?"

"To be honest Al, we hadn't noticed you'd left," she replied.

Alec could hear the laughter in her voice. Her reply was given in a slightly louder tone, obviously for Alex's benefit. She was no doubt hovering in the background.

"I'm taking Alex shopping today. She needs one or two things. Then I thought we'd -"

"Macclesfield?" Alec cut her off, "Aw … c'mon, Ma. Nobody goes to Macclesfield. Even the birds have stopped flying in Macclesfield."

"Then," she came back firmly, "I thought we'd go to Prestbury, to the Old Chocolate Box, for tea and toast."

"Now you're talking, Ma."

"Yes, I thought you'd like that."

She was 250 miles away, but he could see her eyes twinkling.

"Afterwards … assuming it stays nice, we'll probably end up at Gawsworth Old Hall for some nostalgia."

"And cream buns, heh?"

"And, as you say, Alec, some cream buns."

"Look after her, Ma," he said softly.

"Like she was my own, Alec … like she was my own."

"I'll ring you tonight."

"Bye, son."

The phone clicked in his ear, and Alec stood for a moment listening to the dead line. His eyes vacantly roved over the telephone graffiti scattered on the wall. He replaced the receiver.

He continued staring at the wild variety of names and numbers: some scrawled, some neat, some pen, some pencil, some written at an angle that only a circus contortionist could have written and answered the phone at the same time. Amongst all this, someone had neatly drawn two cubes and penned underneath *Picasso's Balls*.

Alec just stared at the cubes. His normally wild sense of humor was untouched. His face impassive, he removed his hand from the receiver and slowly walked to Megan's office.

Why had the phone conversation left him feeling down? Why the planned itinerary for her and Alex? His mother hadn't planned a thing in her entire life. They even joked about his conception.

Alec got the feeling that his mother sussed something. She hogged the phone and never asked if he wanted to speak to Alex. Was Alex okay? Was the planned day to keep her mind occupied?

*Oh shit. Come on … pull yourself together, Al. You can't be in two places at the same time. The sooner you get to the bottom of this thing, the better.*

\*\*\*

He tapped on 205 and entered. The quietness of the room surprised him, especially after the hubbub of the previous day. Megan was standing in a corner, leaning back against a radiator with a group of men seated around her. They sifted sheets of paper and news items.

They were deciding on what stories carried weight, local interest, what to use, and what to discard. Megan looked up and saw Alec. She waved him in with the plastic cup from which she was drinking. She pushed herself off the wall and headed for her small office.

The smile on her face communicated itself to Alec and lightened his spirit.

"Coffee Alec?" she said brightly.

*By God, she's glowing*, thought Alec, as he looked into her smiling brown eyes and the even whiteness of her teeth between her soft open lips. "You are one helluva woman Megs," he said admiringly, "and yes, I will have a coffee."

He lit up a cigarette and leaned forward to turn her *Thank you for not Smoking* sign face down on the desk as she poured the coffee.

The action didn't go unnoticed by Megan. She smiled broadly at him again as she served him. She turned to the map on the wall.

"Right, Alec…" her tone turned a little brisk and business like, though still managing to keep its warmth. Her finger nail dug into the linen map with a sharp crack. "That's about the spot where Rabbie Stewart was picked up. Now where were you?"

Alec crossed to the map while sipping the hot coffee. Seconds passed as he oriented himself. He remembered the length of the hitch that he and Alex had caught during the several hours they walked. It wasn't easy with Megan's eyes playing clinically over his face.

He gently extended a finger from the hand holding the plastic cup. It pointed forward until it touched the map. Alec's fingernail, over long for a man, touched and mated with Megan's.

\*\*\*

"So what's the story, Megs?" Alec's shallow breathing and heartbeat leveled off to a more normal rate. The tendons in his neck relaxed. His lips, pressured into a thin line, opened sufficiently to speak and take a sip of coffee. His mind and imagination were spinning again.

*What the hell has a scuba diver to do with what happened to me and Alex? A scuba diver has an accident, so what? So the accident or whatever happened to him was unusual, so what?*

*It happened more or less in the area where*

178

*we were encamped, so what? So what, you*
*stupid sod. Coincidence is one thing, but this*
*gut feeling is another. The two are linked, but*
*how? Why? Where? Christ knows.*

*What was it Megs said? Rabbie Stewart*
*had turned white ... turned white? Jesus, you*
*read about these things. People have shocks,*
*traumas, and going gray early. But white and*
*almost immediately?*

Alec unconsciously ran his fingers
through his short hair. *I reckon I should be*
*white by now, so whatever happened to Rabbie*
*Stewart must have been something else ...*
*something else.*

He lit another cigarette. His actions were
expert, dexterous, and automatic. They were the
actions of a man who spent most of his life with
a glass in one hand, whilst the other extracted
and lit a cigarette. It was a feat, almost sleight of
hand to the onlooker, but as natural as breathing
to Alec.

He suddenly realized he'd been so deep in
thought that Megan hadn't answered his
question. He looked up at her. She sat behind
her desk, quietly and patiently looking at him.

Their eyes met. The deep brown, gentle eyes
were thoughtful and patient. She was biding his
time and waiting for him to come out of his
reverie. The seconds ticked by in the quiet room.

179

"More coffee, Alec." It wasn't a question. It was a statement; a statement of what was required. The richly spoken words reverberated in the room. Surely, no accent in the world could touch the Scots for depth, character, love, and innuendo. Alec silently marveled and envied the ethereal sounds as he smiled and offered his cup.

# CHAPTER TWENTY-FOUR

Alex drove. It was not that Ma wasn't a good or capable driver, maybe more appropriate, she was. You don't get much of a chance to see the countryside when you are driving and trying to steer down narrow country lanes and bends. Rabbits randomly jump out, and magpies seem to hold their coffee mornings in the middle of the road.

She elected Alex to do the driving. It would also help to take her mind off things. Ma didn't know, but Alex grew much quieter over the last couple of days. The spontaneous chat that bubbled between them, as natural as a mountain brook after the rains, developed into great lapses of silence between them.

She wasn't ill; at least she didn't look ill. She said that nothing was ailing her in answer to Ma's questioning. Her pallor altered though. The shadows under her eyes had a grayish tinge, and the grayness crept under her tanned skin. Hence, Ma was determined to get this lovely and very likeable girl out of the house for a day. What does a girl of any age like doing best, but shopping?

Subject to the weather, Ma told Alec on

the phone what she had in mind, and the day was fine. The hawthorn blossom hung heavy in the air as they started off from the cottage. The sun hung golden in the blue, cloudless sky.

Ken and Ada were rounding up the fat lambs on their smallholding, as Ma and Alex slipped over Danebridge and headed up towards the *Ship Inn*.

One or two hikers were already abroad with maps in hands and packs on backs. With raised eyes, they contemplated the distant walks that disappeared into the surrounding hills.

Alex changed down a gear as they approached *The Ship* and the scarecrow in the field opposite. Frank and Joan were outside, no doubt, discussing the hanging baskets and pots of geraniums displayed outside the pub. They turned as they heard the engine growl, saw Ma, and waved cheerily. Alex joined in and waved back with Ma.

"It's a lovely spot, Alex," Ma said sitting back in her seat.

Alex nodded and concentrated on navigating the car around the bend and down the steep hill past Wincle Church. The car climbed in third gear for the next mile, until they came to the main road between Buxton and Macclesfield.

The road, really no wider than the lane they

just came off and just as quiet, seemed to lie on the roof of England. Ma told Alex to stop the car near the *Fourways Café*, and she alighted. Alex watched her for a moment, and then joined her.

"Have you seen anything prettier, Alex?" Ma asked, pointing down the valley towards Wincle and then moving her arm in a semi-circle. Alex agreed. It was beautiful.

The fields, where the farmers collected their winter silage, were a chessboard of different greens and yellows. Dry stonewalls crisscrossed in neat, straight lines to fade away into the hazy distance. Trees of deep, dark greens were partly hiding the distant, tiny black and white cows. Sheep looked like little, white moving dots around the odd farmhouse tacked into the hillside against the dark blue backdrop of the hills. It was like a painting, a masterpiece.

Ma turned, and Alex followed her eye line down the road they would be taking. The road fell steeply at first and then less so as it melted in to the horizon. Fields on either side rose to hilly heights, giving sustenance to more sheep and cattle. Once more, the checkerboard effect of greens and yellows was repeated. Away in the distance, the nearest town of Macclesfield, known locally as Silktown, could be seen.

Ma took a deep breath and her eyes twinkled.

"Clean air … Mmmmm. Not much of it

around these days, Alex."

Alex was forced to give a little smile and copied Ma's deep breath, but then broke into a hammy, TB cough. "I don't think I'm used to it," she gasped.

They both broke into fits of laughter, and Ma knew the day was going to be a good one. Alex turned back to the view down the valley.

"Where's the cottage, Ma? I don't see it."

"Oh. The trees near the river hide it. It's about … ohh …" She searched for a focal point to use as a marker. "Look. Do you see that old scarecrow? It's in the field by *The Ship*."

Alex peered against the brightness of the day and finally found the tiny brown figure highlighted against the pale green of the field.

Ma continued, "Well, if you take a straight line to the right, then over the river and behind that clump of tall pines is the cottage."

Alex nodded and slowly her eyes reverted to the tiny brown dot of the scarecrow. Her eyes narrowed, but the distance was too far for detail.

Ma laughed suddenly. "You know my eyes aren't what they used to be, but I could have sworn that scarecrow was facing *The Ship* when we passed it. It seems to be facing us now."

Alex lifted her hand to shield her eyes, but it really was too far. The stance and arms lying stiffly away from the body were a fleeting, forgotten familiarity.

She shrugged her shoulders and smiled at Ma. "Well, are we going to buy up the town or not Ma?"

"That we are Alex ... That we are."

The car moved off in the direction of Macclesfield, while Frank and Joan decided which geraniums to repot outside *The Ship*. They were too engrossed to notice that the still, brown-cloaked figure in the opposite field commenced to move over the grass.

They didn't hear the steady slap, slap of its sandals hitting its heels as it strode through the long grass. Nor did they see the impenetrable high hawthorn hedge that separated the tenth acre from the sixteenth acre wilt and wither before the moving figure.

# CHAPTER TWENTY-FIVE

Rod's PA was at the scanner and by the look of things, finalizing some script changes. A thick pile of scanned camera scripts lay nearby as her fingers flew over a keyboard. Her face screwed up in concentration.

Alec tapped on the clear glass panel and entered as she looked up. The concentration on her face relaxed into a big smile as she recognized Alec. "Hi," she said, "Come in."

She pulled her shoulders back and raised her arms to ease her cramped muscles.

"Is Rod around?" asked Alec.

"Popped out for two minutes but due back any second," she replied.

"You look busy."

"We're never anything but busy in this mad world. Everything's wanted yesterday. I've had enough," she said, nodding at the monitor, "I'm almost through … Do you mind if I carry on?"

"Good God, no. Be my guest."

"Great," her head nodded towards a chair, "Sir won't be long … Sit down."

"Thanks."

Alec seated himself in the BBC producers issue and took his cigarettes out. He looked around the office for an ashtray and caught the PA's eye. He held the packet up quizzically, and she nodded assent. The first puff of smoke drifted up to the ceiling, and Alec leaned back in the chair watching it lazily spiral and layer.

Megan's story about Rabbie Stewart was intriguing to him. It lay on a razor edge between laughable and deadly serious. The interpretation depended upon what kind of mind the listener had.

A logical mind gave completely logical explanations and so the loss of a good story and the truth. But to Alec, an illogical explanation of Rabbie Stewart's happening gave a logical conclusion. He'd witnessed and been part of crazy things over the last several days. If it were missed by a newshound, Alec would have missed it.

*Something scared Rabbie Stewart shitless, and something scared me shitless. Could it be the same thing? I've seen it. Did Rabbie see it?*

*Rabbie was in a boat on the water. Did he disturb something under the water?*

Alec blew more smoke, as the keyboard clacking grew more intense. The stone seemed to come from the sea or at least from the direction of the sea. The man, or whatever the hell he is, appeared to be soaking wet the night he arrived.

"Well, Rabbie, old son, it's down to you," Alec murmured.

"Just about finished, Alec." The PA must have heard him. Alec grunted still deep in thought.

*So why didn't Rabbie confide in someone? Because he thought no one would believe him.*

Alec suddenly grew impatient. He needed answers, and he needed them fast. He needed help, but he couldn't go to the helper half-cocked.

He found himself torn between Rabbie and this Phil bloke Rod was putting him on to. Rabbie was here in Scotland, and Phil's address was 250 miles away.

Alec jumped up as a sudden thought struck him. He spoke to the PA. "I don't know what I'm waiting for Rod for. He said he was leaving me an address on his desk. Can you see it, love? No use bothering him any further."

The PA gave a final tap on the keyboard and looked up at him. "There … finished, thank God. Now let me get this lot out of the way, Alec, and we'll have a look-see. Although, he did say for you to wait for him."

She neatened and piled the mess of sheets

scattered over the desktop with a practiced hand and slipped them into several folders. Within seconds, order reigned and she looked through Rod's various papers for the information Alec required.

"Is this it, Alec?" She was holding a sheet of BBC letterhead that had a business card stapled in the corner.

Alec looked over her shoulder. The card read *Dr. Philip Grossman*. A mess of letters followed the name like a dyslexic alphabet. The address was C/O Manchester University, Ancient Studies Department. "That's it, darlin."

A quiet excitement bubbled in Alec's stomach as he looked at the card. He flipped the card and ran his eyes down the BBC paper. It seemed to be a character analysis and CV combined.

What this man had done, or masterminded, was incredible. A list of familiar names, countries, and digs were double-banked on the sheet to make room for them all. Alec whistled softly through his teeth. The man appeared to be part Sherlock Holmes, part Einstein, and part Da Vinci. To Alec, he was pure savior.

He tore the card off the sheet. Impatience was edging through the calm; he wanted to be off. "File this for me, love. Will you?" he said, handing the letterhead to the PA. "I wouldn't like Rod's files to be upset."

"They won't be," a familiar gruff voice growled from the doorway. "Don't dash off, bugger," Rod said to Alec, "I want a word with you."

He looked at the PA, and his eyes said it all. Complete with files, she scampered quickly through the door and closed it gently behind her.

Rod made straight for the coffee pot with cup in hand.

"Now then, first things first. Give me a cigarette and sit down."

Alec, slightly bemused by Rod's manner, complied with both orders. Rod paused whilst he sipped his coffee and lit up.

"Right … I've just had a word with Megan, and I also managed to speak to Phil Grossman. Megan filled in some corners of the picture and also filled me in as to what I'll call your mental state."

He held up a hand to cut off Alec's reply. "No, no. Hear me out. It's important for your safety. I had a long chat with Grossman," he added meaningfully.

Silence descended on the small office.

"What did Megan tell you?" Alec said finally with an edge to his voice.

"Nothing for you to be embarrassed about," Rod threw back.

"Only I can be the judge of that, Rod ... and who the hell are you to be asking a girl what the fella she just slept with was like. Heh?"

Rod looked at him calmly, paused to inhale, and then baldly said, "Her father."

Alec felt the ceiling pressing down on him. He stared incredulously at Rod. Rod nodded affirmation at Alec's questioning gaze. "Oh ... Rod."

"Don't..." came the hard reply, " Don't feel embarrassed. Last night you did all three of us a favor ... Megan, myself, and you." Rod looked at the crestfallen Alec, and continued in quick explanation.

"Megan, well because at a very early age ... twelve to be precise, some bastard raped her."

His voice took on a murderous tone at the recalled memories, and his eyes edged in pain.

"She can't stand a man touching her, or she couldn't stand a man touching her," he quickly added smiling.

"Now you have altered all that ... And me? I'm getting older, and it's nice to think that your kids are matched up and maybe settling down. I was worried, Al. Been living with it far too long ... far too long."

He gave a sigh that told Alec everything and forgave everything. It seemed to come from his soul. "And you …" he continued more slowly as though picking his words carefully. "Well, we have known each other, on and off, for a long time now, Al. Through our work, I think we have come to respect each other. At least, I know I have a great deal of respect for you."

He paused to look at Alec carefully. His eyes gazed steadily and intently at Alec, gauging the effect of each word he spoke almost like the cameras he controlled. "When you walked through the doorway of the bar yesterday, trouble was written all over you. You have a very expressive face, Alec. Your feelings and thoughts show quite clearly. That's why you're in work so much," he added smiling.

He paused yet again and his smile receded. "I believed every word you told me and what's more … so did Grossman."

Alec took out another cigarette and threw one across to Rod. He tried to make the action calm and casual to hide the nervousness in his bowels. Rod's tone of voice and deliberate speech told him something was coming.

"It is essential, Alec, that you don't go off half-cocked against this thing. Mentally, you have to be as sound as a bell because, old son …" The pause was like the silence of the grave, "you have one helluva fight on your hands. I can't help you. No one can … even Grossman might not be able to."

Alec looked at Rod.

"That's right … his own words, Alec. He said something I thought very succinct. He said he was like an old armorer, and given the knowledge of what the enemy was, he could, perhaps, fashion the weapons and find a weakness, but it is your fight."

Alec suddenly felt very lonely. The room seemed to enlarge. Rod, behind his desk, appeared to be a hundred yards away. His speech sounded hollow and echoed around the room. *Jesus, how do you fight a thing like this? … On my own? On my own for Christ's sake!*

"Alec, Alec," Rod's commanding voice broke through his near panic thoughts. Alec grunted and looked back at Rod.

"The important thing is given the knowledge of what the enemy is," Rod repeated Dr. Grossman's words. "In other words, if you're infested with ants, you get out the ant powder. It's no use waving your ant powder under the trunks of a herd of bloody elephants. Do you understand?"

Rod forcefully enunciated each word. He could see Alec had near fallen apart. "Answer me, damn you," he bellowed.

It was a slap in the face. Alec's spinning

wheel brain smacked into cog. He shook his head. Rod was back to being four feet away albeit with a red face.

"I hear you loud and clear, Rod … very loud and clear," he replied with a smile. The tone was cool and calm.

"Good," said Rod gruffly. He was quite amazed at Alec's recovery. "So remember Phil Grossman will want to know the far end of a fart, if he's to try and help. So we'd better get you organized with a hire car, so you can find this Stewart fella."

Rod came from out of his chair to sit perched on the desk in front of Alec. "Pump the bugger dry, Al. Get as much out of him as you can," he said fervently. "A tip from my investigative journalism days, take a bottle with you … You're in Scotland, remember?" he added with a wink.

# CHAPTER TWENTY-SIX

A small town, possibly older than London, most certainly lived here in the Stone Age right through to the Iron Age. The requirements for life were, and still are, abundant: stone, running water, lush fields, and good forests. Roman roads ran throughout the area showing its importance to the Romans.

Kings and queens resided here for years at a time. Edward I (Longshanks) made it his home, whilst he outfought and outwitted the Welsh in the late 1200's.

The Black Prince, warrior son of Edward III, had a great liking for the town and its people. He had a right to, for no where in the world could provide the expertise in the longbow as the young men did from this small town. Proof of what these two hundred archers could do lie in the mud of France at Crecy and Poitiers and later still at Agincourt.

Seven hundred years ago, a boy was considered a man at the age of fifteen. Two hundred such men, lauded by their sovereign, were paid very highly for their expertise. Arrogant and insolent in their lifestyle, they were the medieval version of the SAS and nuclear deterrent all rolled into one.

The modern day town's youth and that of seven hundred years ago were a mirror image. A natural canniness affiliated with a capacity for hard work enabled the town to become an oasis in the world's desert of recession and unemployment.

Throughout the many centuries, the people of the town retained a lot of their character, but not so the town. Alec didn't like the town. Maybe it was not so much the town he disliked, but more of a dislike for what the town planners had, in their poor wisdom, allowed to happen to it.

For instance, the *Marks & Spencer* that Ma and Alex were about to enter was originally the site of a large mansion built in the late 1300's. Original walls existed but, according to Alec, weren't given a chance of revival by the arrival of three feet of concrete that was laid with untimely haste.

"All for the sake of rates," said Alec, "The almighty taxes that produced the wherewithal to finance the wheels of progress. You don't get much income from seven-hundred-year-old walls."

This was the town of Macclesfield. Its folk were a cross section of farmers and industrialists, and its shops reflected their every need. It was a busy little town. Close your eyes for twenty seconds as a passenger in a car. When you open them again, you'll find that not only had you entered the town but you had also left.

Ma liked Macclesfield, and Alex took an instant liking to it. "It's got everything and everybody," Ma said. "Rich people, working folk, writers, TV stars. To cap it all, I've just seen a Buddhist monk complete with sandals."

Alex laughed and then made a beeline for the shop-soiled counter to look for a bargain with Ma following behind like a ship in full sail. They tore through *M & S* like a dose of liver salts. They exited an hour later with the ubiquitous plastic bags. Ma then took Alex around the corner and into the covered market.

The smell of fresh farm cheeses, roast hams, and fresh baked baps made their mouths water. They nibbled a selection of samples of this, that, and the other. They later discovered they made a wild variety of purchases far too much for their needs, but what the hell, it was fun.

From there, they walked the short distance to *John Douglas* and drooled over the fashions paraded before them. Alex was amazed that such fashionable clothing could be found in a small town like Macclesfield. Ma pointed out that if there wasn't a market for expensive fashion in the area, there wouldn't be a shop.

David, the young owner, smiled and waved at Ma. It was obvious to Alex that Ma was a valid customer in the shop. He caught Ma's attention again across the busy shop floor and pointed at one of his assistants walking around in an elegant creation. He then pointed at Alex while circling his thumb and first finger. Alex and Ma caught on to his long distance selling, and Alex mimed opening her handbag and emptying it to explain it was empty. His young face beamed as his shoulders moved upwards in a Gallic shrug.

After half an hour and a few words with the busy and likeable David, they left *John Douglas* and made their way back to the car. Thankfully, they laid their purchases on the back seat of the car, puffed, and smiled at each other for several seconds.

"Prestbury next stop," Ma told Alex, "for a nice cup of tea."

Alex fervently agreed.

\*\*\*

Prestbury, the village annex of Macclesfield and just a good walk away from the town, was a village 800 years old. According to the <u>Sunday Times</u>, it was the richest village in England. Some, of course, would argue this and some wouldn't.

It's tiny, neat, and whitewashed. Its houses are a mixture of centuries-old, tiny Weavers' cottages and old mansions, overlooked by a wonderful old church. The church, set smack in the middle of the village, broods over it like an old mother hen.

The village church is very old; a Saxon cross taken from the wall of the church was found to be over 1000 years old. A neat, stone-carved building just to the right of the church was identified as a Norman chapel. It was proof indeed that Prestbury Church was the mother church to Macclesfield as far as the 1200's. No doubt, Prestbury was as wealthy then as it is now.

Ma told Alex to park the car outside the church. The one lane going through the village was narrow and normally parking was difficult, but Ma's beady eye had spotted a place.

Alex drank in the tranquility of the village as her eyes roamed the lines of the church and the quaint cottages and shops that lined the hundred yards or so that was Prestbury.

Ma looked at Alex as she soaked up the atmosphere, "She's enjoying herself ... good," she murmured.

She called to Alex, and they entered *Ye Olde Chocolate Box.* Ma went through the shop and up the stairs calling out greetings to the staff and owners.

The upstairs room of the *Chocolate Box* was decked out as a tea room with old oak tables and chairs. Jars of jam, honey, and marmalade mingled with oak beams and brassware. The jolly ladies who ran the room welcomed them with a warm smile. "Four burnt … two Earl, Mrs. Sterne?"

Ma nodded and then laughed as she saw Alex's uncomprehending expression. She sat down on a window seat. "It means four slices of brown bread, well toasted, and a pot of Earl Gray tea for two … It's their verbal shorthand," she explained.

Alex smiled at the explanation and followed Ma's gaze out of the window. It was a good spot to see everything. Directly opposite, across the narrow lane, was the *Legh Arms*. Alec once said that you get an expensive meal with a good, but expensive pint there. Legh was a local family name with an impressive history.

Sir Piers Legh fought with distinction at Agincourt and was knighted in the field for his efforts by Henry V. His father, however, was a different kettle of fish. He was executed by Henry IV for siding with Richard II. Playing with kings seemed to be something of a pastime for local folk. Some you won, and some you lost.

The tea and toast arrived; it looked delicious to Alex. The crisp toast, the fresh jam, and the piquant aroma of Earl Gray were just too much for two hungry girls.

Alex leaned across for some jam. The hidden stone fell out from under the shirt she was wearing and hit the table with a thud. Ma looked quickly at the thronged necklace and stone and then at Alex. The jokey repartee she was about to release froze in her mouth.

Alex was positively gray. Ma was shocked at Alex's attempted smile as she pushed the stone back under her shirt. Alex continued eating, unaware of her appearance and the turmoil she caused in Ma.

Ma looked down at her plate, and somehow, the crispy toast lost its flavor. She took her cup and looked back out of the window.

The village was busy with cars toing and froing and villagers walking and chatting on the pavements. The vicar stood by the old village stocks talking to a group of women. A Buddhist monk drifted through the graveyard behind him. The sun shone strongly.

Everything looked pretty and peaceful. Ma took a deep breath. She smiled and turned. Suddenly the toast looked appetizing again. She took a mouthful and looked at Alex.

"Well do you like it?" she asked with her head nodding to the world outside.

"Oh. It's lovely, Ma. It's been a lovely day."

"It's not finished yet, Alex … not by a long chalk." She paused. "I'm taking you to Gawsworth Hall when we've finished here. You'll love it."

The look on Alex's face was reminiscent of a little child's.

"But first, some more tea," Ma said while commencing to refill the cups.

# CHAPTER TWENTY-SEVEN

Alec spun the wheel of the Mitchell Hire car and sent the car onto the new Glasgow bypass that led out to Greenock and Gourock. His mind sifted through everything that happened and was said, especially the last words of advice from Rod; *never broach the subject you want to talk about. Sooner or later, they'll bring the subject up naturally, and you'll end up with more information.*

How the hell do you approach a complete stranger and strike up a conversation without him wondering why? In a bar, it may be possible, but Rabbie Stewart lives a million miles from nowhere.

*I just happened to be passing by wouldn't work. Oh, balls to it. I'll think of something when I get there.*

He looked at his watch; he was halfway into the afternoon. The sun was strong and still fairly high in the sky. It faced him as the road took him around Glasgow and headed out west.

The new road coped easily with the traffic, and driving became automatic and boring. There was no rush. Bullshit, he could feel the impatience welling through him. Remembering Rod and Megan, he deliberately kept his speed in check.

"Don't blow it, Al," he muttered to himself.

He looked down at the two bottles lying snuggly side by side on the passenger seat. The pale amber liquid of the MacCallan malt had formed tiny viscous bubbles in the neck with the movement of the car. It looked, and from past experience was, extremely inviting. He smiled to himself as he remembered Rod's last words to him; *if you're taking coals to Newcastle, take the best.* So the McCallan it was.

He avoided a lorry that pulled out and suddenly found himself at the end of the motorway network. The road came down in size as buildings thrust their dark exteriors towards the blue sky. He passed the great ship building complex on the right.

Huge, silent cranes clawed the midafternoon sky like some giant's arthritic fingers. Large gates appeared in seemingly unending high walls, through which an army of twenty thousand men once marched to do a daily nine-hour battle. The finest engineers in the world were amongst them, uniformed in overalls and armed with lunchboxes. They produced the finest ships in the world.

All was quiet now. The well-planned, broad pavements, built carefully to take the rush of all this pedestrian traffic, were empty. Alec felt a pang of sadness. *I wonder if the Japanese are building wide pavements.* he thought.

He brought the speed of the car down as he went through several built-up areas. Suddenly, on the left hand side he saw the drab exterior of the Gourock Co-op approaching.

"Ah … ah," he murmured as he looked at the grimy upstairs windows that housed the meetings of the Sub Aqua Club.

He turned his attention to the right hand side of the road. Megan said to look out for a pub called *The Thistle*. He pulled the speed of the car down to rolling. There was no traffic behind him, and the road was empty. Sure enough, *The Thistle* lay on the corner of a lane.

Alec pulled across the road and into the lane. He stopped for a moment by the pub. Megan wrote down the postal address, which was really unimportant. The important part was the directions of how to get to Rabbie Stewart's house. She did this in fine detail. Alec glanced at the paper just the once. There would be no need to recheck what his trained mind assimilated.

He paused to clear his mind and have a plausible story ready, should it be required. The seconds passed whilst he composed himself. He was fighting the bubble of excitement spreading through him. He thought fleetingly of Alex and Ma who at that moment were tucking in at *Ye Olde Chocolate Box*.

A sudden doubt struck him. What if he couldn't get the old boy to talk? What if he wasn't at home? If he was in and Alec did manage to strike up a conversation, would Rabbie talk about what happened? Would he talk about what he had seen? He refused point blank to talk to Megan, and she's a very personable, pretty, young lady. So why should he open up to another man?

"Well for the sake of that lovely girl back in Wincle, I'd better get him to talk. Shit or bust … here I go," Alec said as a pep talk to himself.

He put the car into gear and moved up the lane. The few houses there seemed to be in the immediate vicinity of the pub and the main road he just turned off. They thinned out within a hundred yards, and the lane itself narrowed down to little more than a grass track the width of one vehicle.

Thick moorland grass spread away from either side of the track. Grayish green in color, it intermingled with clumps of gorse and heather. The tangy smell of the sea breezed in through the open window.

Alec kept the car in third gear in order to

steer clear of the ruts in the track as he approached a low hill. There wasn't a house to be seen. He checked the rearview mirror, and the ones behind had long vanished from view. He breasted the rise and at once stopped the car.

Laid out before him in all its summer glory, barely a half-mile away, was the silvery Firth.

"This is some sight," murmured Alec.

The hill swept gently down before him. The long grass swayed and rippled endlessly under the caress of the sea breeze. The colors changed constantly. Beyond the ever-changing green sward lay the sea. From this distance, it lay calm and flat like an enormous silver salver under the afternoon sun. The land on the far side of the water appeared shadowy and black. Dunoon disappeared under what could only be a heat haze.

The track swept down the hill and then veered to the right. It was a regular stopping place for beauty lovers at one time. *Of all types, no doubt*, thought Alec. It ended some fifty yards from the sea in a small turning circle for vehicles to turn around or park. Alec could see an old bench there; obviously OK'd at the loneliness of the place.

To the left of the track, setback some twenty yards and placed some similar distance from the sea, was a whitewashed stone cottage.

Even from this distance, Alec could see the front door was open. He couldn't see any movement, but smoke was lazily rising from the chimney.

*A fire on a day like today? No, it has to be for the night, surely*, he figured to himself, *The breeze funneling in off the Firth could be very cold.*

Alec gazed at the cottage for a few more moments and then put the car in motion. Allowing the car to travel under its own momentum with no accelerator pedal, Alec was able to concentrate his full attention on the cottage.

As he drew closer, it was apparent no one was around. The noise of the car in this isolated spot would have somebody come forth from the cottage; human nature was to be inquisitive.

He rolled past the neat cottage. The open door allowed him a quick glimpse of a polished, stone-paved floor, dark oak furniture, a dresser of some sorts, and what could have been a brass ship's clock.

On the seaward side of the cottage, a small, thick, pine table had been placed along side a pine bench. It was there, no doubt, for days such as these, but no one was sitting there.

Alec was in a quandary. He passed the cottage now and no contact. He let the car roll down the track veering away from the cottage to the small, tire-beaten circle of scrubbed land and the battered bench. Stopping the engine, he sat gazing out at the silvery water as he slowly and surely became deeply depressed.

"This whole fucking thing is futile. What am I doing here?"

He looked down at the bottles on the passenger seat. He snatched one up and jumped out of the car. He headed for the rickety bench a few paces away and sat down. He hefted the warmish bottle in his hand as he looked at the familiar label. A cynical smile twitched his lips as a thought struck him.

"I'm in a situation where I should be wielding the Sword of Damocles, and here I am wielding the Sword of McCallan."

He broke the seal and sniffed the rich malt. Raising the bottle to his lips, he took an overgenerous pull. It was as smooth as silk and wonderful. He leaned forward with his elbows on his knees. His eyes looked to the ground as the whisky sang through his veins. He shook his head slightly to clear his thoughts.

*Shit. This is useless ... fucking useless. What on God's green earth could fight this thing? Me for Christ's sake? That's the biggest laugh around. I'm the first to back away from any kind of fight, and the soddin' armorer's going to be a big help ... I can tell."*

Alec shivered slightly under the warm sun as the pervading feeling of loneliness spread through him again. "All alone by the telephone," he laughed cynically again; as he sang the words of the old song pulled out from his memory banks.

He took another pull at the bottle.

"That's an awfu' sad way to drink guid whisky."

Alec started and turned in the direction of the gentle Highland voice. It belonged to the man seated on the bench near him. Appearing from nowhere, he was clad in a pair of green corduroys and a plaid shirt.

The man ran a stubby-fingered hand through his shock of pure white hair. The pale blue eyes looked smiling and questioningly at Alec and then at the bottle.

Alec replied, "Yes, I suppose so. What we need are two glasses."

He led them to Rabbie's cottage to remedy the situation. Alec, psychologically, was on a winner. Rabbie sought him out, not the other way around. He felt a million times better, and it wasn't just the malt. The mental hurdle of accidentally meeting and then talking was out of the way. Alec silently praised his good luck.

Rabbie and Alec introduced themselves. Rabbie, as the host, quickly made some rough sandwiches to compliment the whisky. They ate, drank, and talked at the thick pine table. They finished the sandwiches. Rabbie neatly collected what few crumbs were left and spread them over the short cut grass of his small garden.

"For the birds," he said to Alec in way of explanation, "If I leave them on the table, they'll eat them just the same. That I don't mind. It's what they leave behind I mind." His pale, blue eyes were smiling as his thick, stubby fingers lovingly caressed the smooth, thick pine table.

*Rabbie obviously has an affinity with wood*, thought Alec. The table top was incredibly smooth like velvet. The odds are Rabbie made this table. The man not wanting bird shit on his table was quite understandable.

Alec poured more malt as Rabbie sat down. Megan was right; he was craggy. He was a short, thickset man with powerful arms and shoulders. The plaid shirt was tight across his chest. The open-necked shirt displayed a reddish-brown chest and throat of similar color to that of his face. The color highlighted the silvery whiteness of his abundant, though short, hair.

As Rabbie picked up his glass, Alec could see what his original hair color must have been. His forearms were densely covered in bright red hair. The backs of his fingers, between the second joint and knuckle, each sprouted its own little tuft of red hair.

"Cheers, Rabbie," said Alec mating Rabbie's movement.

Rabbie nodded with the glass already at his lips. "You have a fine taste in malt, Alec lad. You'll have spent some time with us then, I'm thinking?"

"Off and on, Rabbie. Off and on over the years."

There was a moment of pleasant silence appreciated by both.

"And what, are you working on the noo?"

The question took Alec completely by surprise. He broke from gazing over the water and turned to look at Rabbie. "You know who I am?"

"Aye, lad. I don't have a TV myself, but I do get to see it now and then … especially if it's something good. The soft Highland brogue, with its musical undertones and softly spoken cadence, paused for lubrication. "I really enjoyed that period thing, about the Whisky family."

Alec smiled. "Ah yes … I enjoyed working on it too, Rabbie. A good show; well written and well produced."

"An' well acted too."

"Well thank you, kind sir. I'll drink to that

praise, indeed, from a Scotsman."

They both laughed and raised their glasses.

"I'm amazed that you could recognize me, Rabbie, without the beard and mustache."

"Ooh ... I'm used to seeing things that appear one thing, but really they are another."

Alec looked quickly at Rabbie wondering if he'd seen through him.

Rabbie returned the look and started to smile. He stood up. "Here. I'll show you."

He disappeared into the cottage and reappeared moments later. He sat next to Alec. In his hand was a small purse-like green baize bag with a draw string. He opened the neck of the bag and emptied the contents onto the table top. Several stone-like discs lay uninterestingly on the smooth pine surface. They looked like so many rough pebbles on a smooth, sandy shore.

"Now what would you think they are, Alec?"

"Christ knows, Rabbie," said Alec fingering one of the discs. Minute particles of sand and algae rubbed off the crusted disc and fell to the table. "They look like nothing on earth, leastways, nothing to write home about."

"Wrong, Alec."

The smiling eyes told Alec that Rabbie was enjoying this. He smiled back in enjoyment with Rabbie's pleasure. He suddenly remembered what Rod said about letting them broach the subject. These discs could be the opening door.

"These pieces of blackened, circular stone, Alec …" He paused, "are silver. Silver coins to be exact. Look."

He opened the stubby fingers of his extended hand. Lying there on his rough palm was a polished, sliver coin. He placed the bright coin on the table aside one of the gravely discs. "One of 'em cleaned up."

He lifted his glass and emptied it with a smooth movement of his arm. "So you see, Alec. I'm quite an expert at seeing through the bullshit of things that appear to be one thing, but in reality is something quite different."

Alec leaned forward and refilled both glasses. The bottle neck clinked against the side of Rabbie's glass. Alec looked at Rabbie with an apologetic look on his face.

"There's no nicer sound in the entire world, Alec lad."

They leaned back with their glasses in hand. The sun, continuing its westward fall, rounded the cottage and was now bathing them with its hot rays. Alec felt replete. The sandwiches, malt, and the interesting and very likeable company put him at ease for the first time in days. Nevertheless, malt or no malt, his mind was razor sharp.

"Now I find that quite amazing, Rabbie," he said genuinely, but cunningly added, "I know nowt from nowt when it comes to these things, but how on earth can you tell these things apart from all the other pebbles on the beach?"

"Ouch I didna find them on the beach, Alec. I found them out there, laddie." Rabbie's arm waved in the direction of the sea. His voice took on a teacher to pupil, patronizing tone, "In the Moray Firth to be exact."

Alec felt elation. He mentioned the Moray Firth. Now he was getting somewhere. "You mean an old wreck ... a bullion ship?" he calmly asked.

"No, no. It was the remains of a fighting ship from the Spanish Armada. In very good condition ... equally as good as the Marie Rose, I'd say.

You must take in, Alec, that every ship that sailed wasn't a bullion ship. But on the other hand, a fighting ship had to carry plenty of coin in order to replenish its stores on long journeys. So finds like this are inevitable.

Once..." he paused for emphasis, "Once you've found the ship."

"What's it like under water, Rabbie?"

"Yer never been?" The voice seemed to

go up a gentle half octave.

"No. Many things I've done, but diving isn't one of them."

Alec leaned forward and picked up the bottle. He looked inquiringly at Rabbie. Rabbie's eyes twinkled. Alec emptied the remains of the McCallan into the two glasses and then carefully screwed the cap back on the empty bottle.

Rabbie raised his glass and savored the malt reverently. He gently sighed. Alec laughed loudly at Rabbie's actions.

"Now, Rabbie, don't get too mournful. It just so happens I have its twin brother in the car."

"Ouch, Alec. Yer lovely mon," he said, happily clapping Alec on the shoulder and leaving a permanent dent in Alec's flesh.

They happily settled back in each others company. Rabbie's soft, melodic voice broke into the reverie. "It's a different world, Alec. Quiet, free, unfettered, and almost total freedom. But don't get the wrong idea. It's not all buried treasure out there.

The fun is in finding something. You can go a lifetime and see nothing. Most clubs, like ours, have never found a thing. But if you have patience and a nose," he tapped the side of his own broad, lumpy edifice, "you can narrow an area down.

Most wrecks are well documented, even as far back as 400 years. But the sea's never the same two days running. They don't just lie there waiting to be seen and found, Alec.

If they lie at a depth a diver can get to, it stands to reason; it's a depth the weather can get to. It'll whip the sand and silt up and hide a wreck quicker than you can crack the top off that new bottle of McCallan."

"Point taken, Rabbie, old son … Point taken."

Alec rose to head unsteadily for the car as grinning Rabbie watched. His look dropped to the table, and he picked up the polished silver coin. He held it between forefinger and thumb. The coin gleamed as it caught the rays of the lowering sun. Rabbie's eyes narrowed and his lips tightened.

Alec, returning from the car with the bottle, saw the expression on Rabbie's face. *Those bloody coins are part of this mess. We're on the right track, Al … softly, softly, catchee monkey,* he thought.

"Looks like bad memories, Rabbie," Alec said offhandedly as he arrived back at the table, "Here, let me introduce you to a member of my family … Malt McCallan."

He snapped back the cap and replenished the glasses. Rabbie grunted and threw the coin on the table. They sipped in silence for several minutes. Alec bided his time.

"So what brought you out here, Alec?" Rabbie asked, finally breaking the silence.

*Careful, Alec ... we're doing fine. Don't blow it.* "Oh, a few problems, Rabbie. I needed to get away and do some thinking ... quiet spot with a bottle."

The pale blue eyes looked at him gently. "Must be big problems, Alec, seeing as how you brought two bottles."

Alec smiled at the craggy face. "Rabbie, old son, I have found out from past experience that the biggest problem one can have whilst working out a problem is the problem of your bottle being nearly empty and not another one for a hundred miles."

Alec delivered the last words in perfect mimicry of Rabbie's rhythmic cadence. Alec started giggling from a combination of the malt and the look on Rabbie's face. Rabbie's normally unsmiling face cracked and started to chuckle.

Their laughter increased, and their heads moved closer to each other until their foreheads were touching. Their shoulders heaved with unrestrained laughter, and their hands tried desperately to keep the whisky from overflowing the sides of their glasses as they shook in inebriated mirth.

"Ah know exactly what yer mean, Alec," said Rabbie, finally sitting up and trying to regain control. "It's no funny when yer in yer cups and the bottle's dry. I just hope you've solved yer problems."

Alec sniffed and wiped his eyes with the back of his hand. "Well … maybe. Not so much problems, Rabbie, as that it's pressure. People think acting's easy, but by Christ, it isn't," he said shaking his head, "When you get to my stage of the game, you can't scratch your arse without two hundred pairs of eyes watching you and commenting.

You daren't have more than a couple of drinks in a pub, because if you do, you're branded as an alcoholic. Who the hell is going to hire an alcoholic? No one, Rabbie. The name of the game is deliver.

Too much money is involved in this business. If an actor can't deliver because he's too pissed up, then he's out of work. It's a vicious circle really. You drink to relieve the pressure and unwind. Then you apply more pressure, so you have a drink. It's ad infinitum."

He paused to sip the McCallan. "So if I get a bit uptight, I find a nice quiet place like this and release the pressure valve. Cheers, Rabbie, good health to you, old son."

He raised his glass and clinked Rabbie's. "Slancha."

Silence reigned again as they sat back with each other's thoughts. The sun slipped lower, and the early evening shadows started to lengthen.

The McCallan and tranquil surroundings cocooned them with a subtle mist. The Forth almost lost its silver salver appearance. A dark bloom appeared in the water. The hills on the far side were invisible now against the dark, gray-blue of the fading light.

"So when are you taking me down to see the free world of yours, Rabbie?" Alec asked.

There was a pause before Rabbie answered. "I'll show you the rudiments, Alec, but I'll no take you doon." Rabbie's voice was quiet and even.

"Heh. I'm not after your treasure," Alec said nodding his head at the coins.

"I didn't say yer was." Rabbie's voice held an edge.

"I just want to see this wonderful world you romanticize about," Alec continued disregarding Rabbie's tone.

"I'm sorry, Alec. I didna mean it to come out like that. It's just … that I had a bad experience, and I told myself I'd never go down again."

For the first time, it was Rabbie who reached for the bottle. His eyes looked at Alec for permission. Alec nodded, smiling, and pushed his own glass forward. The want duly noted by Alec. *Tread carefully, Alec. This could be the step through the door.*

"Now you've got me wondering, Rabbie. You get me all worked up to see and try this underwater stuff. When I've plucked up the courage, you tell me I might come face to face with a shark or something."

"No, no, Alec … Nothing like that … not at all."

Rabbie didn't sip his malt; he took a large gulp. He was fighting something. Alec waited and then finally Rabbie spoke.

"Do yer think there's more to living and dying … Heaven and Earth, Alec?" His tone was deadly serious.

Alec looked at the grave face of the friendly man next to him and tried to carefully choose the words of his reply. He was definitely through the door.

"Rabbie, I'm sure there is. There are enough preachers, priests, rabbis, scientists, and general run of the mill head bangers who have been telling us so for years, if not centuries. We just don't seem to pause long enough in the race from cradle to grave to take it in."

Rabbie's blue eyes were seriously searching Alec's. *Shit, I hope that's the right answer. It sounded right.* The pause was interminable.

"I'll tell you why I won't go down again, Alec," Rabbie finally spoke, and he picked the silver coin from the table.

"I had researched this wreck for three years, and I was sure I could find it. To cut a long story short, I had to go it alone.

Well, within a few days, sure enough, I found it. It was a fighting ship belonging to the Spanish Armada ... chased by the English, then wrecked by a squall. The ship was called the *San Domingo*."

He breathed deeply for a few seconds and took another gulp of malt.

"The name was clearly visible when I went down," he gave a wry smile, "and I was one very excited diver at that moment.

She was lying against an outcrop, almost upright, but totally invisible from above because of a coral sheath that had grown around her. The sheath had protected her from the heavy movements of the sea, because she was virtually intact ... apart from war damage, that is.

Standing on that deck and looking up at the lace curtain was one of the most beautiful sights I'd ever seen, Alec. It seemed to collect what little light there was and direct it inwards like one of them con-" He paused in search of the word.

"Concave?" Alec supplied.

"Aye. That's right … concave mirror. It was a wonderful, natural sight like nature's cathedral. A sight that, under other circumstances, I would have wanted to spend more time enjoying, but I was deep, Alec. On air, no a mixture … straight air. I had a few minutes at the most, so I looked around."

Rabbie's mouth tightened, and he reached for the malt again. Alec, once again, pushed his glass over.

Alec kept quiet, no banter, he sensed a deep change of mood in Rabbie. It was almost like a girding of the loins, against the impending mental battle of bringing up bad memories.

Rabbie continued, "Just in front of me laid one of the masts broken in battle. The for'ard end lay on the deck, but the broken end was about ten feet off the deck, supported by wreckage in the middle … and impaled on this enormous stump … was the remains of a man."

Alec could see Rabbie's shoulders shudder at the memory.

"I must admit, it didn't mean much to me at the time … air time being short and the man was dead. It's just the manner of his death that somehow gets to you. His skeleton was kept in position by bits of leather still left on his clothing."

Rabbie fell silent and his eyes looked out over the Firth. Alec knew that Rabbie was treading the timbers of the *San Domingo* again.

Alec placed his glass on the table, and the soft chink brought Rabbie out of his memory recall.

"Anyway," Rabbie continued, "it was under his body that I found those," he nodded at the coins.

Alec looked at Rabbie as another silence descended. His thick forearms and stubby-fingered hands were locked straight out on the surface of the polished table. His head bowed to a position where he was looking between his legs at the ground. His broad chest was rising and falling as if he was feeling nauseous. It was nothing to do with the drink. It was recalling, and there was more to come.

"I'd dropped my torch. It was lit, though I didn't need it really, but it made it easy to find. It had fallen near another body. This one was lying at the foot of the only decent mast left. It wasn't a soldier; it was a priest or a monk or something." Rabbie's face was working.

"Around its neck was an amulet or some such. It was the way its hand was grasped around it that made me think it was maybe of some value ... other than its age, that is."

Almost half a glass of malt went into Rabbie's mouth. "I had about a minute of time left, so I decided to have it away. Those finger bones around the amulet were like a gin trap, Alec. I managed to free ... oh, a couple, I think ... when it happened."

Rabbie's voice became cold and totally sober. "Its other arm ... its other arm came around my shoulder and the skull in the hood turned and looked at me."

They drank, almost in unison, as coldness descended upon them. Alec spoke very softly,

"Rabbie, you said you were very deep and on air ... Is it possible you, well ... hallucinated?"

Rabbie turned to Alec, his face working hard. His thick arm came around Alec's shoulder and lay there. "Alec, the arm just didn't come around and lay like this. The bastard thing hugged me," and so saying, he hugged Alec with his face close, showing the full horror of what he felt.

Under the great pressure of Rabbie's arm and the feelings expressed so clearly on his face, Alec felt his stomach turn over. Alec tried to stop the words from coming out, but somehow they squeezed past all commands. "Are you sure?" he croaked.

Rabbie stood up as though bitten. "Sure, Alec? Sure?" Rabbie unbuttoned his plaid shirt and with one swift movement, pulled it out of his trousers and off his shoulders.

He turned his back to Alec. The broad, powerful back facing Alec was tanned to a similar color of his face with freckles across the shoulders intermingling with a fine covering of red hair. Under his right armpit and down as far as his waist ran a deep scar. It was a new scar, but it wasn't the scar that held Alec's horrified gaze.

Across the back just under the shoulder blades, running from right to left, was a weal - a band of dead white skin highlighted by the tanned skin surrounding it. It finished on the left hand side in five deep, bullet hole like indentations that marked the flesh permanently. Whichever way Alec looked at it, it was the imprint of an arm and a hand.

\*\*\*

They sat there for over ten minutes in complete silence. The silence was broken only by the occasional clinking of a glass and the gurgling of the bottle. Alec took out a much needed cigarette. Over the past few hours, he had done without in deference to Rabbie.

It was Rabbie who finally broke the silence. His voice was back to its normal cadence. "Alec, what would you say to some fine smoked ham to chase this fine malt whisky?"

"Well, I wouldn't say no, Rabbie," Alec replied, half smiling. The vision of Rabbie's back was still with him.

"Right y'are," said Rabbie, clapping Alec on the knee and rising. "Let's go indoors."

They rose. Alec collected the glasses and the remains of the McCallan. Rabbie collected the coins.

They entered Rabbie's neat cottage. The peat fire gently glowing in the grate radiated warmth that offset the chill off the sea. Rabbie went over to the Welsh dresser and dropped the coins, now in their green baize purse, into the drawer.

"Sit down by the fire, Alec. I'll only be a minute," he called out from the tiny kitchen.

True to his word and magically, plates appeared with a large loaf, butter, a small bowl of tomatoes, and an enormous ham scored and browned on the outside.

"Come to the table, Alec," he said, "You'll like this. I smoked it myself."

It looked delicious. Rabbie sliced a thick, succulent slab onto each plate. "Help yourself to bread and tomatoes, Alec."

Alec did and again later to another

generous slab of the delicious ham.

Plates were empty and bellies were full when Alec drew Rabbie back. "Rabbie, you said that this thing wasn't a soldier. Why's that?"

Rabbie paused before answering, patting his stomach and sighing. He leaned back and stretched his legs out under the table. "Because it wasn't wearing any chest armor. It was wearing a brown cloak type thing wi' a hood.

Ah know what you're going to say Alec, but even after 400 years, it was still recognizable as such."

Alec rubbed his arm as goose bumps came up. "And the amulet?" he said offhandedly.

"No. I didna get that," Rabbie said quickly. He remembered the total fear that had consumed him at the time. "Anyway, it was just a bit of stone wi' a teensy bit of leather tied to it."

Alec couldn't feel his legs. He was glad he was sitting down. He couldn't clear his brain of the malt. The thoughts and vision of what Rabbie so graphically described spun and intertwined.

*A skeleton? A fucking skeleton? No flesh, no nothing ... comes back to life? Oh sweet Jesus, this has got to be out of someone's nightmare ... out of some horror story.*

"Steady, Alec, steady," Rabbie said from

the kitchen as he heard the heavy chinking of the bottle neck against the glass rim. He finished clearing the plates and food and was putting the last of the cutlery away.

"Living on my own, I have but the two glasses." He halted his flow of words to look at Alec from the kitchen doorway. "Are you alright laddie … You look a bit pale."

"Fine, Rabbie … Fine. It's your lighting. We actors are used to something a little more subtle," Alec lied.

Alec's reference to the pressure paraffin lamp that Rabbie lit brought a smile to Rabbie's face. His cottage had no windows on the west side, and the other windows were tiny. The interior, even on a bright day, appeared quite dim.

"Ah, well, we're a bit too far out for the electricity you see, Alec."

Having his chore over, Rabbie settled his bulk into the old wooden rocking chair by the peat fire. He commenced to poke the fire with the large brass poker that lay in the hearth.

Alec rose unsteadily from the table and handed Rabbie his glass. Alec seated himself opposite Rabbie's creaking chair and raised his glass. The slow, whispering, peat flames distorting in the glass, turned the pale malt a deep, gold color.

"Good health to you, Rabbie L. Stewart."

"Slancha, Alec."

They silently stared at the flames together. The only accompaniment was an occasional hiss from the peat and the creaking of the rocking chair.

"Would you like to stay the night, Alec? I'm thinking you're in no fit state for driving too far ... me as well for that matter."

Alec looked into the friendly, warm face. "I would appreciate that, Rabbie. Thank you very much."

"It's a pleasure, Alec."

"But first," Alec continued, "Let me phone home, and maybe I can get us another bottle."

He rose unsteadily and put his glass down. He reached the open door as Rabbie spoke. "You'll find a phone at *The Thistle* on the corner."

Alec raised his hand in affirmation.

"And Alec..."

Alec turned.

"How did you know my middle initial was L and my surname Stewart?"

Alec froze and flushed with embarrassment.

"I'll tell you when I get back, Rabbie."

"Aye, Alec ... do that," was the soft reply.

\*\*\*

Alec manfully fought the fumes in his head and the twisting wheel of the car as it bucked in the ruts of the track on his way to *The Thistle*. His mind, whichever tiny portion of it that hadn't succumbed to the malt fumes, tried to grasp how and why he'd made that slip. He hadn't noticed it himself, until Rabbie questioned him. There was nothing to do but to tell all.

He shaded his eyes against the setting sun and in doing so, left one hand on the wheel. The front nearside tire hit a deep rut. The steering wheel spun crazily and twisted his remaining fingers off the wheel. Alec automatically stamped the brake. With steering on full lock, it was the worst thing he could have done.

The car spun, juddered over the ruts, leaned heavily, and finally came to rest on its side against a hillock. It happened in a split second. Alec, suspended in his seat belt, was leaning heavily against the window. He looked unbelieving at the sea of green grass pressed up against the glass.

"Oh shit … this is all I need."

He slipped out of the seatbelt and with difficulty, found the window switch to lower the passenger window. That was the easy part. Now he had to get out of the damn window. He managed to turn his body in the restricted space and maneuver his feet against the driver's door. The effort brought sweat down his back. Pushing with his feet, he moved towards the open window.

"Ah ... gravity's a wonderful thing, Alec. The laws of which help to run the universe," Alec grunted to himself, "but when ... *grunt* ... the buggers against ... *grunt* ...you, you sometimes ... *grunt* ... wish the bloody... *grunt* ... apple had gone up, instead of ... *grunt* ... oh thank Christ."

Alec managed to get his body up across the seats and was laying half in and half out of the car window. He panted like a cow about to give birth. The ground looked an awful long way down in his drunken state, but nevertheless he decided he couldn't stay there all night. He eased his way forward.

Alec didn't realize the car hadn't tipped fully over on to its side, but was resting at an acute angle on two wheels against the grassy hillock.

He eased his way forward again, plucking up the courage for the inevitable fall to the ground, when his mind was made up for him.

The car came back from the point of no

return and gravity did the rest. The car slammed down upright on its shocks, and Alec, poised for his fall, shot through the window like a wet cherry stone twixt finger and thumb.

It was a full minute before he could breathe properly. He lay there winded, mentally checking arms and legs. Everything was in place. "Son of a bitch," he muttered, "what the fuck next?"

He staggered back to the car and sat feeling his bruises. Slowly but surely, he pulled himself together. It was then he realized that the car was now facing towards Rabbie's. It was impossible to turn around; the only thing to do was to reverse all the way to *The Thistle*.

"Gordon friggin' Bennett," he swore, "I'm black and blue, and next on the menu is a stiff neck."

The journey backwards to *The Thistle* wasn't without incident. Alec thanked his lucky stars that there was some daylight left. In the dark, and in his state, he wouldn't have made it.

*The Thistle* was a dark pub; its window lamps were already lit and throwing an inviting glow for any thirsty passerby. Alec trod the tartan carpet past one or two regulars to the bar. The landlord put his racing paper and nodded to Alec.

"Have you a phone I could use, landlord?"

233

He didn't bother answering but waved his arm. Alec picked out the phone in the corner.

"Have you a bottle of McCallan, landlord?"

A gleam entered the slaty, uninterested eye of the publican, "That oi have, sir." With a deft flick of his wrist, he produced a bottle of the same from a high shelf. The accent and inflection in the voice told Alec he was from Belfast. *An Irish landlord in a Scottish pub. Christ, what next?*

Alec paid him and slipped the bottle in his jacket pocket. He headed for the phone.

# CHAPTER TWENTY-EIGHT

Five minutes later, he had the operator try the number again. There was no reply the first time. The operator let it ring for longer than usual and was about to interject when it was answered.

"You're through now, caller."

"Thank you … Hi, Ma. It's Alec. Where have you been? I've only just managed to get you."

"Now, Alec. I told you we were going out for the day. We've only this minute got back."

"Well, that's some day you've had. Had a nice time?"

"Ye … es."

"You don't sound too sure, Ma," Alec said intuitively.

"Well, the shopping was lovely, and this afternoon was grand. About an hour ago, something really funny happened at Galsworthy. I can't really explain it, but it seems to have knocked Alex for six."

Alec groaned.

"What did you say, Alec?"

"Nothing, Ma … nothing." A feeling of

dread came over him. "Tell me about it, Ma."

\*\*\*

Alex was joking with Ma as the car approached Gawsworth Hall. Ma put aside what she had seen and felt in *Ye Olde Chocolate Box* and was determined that the day would carry on in the same vein it had started. She directed Alex to park the car in the car park next to *Cream Teas*. They walked over the narrow causeway to the hall. Alex 'ooohd and aaaahd' at the resplendent, black and white, half-timbered Tudor Manor house. It was surrounded by neat lawns, a tournament ground, and a tiltyard all encompassed by a mile long Tudor wall.

Ma waved and chatted to the owners, the Richards, and picked up a glossy brochure for Alex. They walked over the gravel to the entrance of the hall. Ma chatted endlessly about the history of the place. It was fairly obvious to Alex that this was one of Ma's favorite watering holes.

She told Alex that the De Orreby family was the first family to live here back in the 1100's. She jumped from there to the fact that an axe head from 2000 BC was dug up from the lawn. She went on as they entered the lovely old building.

According to Alex's brochure, some of Ma's facts were slightly distorted, but she wasn't far out. Her heart was in the right place, if her memory wasn't. They went into the entrance hall and were immediately hit by the loving care and attention lavished by the owners and custodians in preserving this wonderful house.

"Fancy dusting and polishing this, Alex?"

"I think you'd need a warehouse of lavender for this, Ma."

They both burst out laughing. They both realized the loving care and attention required, plus that certain something more, to keep this four- or five-hundred-year-old house. It was above and beyond the call of duty; it was love.

They passed into the long hall with its large oak beams and Tudor fireplace. Ma turned Alex to look out of the low windows running the full length of the hall overlooking the rose gardens. Some bleachers at the far end of the garden were being dismantled after an open air production of Shakespeare.

"Isn't it a beautiful setting for a play?" whispered Ma.

Alex nodded in agreement and total wonderment. She eventually turned away to head for the dining hall and the chapel. Ma stayed on by the window, watching the men take down the seats.

It wasn't so much the working men that held her attention, more the two figures standing to the right in front of the shadow of Gawsworth Church. They appeared to be looking back at her through the window, especially the one dressed like a Buddhist monk. She shook her head and turned to follow Alex.

"That's three times, or is it four times, I've seen you today," she said to herself, but it slipped out of Ma's mind just as easy as the coincidence slipped in.

She caught up with Alex in the dining hall with its massive refectory table and long oak beams. She showed Alex Maggoty Johnson's fiddle on the wall. She said she was going to have a facsimile made for Alec, her eyes twinkling madly.

"Because," she said in answer to Alex's nonplussed expression, "Maggoty Johnson helped found the Firm of Justini and Brooks, and Alec drinks so much J & B whisky. He's just got to have shares in the company."

Alex laughed, and they left the dining hall to enter the tiny chapel.

The chapel, first licensed in Edward III's reign in 1365, was a domestic chapel and therefore, tiny in its proportions.

"Fancy, Alex, you had to have a license.

Just shows you they were mad on taxes back then, so this government's nothing new."

Ma entered first, intent on being able to point out items of interest to Alex. It wasn't until she paused from speaking and stopped in the doorway of the ambulatory that she noticed Alex hadn't moved from the spot just inside the chapel doorway. Her eyes were wide and staring. She was pleading with Ma.

Her face was flannel gray and her mouth was open trying but unable to speak. Her fingers went to her throat as she fell to her knees. Ma, totally distraught, dashed across the chapel calling to her. She fell to her knees in front of her as Alex's eyes pleadingly moved from Ma's face and then to the door.

Ma acted quickly. She was small, but strong for her age. She dragged Alex through the chapel door to a chair in the corridor on which a *Please do not sit on the chairs* sign was placed. She lifted Alex up and sat her on the cardboard sign.

The air whistling into Alex's lungs sounded like a dying steam kettle. Ma caringly fussed and rubbed the backs of Alex's hands as her breathing became more settled. She undid the buttons of her shirt in order to massage her back and shoulders. It was then that Ma noticed the thick, red weal around her neck. It was so deep that it had almost brought blood.

Ma paused with shock of the sight. The only thing around Alex's throat was the leather thong attached to the stone thing she wore. Her fingers tentatively touched the leather; it was quite slack and free.

After ten minutes or so, Alex regained her composure and was feeling better. She smiled at Ma, but Ma noticed the smile didn't touch her eyes. Alex apologized profusely for the fuss she caused. Ma suggested they go for some tea and cream cakes. Alex nodded in agreement as though not trusting the strength of her voice.

\*\*\*

"And then it happened, Alec."

*Oh, Christ, not more, Ma.* "What was that Ma?" he said as calmly as he could.

"We left the hall and were walking across the gravel to the causeway. I was chatting away as usual, when suddenly; I found I was talking to myself. I turned around, and Alex had stopped about twenty paces behind me. She was looking at two men - the two men I told you about earlier."

"What were they doing, Ma?"

"Nothing, Al. Just looking at Alex. No, staring at Alex, and she just stared back."

"Then what?" *Christ, this is like pulling teeth.*

"Well, the monk nodded his head, and the one with the white hair walked towards her."

"White hair, Ma?" Alec cut across her.

"Yes. He walked towards her and then lifted his hand as though asking for something. The most horrible thing Alec … It looked as though he'd recently lost two of his fingers in an accident … as though they'd been ripped out at the knuckle."

Alec could taste the bile in his mouth. "Go on, Ma," his words tinny in his ears.

"Alex started shaking her head, and she grabbed that stone thing she wears. I saw her lips tighten and her chin stick out.

It was obvious to me then that he was asking her for something, but there was no way he was going to get it. I started forward to help her, and then I noticed the Buddhist monk walking towards them.

He didn't raise his hand, but he must have asked for the same thing because I saw Alex's head shake again."

"Didn't you hear or see him speak, Ma?"

"No, I couldn't, Alec. He was wearing a kind of cowl."

Alec felt like vomiting. His breathing went shallow. "Ma, Buddhist priests don't have cowls and their robes are saffron. What color was this one?"

"Dark brown, Al."

*Oh ,Jesus ... sweet Jesus.* "What did the white-haired man look like? What was he wearing, Ma?" Alec tried desperately to keep the panic out of his voice.

"I think ... yes ... he was smallish, but broad ... chunky, like a boxer. He was wearing a short-sleeved tartan shirt and baggy green cords."

The phone fell from Alec's fingers as he dashed into the toilet to vomit. Beads of ice cold sweat dripped from his brow as he retched over the urinal. Total despair sapped his muscles and weakened him. Ma just described Rabbie L. Stewart to a T.

# CHAPTER TWENTY-NINE

The brown saloon car swept onto the motel car park and pulled gently to a halt, belying the speed of its entrance. Rod and Megan exited the car; Megan moved more quickly than Rod.

Rod called to her, "Megan, keep it cool. It's two am, and we don't want to arouse any interest at this time of morning."

Megan nodded and with controlled impatience, waited for her father to catch up to her.

He smiled at her assuring and squeezed her arm. "This isn't the first time."

"With Alec?" Megan's tone was one of outrage.

"No, no. Other actors middle of a series. Pressure building up, so they go walkabout on a drunk. They have to be handled carefully, firmly, but carefully. This one's different."

"This doesn't sound like a drinking jag to me, Dad."

"I know. That's why I said, this one's different."

They entered the motel and crossed the

carpeted floor to the reception desk. The motel was quiet, and the night receptionist cum hall porter was just returning from the bar area. "Good evening, sir, madam, or should I say, good morning?"

The token greeting bypassed Rod; he grunted and half smiled. "A friend of ours has just phoned us. He's only in the area for a couple of hours ... Mr. Sterne, an Englishman."

It was a statement, not a question, and delivered in such a manner by the big man that there was only one answer. "Yes, sir. Room 117. As a matter of fact, I was just going there myself with this," he said and held up a bottle of Glenmorangie.

Rod held his hand out. "For us, no doubt. I'll take it." He spun on his heels and headed for room 117 with Megan following.

The night porter looked after them and then shrugged his shoulders. "If he says it's Tuesday, it's bloody Tuesday," he muttered.

He suddenly called after them, remembering, "Would ye tell him there was no any McCallan, sir?" Rod just waved his hand without altering pace.

The door to 117 was slightly ajar. Rod eased the door open fully with an extended finger. The room layout was the same as in motels the world over. Whoever designed the first mass-produced motel room forever conformed the traveling populace of the world.

Rod and Megan knew exactly what they were stepping into. The bathroom was to the left or right. A short, two paces was the square bedroom. Two single beds and opposite was a long shelf that doubled as a dressing table and TV shelf, plus the usual makings for tea and coffee. A large window at the far end had full-length, beige curtains that one could draw for privacy from the outside world.

It was the same, whether you were in Shanghai or Stockport. A room is a room, is a box is a box.

Rod stepped inside. The bathroom light was on, throwing its glare across the passageway and entrance. The main bedroom lights were off, but the bathroom light was sufficient to throw it into pen umbra.

"Alec," Rod called out. The room was silent apart from a soft moaning. They entered the bedroom. Rod scanned the room; it appeared to be empty. He heard the soft moaning again.

"Dad?" Megan's disturbed voice came through the quiet room.

Rod lifted his hand to silence her, and he walked to the end of the far bed. "Alec," he called again, and again the soft moaning responded.

"Oh, Dad, look," Megan said softly at Rod's shoulder.

He looked down. In the corner of the room, hidden by the TV set, was Alec. An empty bottle of McCallan lay on its side in front of him. He was squatting, knees up to his chin and rocking to and fro with a section of the curtain held to his face. His eyes were vacant and spittle drooled from his open mouth. The keening sounds they heard were coming from Alec's throat.

"Oh … my … God," Megan said brushing past Rod.

"No," came the firm command, "Run a bath, girl … hot, and get that bloody thing set up for some coffee."

Megan stopped in her tracks and spun around at the commanding voice. Rod soon heard the heavy splashing of water into the tub as he approached Alec. He sank to his knees in front of him. Alec's vacant stare didn't alter.

"Alec," Rod said softly. The name was almost choking in his throat as he filled up. The sight of Alec like this was too much even for Rod.

This strong, very capable, and intelligent man knelt in front of his friend and beheld a sight he never thought possible - abject terror. Rod let the seconds slip by as moisture built up behind his eyes and alien tears formed. Rod quickly sniffed them back.

He turned and threw the bottle of whisky he was still carrying on to the bed and then viciously backhanded Alec across the face. The blow was stunning, and Alec's eyes rolled around his head, fully expecting the pain to follow. Alec was anaesthetized; the McCallan saw to that. His eyes started to focus. That was the signal Rod was waiting for, and he lifted Alec to his feet.

"Megan, how's that bath?"

"Ready, Dad."

"Good. C'mere and give me a hand with Alec."

Megan and Rod eased Alec out of his jacket and shirt, and then Rod seated Alec on the foot of the bed. Megan removed his shoes and socks.

Alec slowly raised a hand to his face. "Jesus, that fucker hurt," Alec mumbled.

"Twas just a love tap, Alec," Rod replied trying to remove Alec's trousers.

"Yeah, well remind me never to make love to you."

Rod laughed. The Alec they knew and loved returned. He bundled Alec into the bath.

Twenty minutes later, Alec emerged with his hair still wet and wrapped in a bed cover.

Rod couldn't find a dressing gown, so he used the next best thing.

Megan had hung Alec's clothes up and had some coffee ready. As soon as Alec seated himself on the pillows of the bed, looking like a latter day Gandhi, she pressed a cup into his hands.

He looked pale, his face drawn. A bright scarlet imprint on his right cheek from Rod's heavy backhander glowed painfully as did his skinned shins.

Rod and Megan kept silent; their eyes taking in the change in Alec. They were in disbelief that a man's physical and mental makeup could alter so drastically in less than twelve hours.

Megan was appalled. Rod looked at her and shook his head gently. The movement told her to keep quiet and cool. Rod bided his time, allowing the seconds to slip into minutes, and then judging the moment right to speak.

"Tell me, Alec." Rod kept his voice gentle but weighted.

Alec continued to stare into his cup and then slowly raised his eyes to look at his friend. His eyes were brimming with tears. They ran silently down his face and fell onto the bed cover as he shook his head slowly. Pain and agony was etched on his face.

It was too much for Megan. Her eyes filled in sympathy. She started to rise to go to Alec, but Rod firmly held her arm keeping her seated.

"Tell me," Rod repeated the softness still there.

Alec swallowed; it was an effort. His larynx tightened under the strain, but he finally started speaking. The words croaked their way out. He told Megan and Rod all that happened, from the very first fortunate moment he accidentally met Rabbie Stewart.

He stumbled and paused. Sometimes his voice was so low that they had to lean forward to catch the words. The tears stopped running as his memory automatically brought back every little detail. The details made it obvious to Rod and Megan that one of those wonders of human nature had taken place.

It was a rarity that happens, just maybe once in a lifetime for anybody. An instant rapport and liking for someone else, someone of the same gender, that was all based on body language, a look, a grin, and total respect.

Megan filled his coffee cup twice during the telling. His voice was getting noticeably weaker, and the words were further apart. He began to rub his sore shins as he retold the accident with the car.

Megan kept biting her lips, and it was only the calm strength of her father that stopped her from going to comfort Alec.

Rod could sense that the traumatic happening wasn't far away as his eyes and ears took in Alec's manner and speech delivery.

Alec paused and deliberately altered his shallow breathing by taking several deep breaths. He continued. His voice was no louder than before, but it was more controlled as he told them of the telephone conversation with his mother. He delivered the last line of his mother's conversation verbatim.

He looked up at Rod, and even Rod was shocked. "How can a man I left no more than twenty minutes previously ..." Alec paused, more for strength to carry on than for breath, "How can he possibly be 250 miles away?"

There was no answer. There could be no answer.

Rod turned and took a glass off the shelf. He snapped the cap off the whisky bottle and poured himself a large drink. He ignored Megan and Alec. He allowed the malt to sift through his veins in the silence that followed.

The silence gave him time to think and time to compose himself. He looked back slowly at Alec. There was more to come, possibly worse to come, God forbid.

"What did you do then, Alec?"

Alec's eyes started to fill again, and his head moved slowly from side to side. "No Rod," his voice croaked in disbelief. It was a disbelief that anyone should ask him, not just a friend, to recall the events that happened next. "No," he repeated.

An unseen fist twisted Rod's vitals as he looked at Alec's face, but he steeled himself. It was all too much for Megan. She rose quietly and stood in the little hallway. She turned and leaned against the doorway looking down on Alec and her father. Tears rolled uncontrollably down her face.

"What did you do then, Alec?" The voice was still soft, but there was no missing the edge in it.

Alec visibly winced. The pain on his face was all too apparent to Megan and Rod. Alec looked down at his cup, but Rod was walking with him side by side in his thoughts.

Rod leaned forward in his chair, elbows on knees, and his face as soft and gentle as Megan had ever seen. "Later, Alec … when it's needed old friend."

Alec picked up the courage, attempted a half smile, and nodded. "I felt like death when I came out of the pub. A large brandy hadn't helped. I felt as though I was a piece in some

vast jigsaw puzzle, but I was upside down ...
white ... the picture on the other side.

I sat in the car a few minutes. I knew I was
heading for something, júst what I didn't know.
My intestines were tied up in a granny knot, and
it wasn't the whisky."

# CHAPTER THIRTY

Alec started the car and set off down the track for Rabbie's cottage with his mind in total turmoil. Ma had just described Rabbie perfectly, saying he was in Gawsworth. He couldn't be. He was here in Gourock. Not only did she say he was in Gawsworth, but he was in the company of the thing.

Is Rabbie in league with that thing or was Ma wrong? She had to be wrong. It's got to be sheer coincidence. *Could be a familiar,* he mused. Either way, if true, it meant the thing followed him to Rabbie's. Alec had been the Judas goat. *It had shown itself to Alex and possibly spoke to her. Christ Almighty, what if it had touched her?*

The awful memory of Rabbie's scarred shoulder blade invaded his thoughts. He shivered and hung on to the steering wheel as it topped the small hill that led down to the Forth and Rabbie's cottage.

A full moon rose early and hung over the dark landscape. Torn ribbons of white clouds scurried lengthily in front of it, but did little to prevent it from eerily illuminating the slope and the track. Rabbie's cottage appeared as a square, darker blob against the dark background. No light shone from Rabbie's windows.

Alec rolled down the hill. The beams from the car flickered across the cottage for a second or two, but didn't induce Rabbie out. Alec passed, turned the car around, and came slowly back. There was something strangely quiet about the cottage, something different.

He turned the engine off and looked again at the moonlit cottage. There was no smoke coming from the chimney. *Rabbie must've gone to get more peat for the fire.*

Alec jumped out of the car. His stomach settled down, and he was feeling a lot better, still whisky groggy, but better. He walked up the pathway to the cottage and remembered Rabbie's question as he was leaving.

*Tell him the truth*, Alec thought. *There's no other way, and he deserves the truth.* He took the bottle out of his pocket as he approached the near-closed door. He pushed the door open with the flat of his hand, calling out Rabbie's name. His hand was tacky. *Don't tell me he's been varnishing the door in my absence*, thought Alec as he entered the dark room.

He called Rabbie again, but there was still no reply. He heard a hissing noise. Alec waited some moments for his eyes to become accustomed to the gloom and to find out what the noise was.

The moon angled in through the small windows, and Alec's eyes could make out the table. He crossed to it gingerly. He put down the bottle he was carrying and found the hissing noise was Rabbie's paraffin lamp. It was out but still pressurized. Alec shivered as he found his lighter. *Christ, the room is cold.*

Alec clicked the lighter and burnt his fingers on the still hot lamp. "Shit," he muttered, licking his burnt fingers. It must have only just gone out. It hadn't been turned off. It was still hissing. *Maybe it's out of fuel*, he thought.

He clicked his lighter again but more carefully this time. He attempted to light the lamp. It caught immediately. The dazzling white light of the gas mantle glared across Alec's retinas. He turned away closing his eyes and blinked a few times to bring his eyes back to normalcy.

Nearing normal, Alec opened his eyes to find himself looking at the fire grate. It was several seconds before Alec realized the fire hadn't burnt out of fuel. It was still well banked up. This kind of fire lasts all day, but it was out. Alec shivered again. The first glimmer of something wrong started to worm its way into Alec.

The cold, the fire, the lamp, and then he noticed the big brass poker Rabbie had used to poke the fire. It was lying just in front of the hearth. Alec walked towards it and knelt down. It was twisted into a large U shape. The working end of the U was melted away. Spats of molten brass surrounded it on the cold, polished stone floor.

Alec looked at it in silent amazement, and then he raised his head to look around. It was then that the full horror of the room hit him. The bright, harsh light from the lamp brought out every nook and cranny of Rabbie's once neat cottage.

It was no longer neat. It was no longer a picture of white-painted walls and dark oak beams. It was no longer anything that resembled a neat cottage room, where two newly acquainted friends enjoyed a dram and a laugh.

It more resembled the killing room of an abattoir. The walls ran with blood. Huge thick cloying streaks ran around the room. They were not the thin streaks as one would mark a wall as a child with a cut finger. They were two feet wide smears that ran the length of the walls. The smears could only have come from a human being ripped apart and callously smeared around the walls.

The light from the lamp played across the

open door, and Alec's disbelieving eyes could see that a huge cross was painted there. He looked down at his still tacky right hand. It was bright red.

Alec turned on his knees and threw up in Rabbie's fireplace. He wretched until nothing but green bile came up. Mentally and physically ripped apart, he cowed, shivering as his heaving subsided.

He tried desperately to pull his thoughts together, but he wasn't given the chance as a small object fell to the floor by his right hand. He last saw Rabbie putting the object away into a drawer of the Welsh dresser.

He looked at the small green baize purse with its draw string through tear-filled eyes. His finger jerked spasmodically out to touch it. He didn't wonder how it came out of the drawer to be near his hand. What was left of his battered mind could only cope with what he knew the contents were - pieces of silver. Alec snapped.

# CHAPTER THIRTY-ONE

The horror of what Alec just related left Rod and Megan cold. Megan, to all intents and purposes, stopped breathing. She shook her head in disbelief as she looked at her father and then at the poor beaten figure of Alec.

Rod moved to the bedside with the bottle and poured a generous amount into Alec's cup. Rod looked at Megan, who rose from her chair in answer to the look in his eye. She didn't need telling. Sitting on the edge of the bed, she cradled Alec and rocked him. Her tears joined his.

Rod paced the room in silence, pausing once to pour him another whisky. As he sipped the whisky, he looked into the long mirror at the two figures behind him. His mind filed every word, nuance, and reaction Alec just told them.

The boy needed help; nothing was more certain. Boy? There was barely ten years difference in their ages, but he looked very childlike and vulnerable now cradled in his daughter's arms. *Good help ... professional help. Sandy! Yes, Sandy's the man*, he thought.

He put the glass down and reached for the phone. He barked a few orders in the mouthpiece to the night porter, and shortly he was through to his number. The night porter behind the reception area looked at the mouth piece of the phone and nodded his head knowingly. "It's Tuesday," he said cynically and wished it was morning.

Half an hour passed, during which Alec fell into a fitful sleep. A half of an hour in, Rod tried to answer Megan's whispered questions without a hope in the world of succeeding. He was as baffled and bewildered as either of them.

Things like this just don't happen. They're written about as the product of some horror writer's weird imagination, but they just don't happen. Yet here they were, totally involved and believing every stuttered word that came out of Alec's mouth. He'd known Alec too long. He was a good actor, but what Rod just witnessed was no bloody performance. It happened.

The pain on the wretched man's face as he pulled out each descriptive word was proof of that. *If it's true, what the hell happened to Rabbie Stewart? Like Alec said, a man can't be in two places at once. No human man, that is. This thing must have followed Alec to Rabbie's. Being instrumental in Rabbie's death is breaking Alec up.*

"That's a bastard trick," muttered Rod to himself as he thought of the silver payment. *If he followed Alec to Rabbie's without being seen, how the hell does it move around? It just appeared in front of Alec when he was camping, at the station, then at the chapel in Wincle. They were all miles apart from each other.*

*What kind of power must it have to annihilate a person and then resurrect the body hundreds of miles away within the space of twenty minutes? What the hell does it want with Alec?*

His baffled thoughts were disturbed by a discreet tap on the door. Megan quietly opened it to reveal a tall, gaunt man in his early sixties. A rather large, doctor's type case was suspended from a long thin arm. The other caressed and rasped across his unshaven chin while he stood in the doorway.

"Come in, Sandy. Come in," Rod said in a voice just above a whisper, "Megan, this is Lyle Sanderson ... Doctor Sandy to his friends. This man has helped me out times without number. Sandy, this is my daughter Megan."

Sandy shook hands with Megan. His eyes flickered over her in more than a professional manner. He might have been in his sixties, but his eyes were definitely in their twenties.

"Same old problem, Rod?" Sandy said using Rod's voice level. His eyes took in the intended patient.

"Mmhm … but with a twist. He thinks he's responsible for his friend's death. It was quite traumatic."

Sandy took Alec's wrist to check his pulse.

"What's his mental state under normal circumstances?"

"As strong as you or I, Sandy."

"Hmm," his eyes twinkled at Rod, "that's not saying much, considering our actions at the last Golf Club dinner." He turned his head and winked at Megan.

Megan turned to look at her father who coughed in embarrassment. For the first time that morning, Megan allowed her self a half smile.

"You say he took it bad, Rod?" Sandy said replacing Alec's wrist and checking his pupils with a deft, gentle touch.

"Very bad."

"How much booze?"

"Hard to tell. Two, maybe three, bottles."

Sandy whistled softly as he opened his case. "Well his pulse rate is up and very erratic … to be expected. He needs sedating quickly. How soon do you need him back on the studio floor?"

"Not for a week. I can work around him,"

Rod calmly lied.

"Good. I suggest I sedate him and we keep him that way for at least three days. That will give his mind some rest and time to repair."

He looked at the two bottles of whisky; one empty, the other broken into. "His body as well," he added.

He took out a bottle of tablets labeled *Heminevrin* and with Megan's help, ladled some of the pills down Alec's throat.

"What about a nurse?" Sandy questioned.

"No, Dad. I'll look after him," Megan said cutting across Rod's reply, "I'm due some leave. I'll take it now."

Rod nodded. The look on Megan's face wouldn't allow him to do anything other than comply.

Sandy left the *Heminevrin* with strict instructions on how many and when. A drip would be necessary, and that too, he would organize.

To back up his verbal instructions, he wrote every thing down including his phone number. He told Megan he would be back in three days, unless she called for him. She was to keep him comfortable, quiet, and hydrated.

"Sandy?"

"He'll be fine," Sandy said in reply to the concern in Rod's eyes. "How many times have I told you? The human body is a wonderful machine. If only people wouldn't push it beyond its limits. Believe me, three days totally knocked out … no worries," he laughed, "I wish somebody would knock me out for three days."

Rod smiled. He trusted this man, and Sandy had never let him down.

"I'll give him a shot of *Parenterovite* when he comes out of it. Not necessary, just belt and braces, so don't worry. He'll be a new man, and you owe me a large one," he added waving a finger at Rod.

The gaunt figure of the likeable and very professional Dr. Sandy left the room with a warm smile on his face and a last twinkling eyeful of Megan.

Rod looked at the closing door for a few seconds, then turned and sought out his whisky glass. He thought better of it and replaced the thought with a coffee.

Sitting at the bottom of the companion bed, he looked at Alec. The *Heminevrin* was taking hold. The ravages of the happenings and memories of the past few hours were slipping off his pained, sleeping face. His body was curled up into a semblance of the fetal position.

Rod looked across at Megan. "Sandy's right, girl. Three days will sort him out, but God only knows what the future holds for him."

"He'll be okay, Dad?" Megan's face held a million questions apart from the one she just asked.

Rod looked at her. His shoulders rose and his free hand flapped the air, the unspoken *Who knows?* written on each gesture.

Rod rose and put down his coffee. "I'll be off, girl. There's a lot of phoning to do." His head nodded in Alec's direction. "He has relatives who'll want to know where he is, an agent, and I have to get in touch with Dr. Grossman."

He crossed to the door and paused, "We'd better have a cover story. Something simple that won't arouse the curiosity of the hotel and, more to the point, the bloody press. We don't want those nosey bastards horning in."

"Heh, heh. I'm one … Remember?"

"Except present daughter," he added with a rueful smile.

"Right, what's the story? Flu virus, mumps, AIDS?"

"Anything but AIDS, Dad. Let's go for flu virus. Three or four days is about right and no hospitalization required. Anything more serious and they might wonder why he's not in hospital."

"Flu it is then. I'll leave you to phone your office about your leave of absence. What about clothes, money, and things?"

"Get your PA to phone me, Dad … and here." She crossed to her handbag and gave Rod a bunch of keys. "These are the keys to my flat. If you can spare her, she can pick me up some things."

Rod took the keys and looked at his daughter's face. A feeling of pride swept through him as he looked at her. She looked and sounded like a new woman. He leaned forward and kissed her on the cheek, something he hadn't been able to achieve for an awful long time.

"Thanks, Dad." Megan said gently.

"Anytime girl," Rod relied smiling, "Now money?"

"I'm okay, Dad. I'm well plasticed," she said and then added, "Besides I want you to do something for me."

Rod raised his eyebrows and waited.

Megan's voice took on a different tone. "I want you to get John from my office down here no later than five am with his camera."

"For what reason?"

"We're forgetting one very important thing Dad … Rabbie Stewart's cottage. I want it filmed before the police get there."

Rod's eyes narrowed as he looked at his willful daughter. "You're treading dangerous ground, girl."

"I know, Dad, but not for the first time. If this turns out right, there's a good story here. We will also have a record to help Alec," she added.

She was serious, and she was right on both counts. He nodded. "There's going to be an awful lot of questions asked, my girl. You be careful."

"I'll be in and out without touching a thing. They won't even know I've been there," she said confidently. "But," she added, "only if I can get John down before people like milkmen, postmen, and the like start arriving. If I can't, then it's a no go."

"Remember, Megan," Rod nodded at the sleeping Alec. "He's your main responsibility. Don't get sidetracked."

"I won't, Dad. Trust me."

Rod gave her one last searching look and then quietly slipped through the doorway closing the door behind him.

*** 

It was midday and the motel restaurant was busy. Megan sat for the past ten minutes looking at her chicken salad. She picked aimlessly at the lettuce with her fork.

She should be hungry. She had a big frame to

feed, and her metabolism cried out for sustenance. She couldn't get the food to her mouth, let alone down her throat.

Alec was right in his description of Rabbie's cottage. If anything, it had been underplayed. It hadn't affected John at all. She told him she had found an animal fighting club's headquarters: dog fighting, cock fighting, badger baiting, etc, and the Animal Rights people got to it and messed it up.

John had not been part of the crew when Megan first tried to interview Rabbie, so he didn't suspect anything. Had he known that the thick brown stains, some almost black in parts, running deep around the walls and across the front door were human blood, he might have acted differently.

Under Megan's direction, John carefully recorded everything minutely from different angles, interior as well as exterior. It was thirty-five minutes from arriving to leaving. With the sun breaking through as they left in John's camera car, all was still quiet.

He dropped her off at the motel and sped off with Megan's explicit instructions as to what to do with the tape in his ears. All his equipment was stored back at the BBC. To get from his home to the Beeb, then from there to Megan before five am was impossible. No HD, he would have to rely on his back up, a plain and reliable analogue tape.

Megan went straight to 117 and checked on Alec. He was still sleeping peacefully and wouldn't require more medication for at least a couple of hours.

Rod's PA rang. Using some foresight, she waited until she was at Megan's flat before phoning. Megan was able to direct her to her overnight bag and what to put in it, missing nothing she thought important or necessary.

Megan put the phone down and then quietly ran the bath. The hot, steamy water cleansed and relaxed her. It cleansed the skin, but couldn't cleanse the memories of that violent, quiet cottage.

The phone rang again; it was Jean from London, Alec's agent. It seems that Rod asked her for Alec's home phone number.

Alec had been with Jeannie far too long for her to submit that information over the phone, even though she recognized Rod's voice. He respected her for it and suggested she phone the motel.

Megan answered her questions and put her mind at ease. Jean would phone Rod back now and no doubt, give him the information required.

She rubbed herself down vigorously with the large bath towel and then looked longingly at the empty companion bed next to Alec. She felt exhausted. She looked closely at Alec sleeping peacefully and then phoned reception.

"Do not to put anymore calls through for the next two hours. When the PA arrives, please show her to 117 and let her in." With that, she slipped between the sheets of the bed and fell immediately asleep.

***

It was a long sixty seconds or a short two hours, whichever way you want to look at it. To Megan, it felt like the shorter of the two when Rod's PA was pulling gently at her shoulder.

A quick look at her watch told her it was two hours or more since she fell asleep. She thanked the PA, who left hurriedly, saying she was on the floor at two pm with Rod's show.

Megan dressed from the clothes that were brought for her and then gently ladled more medication down Alec's throat. He gagged passively as the tablets went down but didn't rise from the depths of the induced sleep.

Megan's fork played with the lettuce again, and then she dropped the fork and pushed the plate away. She finally realized the food wouldn't and couldn't get eaten.

It wasn't until Alec's third full day of

enforced rest that her appetite recovered and was back to normal. Dr. Sandy phoned several times, checking on the patient. He was due around six pm. He wanted Alec awake, so no more medication.

She enjoyed the three days looking after Alec. She caught up on unread books and generally fussed around him. She bathed his face, neatened his bed, and fluffed his pillows. Now a little flush of excitement was running through her, because he would be coming out of his induced sleep.

She was just about into the third chapter of her book, when almost simultaneously, there came a discreet knock on the door.

"Christ ... I could murder a cigarette," Alec's voice chimed with the knock on the door.

Megan didn't know which way to look. Alec won, but her body was heading for the door.

"Good evening, sir," she smiled at him as she opened the door for Dr. Sandy. "Your timing's perfect, doc. The patient has just surfaced."

Sandy's gaunt face smiled and nodded, "Aye, lass. That's why I'm here," he said confidently as he moved past Megan to Alec.

For the next twenty minutes, he went over Alec with a fine-toothed comb. His pulse, blood pressure, eyes, nose, throat, and chest were all checked.

Sandy plugged wires onto Alec that led into a small black box that made a small whirring sound. It was left there during his various examinations, and then a button was pushed. A paper readout came issuing forth. Sandy tore off the readout examining it carefully,

"Mmmm … yees … mm. Just as I thought, as strong as a bloody ox."

Megan looked at Alec smiling and nodding her head.

"Not quite finished yet," said Sandy wielding a little instrument.

"Oh doc, not the little hammer," Alec said in mock horror.

Megan laughed out loud. It pealed around the room infectiously.

Sandy finally reached into his bag and began preparing a hypodermic needle. Alec looked up at Megan and winced. She smiled back. Alec held his arm out to Sandy, who looked at it with disdain, slowly shaking his head.

"No, no, son … not that simple. Roll over onto your stomach."

"Aw c'mon, doc, not in my arse?"

"Aye, that's right," he winked at Megan. Sandy was enjoying this.

Alec rolled over with a complaining grunt and bared his backside.

Sandy slapped the buttock hard with his left

hand and hardly had his hand landed with the stinging slap when the needle of *Parenterovite* entered Alec's flesh totally unfelt.

"Sadist," muttered Alec quietly into his pillow. He was unsure of what Sandy might do next.

Sandy cleaned up in the bathroom whilst telling Megan Alec was perfectly fit, and the three days of enforced rest had worked well.

Turning to Alec, he said, "Food and some exercise now, my lad … er … The right kind of exercise." He took a sidelong glance at Megan's breasts.

"You'll be a bit wobbly at first, but that will pass with walking. Now go and have a bath. You smell."

With that Dr. Sandy said his goodbyes and left with their thanks ringing in his ears.

Dr. Lyle Sanderson was right with his prognosis. Alec's legs were like jelly. He walked up and down the room until feeling and strength returned to his legs. He was finally able to walk without holding on to something for his balance.

He walked up and down talking to Megan, totally unaware that he was as naked as the day he was born. It wasn't until he reached the stage that he could stand without support that he turned his head coming up from looking at his feet on the carpet. He saw Megan seated and stifling her laughter. It was then he looked down at himself and saw his nakedness.

"Woman," he said warningly. Then he added with a smile, "Run me a bath, Megs."

It was a half of a chapter of Megan's book later when he emerged from the bathroom pink and glowing. Megan smiled and walked to the wardrobe. She handed him his clothes. They were all neatly cleaned and pressed which didn't go unnoticed by Alec.

"Thanks, Megs," he said softly.

He was buttoning up his shirt when she pressed something into his hand. "I thought you might like to use this again," she said.

Alec looked down at the object. It was her tiny battery razor.

"On this … this time," she said laughing as she rubbed his rough chin. Alec feigned disappointment and then thanked her again.

Megan sat down watching him going through the motions of shaving and dressing. She wondered why he never questioned the obvious. How long was he here? Why the doctor? How did she get here?

She looked at the strong face, the slightly overlong nose, and the reflection of the intelligent eyes in the mirror. Then it dawned on her. Alec was one of those people who posed questions to himself and then quietly and mentally worked out the various possibilities. If in doubt, then and only then, would he ask for answers. *He's probably worked it all out by now*, she thought to herself as Alec gave a final look in the mirror and turned to her.

"C'mon, girl. I'm starving, and I owe you a good meal. I don't know what was in that shot the doc gave me, but I feel like a sixteen-year-old."

"You'll just have to make do with a twenty-nine-year-old," Megan said laughing.

The old gag brought a smile to Alec's face as they went through the door arm in arm.

The motel restaurant took on an entirely new ambience at night. It was quiet and intimate. The lighting was pleasantly dim.

The canned music that one is normally subjected to in these establishments was not playing. The management with a little heart and foresight went through a variety of old Nat King Cole melodies, backed up by some Johnny Mathis and Sinatra songs for swinging lovers. They complimented the restaurant's intimacy extremely well.

To cap it all, and to Alec's delight, they served an incredible Aberdeen Angus steak, succulent and full of magical taste. He went through the menu like a refugee from

Buchenwald. Much to Megan's surprise, her appetite for food returned.

The meal was simple and superb. They washed it down with half a carafe of house red for Megan and a bottle of Buxton spa water for Alec.

After the coffee was served, Alec asked Megan how long he had been out. She told him all, simply and without her voice showing any seriousness or deep emotion. He nodded, lit a cigarette, and listened.

When she finished, he thanked her for contacting his mother and Jean, his agent. He told her to tell Rod that he was extremely grateful.

"Rabbie wasn't a nightmare," he said quietly.

"No, Alec, no nightmare. Police are involved now ... Of Rabbie? There's no sign."

"No, there wouldn't be, Megs," he said grimly, stubbing his cigarette out. He reached across the table, and rising from his seat, he took her hand. "C'mon, girl. I'm taking you to bed."

*\*\*\**

Although the air was cool, the sun was strong on Alec's face as he stood in the entrance of the motel. The dew glistened on the night damp grass as he filled his lungs several times with the cool air and cleared his head of sleep. He didn't have much; Megan saw to that. The girl was an animal.

Megan rose early. After showering and kissing him, she left for the BBC. There were no awkward goodbyes.

He lay in bed for several minutes looking at the door that closed on her departing back. *I'll see her again*, he told himself, *but at Alex's expense?* He had that gut feeling.

He breathed deep again and walked across to the hired car that had been parked there for four days now. It had been unused and unpaid.

Megan phoned Mitchell's Hire Car people and spoke to Mr. Smith, the Advertising and Public Relations Director. She told him the circumstances and suggested they pick the car up and deliver another one in three days time.

Smith, ever with an eye and ear for good follow-up business, suggested they leave the car at the motel and deduct the four unused days from Alec's final bill.

Megan thanked him on Alec's behalf and then did something that she didn't tell Alec about. On the spur of the moment, she gave the affable Mr. Smith her plastic card number, telling him to send the bill on to her C/O the BBC.

Alec started the car and revved the engine. It

was cold in the car, sun or no sun. The chill brought back memories that he quickly pushed into the corner of his mind. His lips tightened, nevertheless. He stayed in that position until the warmed engine gushed hot air over his feet and into the cabin.

"Right," he muttered pushing the stick into gear, "Let battle commence. I'm on my way, Dr. Philip Grossman."

# CHAPTER THIRTY-TWO

"Dr. Philip Grossman? Certainly, sir. Is he expecting you?" the old dear with the easy face asked.

Alec was nonplussed for a moment. *Rod had phoned Grossman, but an appointment?* He smiled quickly. "Yes." If he wasn't expecting him, he is now.

The old dear reached for the phone and looked at Alec. "The name, sir?"

"Alec Sterne," then added as an afterthought, "BBC Glasgow."

The old dear diplomatically slid the glass door as she started to speak to someone. Alec turned his back to the window and once more looked at the message wall with its hundreds of notes pinned to it.

He noticed something he hadn't seen before. It brought a smile to his face. Partly hidden by several tacked up pieces of information, but still clearly readable, some wag had boldly written in black marker pen *The Wailing Wall*.

*True*, Alec thought, *very true*. He was still smiling to himself when he heard the glass window slide open behind him.

"Mr. Sterne?"

Alec turned to the old receptionist who immediately picked up the smile from Alec's face.

"Dr. Grossman has asked me to tell you to please go to the canteen and help yourself to a coffee. He'll be with you as soon as he finishes his seminar. Ten minutes, no more."

Alec felt relieved, although his face didn't show it. This was obviously one hell of a busy man.

"The canteen?"

"Through the swing doors, turn left, straight down the corridor, and it's on the right," then those infamous last words, "You can't miss it."

Alec thanked her with a smile and left. She was right, he didn't miss it. For the first time in years, after hearing those fatal last words, he'd actually found the place he was directed. Alec always considered those words to be the kiss of death in location finding.

He bought himself a coffee in the busy canteen and marveled at the cheapness of it. *Subsidized by my bloody taxes, no doubt,* he thought.

He sat down and looked around. The variety of hair styles and clothing were unbelievable. Some of the kids looked as though they'd been dragged out of bed kicking and screaming.

One or two were looking at him. No doubt, he stuck out like a sore thumb being conservatively dressed, but he knew the look. He'd been clocked. It's the one thing you forget about when you walk into a strange room. He was about to be visited.

Sure enough, one of the kids came across. She could have been halfway to being pretty if she made an effort of putting a brush through her tangled hair.

"Excuse me, but aren't you Alec Sterne?" the tangled hair girl asked.

Alec looked up, feigned being startled, smiled, and nodded.

Tangled hair, her face triumphant, turned and waved to her table.

*Oh , Christ*, Alec groaned inwardly, *the whole bloody table.*

The kids rose en masse excitedly and encamped around Alec, pushing the table and spilling his coffee in the process. After the clamor, the questions commenced. They were obviously drama students and the very types he'd been discussing with Rod and his director in the bar in Glasgow. They were the naïve rose-colored glasses, going to set the acting world alight types.

Alec looked at each one in turn. Their special stars oozing out of them: the Johnny Depps,

Sharon Stones, Brad Pitts, but no Schofields, Geilguds, or Oliviers. He'd seen it all before.

They'll learn the bloody hard way, but meantime, he wasn't going to knock their wonderful enthusiasm. He answered their many questions as carefully and as fully as he could.

He tempered his answers slightly with a few hard facts of life. He was in full flow and enjoying himself. They were hanging on to every word, when he felt someone other than the kids looking at him. He looked up in the direction of the gaze at the small man standing by the coffee bar.

He was neatly dressed in an expensive blue pin-stripe with a large folder under one arm. The small man nodded and smiled at Alec. His nod was telling Alec to carry on with the kids. *So this is the armorer, Dr. Philip Grossman,* thought Alec as he pulled himself back to the questioning pack.

Two or three more minutes of intense questioning passed until one of the kids checked his watch. *Christ, a bloody Rolex*, thought Alec, *no doubt this is one of the hairy arse Porsche brigade.*

Rolex muttered something, and the group rose as one. They said their goodbyes as they exited for a class. Alec released a deep sigh. The Irishman was right; youth is wasted on the young.

Alec turned to look at Dr. Grossman. Grossman smiled and put his cup down. He crooked a finger at Alec and left the canteen.

Alec rose and followed him. He followed the neat, small figure down corridors, up stairs, and down more corridors until Grossman finally stopped at a double swing door.

He paused for the first time to see if Alec was behind him. *Now there's confidence for you or arrogance*, thought Alec. It turned out to be far from either.

Grossman went through the swing doors with Alec a pace behind. It was a large room built in the style of a Roman amphitheater, semi-circular and decked downwards to a stage area. It was an old design that was simple and brilliant; a room that could double as a small theatre and contain lectures. No matter where one sat, there were no chairs, just steps. One could see and hear perfectly.

Grossman went down the terraced decking with an ease that told he had done it a hundred times before. Alec followed more slowly as the height of the steps was deceiving. Grossman reached the stage area and crossed to a desk throwing his folder onto it. With a swift and graceful movement, he jumped and sat atop the desk facing the descending Alec.

Not a word had been spoken during the walk from the canteen, and he was still silent as Alec reached the stage area. Grossman nodded his head in the direction of the first step indicating where Alec should sit. Still, there was not a word. Alec sat.

Grossman's eyes lay on Alec light and warm like a winter duvet. Silent seconds passed as they searched Alec's face. If Alec would have been anything other than an actor, the gaze would have made him flush.

"Sterne?" came a hoarse question. The voice of a boilermaker coming from a 2000-pound suit was quite a contradiction. "Jewish?" the hoarse voice asked.

Alec smiled and shook his head, "No."

"With a name like Sterne?"

Grossman took out a packet of Park Drive cigarettes and lit up. He offered the pack to Alec. Alec declined and took his own filtered brand out. *No wonder he's got a bad throat, smoking them*, he thought, and then he said out loud, "It's a stage name. My birth name is already in use by another."

Grossman nodded, accepting the anomaly, his gray eyes never leaving Alec's face. He paused for a moment whilst he sucked on his cigarette. "Graeme phoned me from Scotland."

The statement hung in the air for several

seconds as the eyes honed down to twin gray lasers. For the first time, Alec started to feel uncomfortable. He couldn't read anything in the gray eyes or on that babyish face. *When in doubt, say nowt*, his mind said.

"It seems you have had a very interesting time, Mr. Sterne."

"That, Dr. Grossman, is a great understatement," Alec said. The gray eyes picked out the tightening of the jaw muscles as Alec spoke.

He nodded understandingly. The ash that grew to a dangerous length on his cigarette suddenly collapsed on to the front of his expensive jacket. Alec thought it was unnoticed and then changed his mind when Grossman's hand came up and automatically brushed it away. It left behind a worse mess than had he left it alone.

"You recovered well."

"Thanks to good friends, yes."

For the first time in ten minutes, the gray eyes looked away. Silence descended momentarily. Grossman coughed to clear his throat, and the eyes returned. "From this moment on, Alec, you will no longer have any friends. Understood?" The grating hoarseness of the voice gave the words of the statement a somber finality.

Alec felt that bowel turning fear that he experienced too many times in the last few weeks flush through him again. *Alone? I have to stand alone?* Alec paused, before slowly nodding agreement. "Understood," he replied.

"Good," Grossman said perkily and jumped off the desk.

He extended his hand towards Alec, and a smile spread across his babyish features. Alec took the hand thankfully. It was a small hand as smooth as silk but with a grip like a docker.

"First and foremost, we'll cut out the Dr.'s and the Mr. You call me Phil, and I will call you Alec."

Alec agreed wholeheartedly. The meeting stepped up a gear. He was not completely alone.

Phil returned to the desk and pulled open a drawer. He extracted two plastic cups and a bottle. Without asking, he poured two generous tots and pushed one towards Alec.

"Kosher Rum. You'll like it. Puts hair back on a bald man," he said.

They both sipped their drinks in silence. The rum slipped down easy. Phil refilled the cups. As Alec reached for his, Phil put his hand on the top to prevent him. The gray eyes rested full on Alec again.

"Now you tell me all from the beginning. Do not leave out the slightest thing. What you saw, what you felt. Every tiny, insignificant detail from the second you saw the stone in the sky falling earthwards."

Alec did well. It took longer than he thought. He didn't gloss over it as with Rod, just giving Rod the salient facts. His excellent memory recalled everything just as Phil requested it.

Phil sat leaning back in his chair looking at the ceiling. Every now and then his chair would tip forward as he made a note of something Alec said and then returned to its original balancing act. He asked no questions. He just listened.

They were disturbed just once, when the doors behind Alec opened and voices came into the room. Alec paused as Phil, still looking at the ceiling, called out commandingly, "Out."

The doors closed immediately. It could have been the dean, and Phil wouldn't have known. Alec got the feeling that he wouldn't have cared either.

Alec continued. His calm matter-of-fact voice painted the pictures. It was only near the end in trying to recall his return to Rabbie's cottage that he stumbled and paused.

Phil listened quietly to the broken and pause-ridden description for a few seconds. Then he allowed his chair to return to its natural, four-legged stance with a thump.

"Enough, Alec," he said diplomatically, "I've

heard that bit from Rod's daughter."

It was far too soon to ask Alec to recall something that almost blew his mind. He looked at the notes on the pad in front of him as Alec lit a cigarette. The sound made Phil automatically start looking for his own cigarettes.

"The stone," he mused to himself, "Everything seems to revolve around the stone."

He looked at Alec and asked, "Rabbie said the stone was around the neck of the skeleton in the remains of a brown robe?"

Alec nodded.

"And the stone is now?"

"Around the neck of Alex," replied Alec.

"And it can't be removed." It was a statement, not a question.

"No, it can't be removed."

Phil puffed on his cigarette and more ash joined the front of his suit. His gray eyes returned to Alec. "I don't like it. It means but one thing." He paused to see if Alec grasped the point. He didn't.

Phil continued as gently as his hoarse voice would allow him. "It means that it can only be removed when she's dead."

"Jesus, Phil." Alec's whispered tone reflected the horror on his face.

Phil nodded and then became even more thoughtful. "There are dozens of questions that, at this moment, we can't answer, Alec. What is so important about the stone? Does it have a power we don't know about?

We know it has a peculiarity in water. We know he has incredible powers. So if the two get together, would they combine?"

Alec shivered at the thought.

"If the stone is important to him, why doesn't he just take it? He's had opportunities. Maybe he can't. Maybe it has to be given to him, hence the asking of Alex at Gawsworth.

One thing is most certain. He needs that stone, and he'll be around until he gets it."

Phil paused to put out his cigarette.

"Which," he continued, "gives us little time. Time to put in some research. Time to put some flesh on the bones of this character and to find out what it is or who it is and whether mortal or a continuum."

Phil paused looking at the jotter in front of him. "Describe the … No, better still." Phil turned the jotter over and pushed it towards Alec. "Draw the stone for me, Alec, as near actual size as you can."

Phil looked on as Alec drew a facsimile of the stone, complete with faint etchings on the face. Phil brought the finished drawing towards him and pursed his lips.

"I agree with you. These faint markings could

well be an inscription." He looked up. "That inscription could unlock the door and tell us what and who we are dealing with.

Now then, there are several ways we can highlight these markings, but we need the stone and that we can't have."

"I could bring Alex down here, Phil."

Phil shook his head. "No, some of the techniques could be highly dangerous with a human being less than twelve inches from the source. No, but a closer inspection is a necessity."

Silence fell again as Phil rubbed his chin with his hand, and he looked at the drawing. "Photograph," he said suddenly, "Have you a photograph we could blow up?"

"No, Phil. I didn't ta- Just a minute," Alec added excitedly, "I did take a couple of the campsite as we left, and Alex was smack in the middle of one of them."

"Good," Phil said calmly, "Where is it?"

"Christ, it's still in the camera. It's film, not digital."

"No bother, just bring me the camera. I'll get the lab to process it very carefully. Spot of luck that, Alec, it still being in the camera. A commercial lab wouldn't take the pains that we do." Phil looked at his watch.

"Am I keeping you, Phil?"

"No, my stomach was telling me it was time for food. Fancy something to eat?"

"Sure, why not?"

"Right then. Let's go to the canteen. It will be quiet now … No autograph hunters," he added with a twinkle, "We can eat, and I can ask you more questions at the same time. They do a passable roast by the way."

\*\*\*

Phil was right; it was a passable roast. The Yorkshire pudding had the same aerodynamic lines as a Frisbee, but otherwise excellent value.

They finished their meal and at Phil's behest, garnered two large coffees. They headed for a small staff smoking room nearby. Phil lit up immediately, whilst Alec preferred his own filtered brand.

"No wonder your voice is going Phil … smoking those sticks of dynamite."

Phil smiled ruefully.

"It's possible the root cause is this," he said waving the little cigarette about, "but I have had cancer of the throat, and the ray treatment has a tendency to burn away some of the vocal chords."

Alec just looked at him. Phil shrugged his shoulders. "Gets a little hairy at times during lectures."

"And you're still smoking?" Alec asked with quiet incredulity.

Phil smiled again. "Now, Alec, I don't need you to lecture me."

Ash fell onto the front of his jacket again as he deftly changed the subject. "The coins, Alec. You have them?"

Alec nodded and reached into his anorak pocket, where he'd found them whilst looking for his cigarettes about a hundred miles from Glasgow. He knew he hadn't brought them out of Rabbie's cottage. He couldn't have. It was Megan, knowing full well they were evidence and that they might possibly help him.

He dropped the green baize purse onto the table in front of Phil. Phil looked at the purse without touching.

"Now, Alec, cast your mind back to when you entered Rabbie's cottage after leaving the pub. Am I right in saying that virtually everything was in its place, apart from the poker that is? No sign of ransacking?" His gray eyes lay steady on Alec's face.

"That's right, Phil."

"No drawers open?"

"No."

Phil took a moment and looked down at the green purse. He picked it up. "So this came out of a closed drawer across the room and came to earth by your hand?"

Alec swallowed before he answered, "Yes."

"Mmm … so we must assume, Alec, that he was in the room with you." The gray eyes saw the brief flash of fear in Alec's eyes. "Rather a macabre sense of humor, don't you think, Alec?"

Alec nodded, and Phil continued, "But he didn't harm you. Now why?" Phil shrugged again and drank from his cup. "Another question that needs answering."

"Phil," Alec's voice held a note of anxiety, "all these questions and no answers; the who, what, why? Look, I've got to be honest with you. I'm scared shitless.

I want as far away from this as I can get. I've been with it, and I know what it can do. I'm not interested in putting a yardstick against it to find out how much it can do. The only trouble is somehow I'm involved. Why it should do that to Rabbie and not touch me? Well, God only knows."

"Easy, Alec, easy," the hoarse voice dropped several tones and was just above a whisper. His hand reached across and gripped Alec's wrist.

"Questions have to be asked, and what's more important, Alec, answered. The identity of this character must be found to give us a semblance of a chance."

"Us, Phil?" Alec questioned sardonically.

"Us, Alec." The gray eyes honed down to lasers again. "It might have slipped by you, but you went to Rabbie's for help, information, call it what you will, and Rabbie Stewart is dead."

He paused to inhale, and his eyes never left Alec's face. "Now you come to me."

Realization hit Alec as Phil added, "So that makes it us. Doesn't it, Alec?"

"Oh, God. What the hell have I got you into, Phil? And what about Megan and Rod Graeme?"

"No," Phil came in quickly, "about them you don't worry, unless they have done something that appears to be a threat. Rabbie imparted information."

He raised his hands to cut off Alec's words, "He did impart information. Believe me." Phil hefted the green baize purse. "The coins will give us a starting date."

"Of course. Why the hell didn't I think of that?" Alec's mood changed. There was something tangible to go on.

Phil smiled at him. The soft, baby face belied the strength behind it. "Well, Alec … In all fairness, we already know the date. The coins will just verify it. Rabbie told us the ship was part of the *Great Armada*. He even told us the name." Phil was forced to smile again at the look on Alec's face.

"I'm an actor, Phil, not a historian," Alec protested, "If you say a not too bright one, you'll be checking the dates on those coins from a very peculiar position."

They wandered back to the canteen for a coffee refill, and Alec asked what the plan of action would be.

"The coins will give us a date to work back from. Back, because we know this thing has been underwater for the past four and half centuries. And back further because there is something vaguely biblical in its actions.

The warnings before the ensuing actions: It warned Rabbie; it warned you. And back possibly even further because somewhere in my learning, my reading, my digs ... I have a feeling that I have come across this being before."

"Aw c'mon, Phil. It's hard enough trying to make myself believe this thing is still alive after 400 years. Are you trying to tell me that it could be older than that?" Alec asked incredulously.

"I think the stone will tell us, but it could be four, maybe five, thousand years old ... possibly as old as thinking man."

"Jesus H. Christ!" Alec was flabbergasted.

Phil stubbed out his cigarette and breathed out the last of the smoke. "Alec, does it not throw some questions up in your mind that whilst you are amazed and dumbfounded regarding the existence of such a being, I and many others like me take the possibility of such a being for granted?"

"I just thought you were being cool and laid back, Phil."

"Far from it, Alec," he said flatly, "I take it you don't have a faith … in a God, that is?" he added.

"No, not really."

"Then this would be a good time to find one," Phil remarked flatly, "You see, Alec, my faith is my religion, my people, and my race."

Phil took a sip of his coffee. "Sunday school as a child?" he queried.

"Yeeess."

"The Garden of Eden. Four entities are involved. Name them? I'm serious. Name them."

"Alright, alright. Adam. Eve," Alec paused, searchingly, "God."

He looked at Phil, who nodded, "The fourth?"

Alec paused, "Well, I suppose you must mean the snake."

"Serpent," corrected Phil, "Satan in the guise of a serpent. Satan, Alec. Do you understand?

Thousands of years ago, even in the very

beginning, allowances were made for evil to exist, because it did exist and," he paused momentarily, "does exist.

The various Tribes of Israel recognized the existence of evil. The very name Satan is a Hebrew word, so why should something that doesn't exist have a name?"

Phil started to dust down the front of his jacket but lost the battle and lost interest. "You say you have no faith, Alec. No faith as such, that is. Yet deep inside you, you must have a belief. Did you not reach for the cross in the little chapel when he enticed you inside?"

"Yes, I bloody well did," Alec said fervently.

Phil nodded and continued, "Don't get me wrong, Alec. I'm not trying to convert you or anything. I'm just trying to explain to you why it's easy for me to accept all that has happened to you."

Alec's mind was back in the chapel as he looked at Phil. "Phil, my knowledge of these things is zero, apart from what I've read in novels and seen at the movies. All, I might add, from someone's weird and wonderful imagination. This is fact, but how come this thing took the piss out of me in a church on sanctified ground?"

"I'm afraid, Alec, that's exactly what it was doing. That and showing you its strength."

"What? You mean like a bloody peacock spreading its tail?"

"Precisely. Rather animal like, don't you think?"

Phil suddenly stood up. "Look. No more questions, Alec. I have a tremendous amount of work and thinking to do and precious little time. If we are to achieve anything and getting back to a plan of campaign that negative, I need it … like yesterday?"

Alec stood up and returned Phil's confidant smile. "Right, but this research ... can I help?"

"Alec, in the Central Library alone, there are over 600 various testaments, etc. That's without the works I have in my own library. Plus there are parchments and scrolls … some 2000 years old."

He steered Alec to the door with a friendly arm around him. "Now at some time or other, I have gone through them all. What I need is a trigger … that little piece of jigsaw knowledge, that little piece that's starts the whole picture.

Understand me? I think the stone could provide it." The husky, condescending voice ended firmly with, "So go and get me that negative."

# CHAPTER THIRTY-THREE

Alec rolled down the hill past *The Ship* at an easy pace. The lane was narrow, and nine times out of ten, there was always someone trying to pick up speed coming from the opposite direction. It paid to slow down.

His reduced speed also gave him time to look across the valley over the Dane and see his cottage. The sight never failed to gladden his heart. He just loved coming home. He already felt uplifted.

The session with Phil, the armorer, he laughed to himself, had given him strength and cause for hope. The little man was definitely what the Jewish Brethren would call *Ein grosse mensch*; a contradiction in physical terms, but in intelligence most definitely a big man.

Alec was no slouch in the brain department, but it was damn good to have a man of Phil's caliber on his side. Phil hadn't painted a pretty picture with his questions and observations, but the strength and belief in the man came through and wrapped around you. Those eyes at times made him feel as though some x-ray machine was scanning him.

Alec changed down a gear as the declination became more acute.

If it could be fought, fighting this thing wouldn't be easy. If there were a way, Phil, he was sure, would find it.

He looked across the valley through the trees. He could see his cottage for a split second. His car wasn't there; the girls were obviously out.

"Sod it," he muttered to himself, disappointed. He picked up a box of Ma's favorite chocolate liquors and a large bunch of flowers for Alex. Now he was going to miss the look on their faces.

He navigated the narrow bridge over the river Dane and pulled up by the side of the cottage. No car.

The door of the cottage was locked; a thing never done unless the intention was to be away from home longer than a couple of hours. His surprise was ruined.

He found a note from Ma on the hall stand:

*Al,*

*Taken Alex to doc's. Back, who knows?*
*You know what doctor's surgeries are like.*
*Left a nice salad in frig.*

*Luv, Ma.*

*P.S. Fix the boiler. This place is like an igloo.*

Alec laughed at the note as he put the presents on the hall stand. He looked at the postscript again and automatically reached out to touch the hall radiator. It was red hot.

His brow furrowed as he looked around the hall. It was cold in here, like a November day. It was a damn sight warmer outside. He touched the radiator again. With radiators that hot, they should have been walking around in bikinis.

He walked through the rooms of the cottage. Every radiator was near glowing, and Alec shivered under his anorak.

He came back from checking the boiler. It was well logged up and working perfectly. There was nothing wrong with the system.

There was nothing amiss in the cottage. The only thing he noticed out of place was a large comfy chair. His TV chair had been turned to face the window. He looked at it and shrugged his shoulders.

Ma was garden mad. She probably sat there and tut-tutted at what Alec flippantly called his herb garden. It was his euphemism for being a lazy gardener.

He went upstairs to find his camera. It was whilst he was there that he heard the noise. It slightly shook him, knowing he was alone in the house.

He stepped out of the bedroom and stood on the small, decked landing that separated the upstairs rooms. The strange, muffled thrumming noise stopped. The acoustics and the two-feet-thick walls of the old property made it virtually impossible to trace the source.

Alec took a step forward and cocked his head. His breathing was quiet but his exhaled breath hung mistily around him on the unusually cold landing. The only sound was the occasional gurgle of water in the pipes, and there it was again.

This time there was no mistaking the direction from where it was emanating. It was coming from the spare bedroom that doubled as Alec's office.

He crossed the landing and opened the stripped pine door. The noise stopped. He stood in the room and looked around. Nothing stirred, and nothing had been moved. Ma had opened the window slightly to air the room, but that was all.

"C'mon, Al. You're hearing things now," he muttered and shivered again at the coldness of the room. He turned to go but froze in the doorway as the sound started again.

His heart missed a beat. He turned his head to

look over his left shoulder in the direction of the sound. It came from his electric typewriter. It was literally a museum piece whose golf ball was going mad. It was whirring and striking the platen like a thing possessed.

Alec breathed out, relieved. "Christ," he muttered, "must have left the bloody thing switched on."

He crossed to the machine to switch it off but pulled up short. He realized the machine was switched off. He checked the platen and the paper. There was a mass of gibberish in printed half strokes. It was circles and squiggles equaling unreadable gibberish. It had to be a short in the wiring.

He rolled another sheet of paper into the machine and quickly typed his name. Perfect. It was a glitch and nothing more. Can you expect perfection from a museum piece bought at an auction?

He turned to leave, and the machine went berserk again. "Christ. I haven't got enough on my plate. I've now got a runaway typewriter."

It stopped as suddenly as it started. The gibberish-filled page spun out of the machine and lay atop Alec's makeshift desk. "You are going back to the repair shop, bugger, as soon as I find the time."

Alec pulled the power plug from the wall.

He collected his camera and went downstairs into the kitchen.

His mail had been neatly stacked by Ma and put on the tiled windowsill overlooking the valley. He sifted through it and found a slim, brown, cardboard box with his mail.

It was unmarked and about the size of a pen presentation case. He shook it, looked at it again, and then threw it back with the rest of the mail. He'd sort it all out when he returned.

He turned to the kitchen message pad to see who had phoned. There were several messages in Ma's neat writing. None were too serious, and they could wait a few more hours. Only one stuck out. In the middle of the list was one for Alex from her agent.

*Now why on earth did she not reply? Come to think, why has Ma taken her to the doctor's? Could be something and nothing, I suppose*, he thought, *Woman's complaint ... never mind. I'll see them when I get back.*

He pulled the kitchen pad over and tore off a sheet of paper. He scribbled a short note to them both, saying he'd be back in a couple of hours. He raided his cigarette cupboard for a few packs, and then he placed the note with the flowers and chocolates. He left to take the negative to Phil.

The journey from Wincle to Manchester

takes on average of about fifty minutes to an hour. Alec found out from past experience that, whether clogging it or taking it easy, he could only expect a five-minute difference from par. Driving fast would prove and save nothing.

He looked at his watch. It was already 6:30 pm. Phil must have planned a long evening. Alec just hoped to God it wasn't in vain and that his camera work was worthwhile.

He couldn't remember much about taking the shot, just that he did. It was one of those automatic gestures that one makes. He did remember seeing Alex in the lens, so there was at least one shot. Whether it was up to the standard Phil required was a dog with a different collar.

Parking outside the university proved fairly easy. Quite a number of cars had left the vicinity. *Lecturers, no doubt*, thought Alec.

The cars that were left, obviously, belonged to the students who were imbibing their subsidized ale in the students' bar.

Alec paused at the reception window, and the night porter told him Dr. Grossman was in the little amphitheatre, expecting him. He instructed Alec on the easiest way to get there and retired to his little corner with a dog-eared novel.

Alec espied the lurid back and the author's name, Hank Janson. *Christ, I haven't seen a*

*Hank Janson since I was a kid*, he thought, *That's progress for you. Emancipation gone mad ... too many Jackie Collins and the like have killed the male domination in the sexy book market.*

Alec found the double doors to the amphitheatre and swung in. He took three steps down to the stage area before he realized Phil had company in the shape of two men. All three looked up from their conversation at the sound of Alec's footsteps.

"Ah, come on down, Alec," Phil's hoarse voice called out as Alec paused, "I see you have the camera. Good."

Phil rose from behind the desk and went to meet Alec. It wasn't easy. Phil wasted no time and obviously had been very busy.

The stage area was littered with books. Some books were open and some stacked. His desktop, by which the two men stood, was also littered.

Alec looked at the two street-attired men. One was wearing a fawn-colored raincoat and the other, older and more portly of the two, was wearing a light overcoat.

They weren't colleagues of Phil's. The look on their faces, whilst not grim, was certainly not the look that a colleague has when about to be introduced to a personality. There was also wariness about them.

They worked as a team and were very professional at the way they separated at Alec's arrival on stage. They casually placed themselves nonchalantly at either side of him. They were not too close, but there was definitely a feeling of being shepherded.

Phil put his small hand on Alec's elbow and led him to the desk. He sidestepped the self-made obstacle course in the process.

"See what I mean, Alec," Phil said with his head bobbing at the books, "Almost a needle in a haystack, eh?" He shook the camera. "This will give us a clue. I'm sure of it."

The younger of the two men coughed politely, and Phil's head swiveled at the sound. There was a brief flash of annoyance that rippled across his face. It disappeared as quickly as it came.

He looked back at Alec. "Alec, I'd like to introduce you to?" His face turned to the younger of the two men to query their forgotten names.

"Detective Sergeant Muir, sir and this is my superior, Detective Chief Inspector Black," came the answer, but they were looking and talking to Alec.

"From Glasgow C.I.D, Alec," Phil added quietly.

Alec must have made a small movement

without being aware of it, for Phil continued, "Easy Alec. I've been talking to them for over an hour. It has been a difficult and somewhat enlightening conversation. Has it not gentlemen?"

"It has indeed on both counts, Dr. Grossman," replied the portly Inspector Black. He turned to Alec, "Mr. Sterne we would like you to accompany us back to Glasgow."

Alec felt the adrenalin start to flow as a feeling of guilt flushed through him.

Black continued, "I must point out to you that you are not under arrest, and your return with us will be of your own volition. However," the thick Glaswegian accent ploughed on with the terminology, "should you refuse to do so, I am empowered to arrest you."

"Cer-," Alec coughed to clear his throat, "certainly."

"Good." Black turned to Phil, "Well, Dr. Grossman, I thank you for your time, and as a God fearing person, I can only wish you all the best." He glanced at Alec. "I'll have him back as quick as I can. You have the problem, but unfortunately, I have the paperwork."

Phil looked at Alec and smiled at him. The smile spoke volumes.

*Thank Christ*, Alec thought, *of all the hard-nosed coppers I could have got, I got a Scottish*

*Presbyterian. No one firmer in their Faith.*

But Muir was a different kettle of fish. It was obvious by his tone of voice that he didn't go along with his chief's interpretation. "Is there anybody you want to phone, Sterne, before we leave?"

*Hard-nosed bastard*, thought Alec, but aloud said, "No, Sergeant, there isn't."

Alec turned to Phil and handed him the Hire Car keys. "Phil, could you ask Mitchell's to pick up their car? It's outside, and if you have the time, phone this number."

He scribbled a number on Phil's jotter. "It's home. My mother and Alex are expecting me. Tell them … oh, that I've had to return to Glasgow for an audition … Back, well?" He looked at the C.I.D. men.

"Thirty-six hours," Black interjected.

Alec smiled at Phil and shrugged his shoulders. Phil nodded.

# CHAPTER THIRTY-FOUR

Megan finished the morning news conference and sat in her office, deep in thought. *Four days passed since Rabbie Stewart disappeared ... yet no news story.* She opened her desk drawer and looked at the twenty-minute video cassette that John put there.

*Why no news story? The News Department contacts in the Police HQ mentioned nothing. By now this story should be front page headlines, but the police are keeping it under wraps. Unusual for the police. They must have someone on the case that doesn't go by the book. Who the hell could that be?*

Her mind ran through all the faces and characters she knew personally or by reputation. It came up blank.

She closed the drawer on the tape. That thing was becoming dynamite. The quieter this game was being played, the hotter this property became.

Under normal circumstances she could have brought it out as a scoop, amongst a welter of other newspaper and television news, but by doing so, it left the door open for the police to make enquiries. Whose door would they be knocking on first? Why hers, of course.

But timing it right, it would have been accepted. *So, who the hell is keeping this quiet? Who the hell is handling this case?*

On impulse, she reached for the phone and punched a number. "Glasgow C.I.D.," a voice answered.

Megan's own voice sweetened and became more lilting. "Is that you, Mac? … It's Megan."

"Oh … Hi, Megan. How's the world of television?"

"Quiet Mac … too bloody quiet."

"Quiet enough to take me out to dinner on your expense account?" Mac laughed down the phone. The braying sound made Megan wince as she moved the receiver away from her ear.

"Now, Mac, what would your lovely wife say?"

Megan heard him groan at the other end. "Don't remind me … Don't remind me."

It was Megan's turn to laugh at his discomfort. "Anything happening, Mac?" she slipped in easy.

"Just the usual run of the mill, Megan. I'm sure you've been told."

"Yes, we have."

Mac's flippant, usual run of the mill description of Glasgow's crime rate grossly under read the enormous number of crimes committed daily in the city.

"I was looking for something interesting … something for a future story … something I could work on for a few days."

"You getting bored Megan? … My offer still stands."

"Heh. C'mon, Mac. I can't have dinner ten hours a day. I'm in this office now, and I need to work on something. Is anything happening outside the area?"

He eyes narrowed as she asked, and then more so as Mac paused before he spoke.

"No, not really … D.C.I. Black was called out of town on something. He's gone down South. If it's something, no doubt, you will get to know when he gets back."

"South, Mac? …. You mean London?"

"No, not as far … Manchester, I think or around there anyway."

*Jesus, they're on to Alec*, thought Megan. "Did you say, D.C.I. Black?"

"Yeah. Black."

"I thought he'd retired?"

"No, next month."

"Last fling before throwing in the towel?"

"Could be, Megan … could be."

Megan made small talk for two more minutes and then replaced the receiver. She sat looking

311

at the phone for several seconds.

Mac had been evasive and dead-panned about Black, but she got what she wanted. *D.C.I. Black* … She riffled through the pages of her mind. *Got him. Gray-haired, large face like chiseled granite, rarely smiled, talks little … church man.*

*A very interesting background. Queen's bodyguard many years ago. On easy terms with M.I. 5 and 6. Rumors of him being in Intelligence. Certainly escorted an exchange of spies some years back.*

*All this and never seemed to leave Glasgow C.I.D.? The man's an enigma*, thought Megan, *But if he's gone to Manchester, he's after Alec. This is where Dad said we were on thin ice.*

Megan's brow furrowed. She reached for the phone again, and contacted the video editing suite. After finding out when the suite was liable to be quiet, she booked it for 9:45 that evening.

# CHAPTER THIRTY-FIVE

The black Jaguar slipped onto the M6 Motorway and sifted through the traffic into the fast lane. Once there, Muir toed the accelerator, and the car powerfully nosed up, thrusting Alec and D.C.I. Black deeper into the comfortable grained leather upholstery.

Black spoke for the first time in thirty miles. "You surprise me, Mr. Sterne."

Alec turned his gaze away from looking at the back of Muir's thick, almost nonexistent neck to look at Black. "Why is that, sir?" Alec didn't know why he said sir, but Black certainly commanded the title.

"You haven't asked one question."

Alec turned his head to look back at Muir. He noticed Muir imperceptibly angled his head to catch the conversation.

Alec looked into the rearview mirror and looked into Muir's eyes. They were case hardened. "Tantamount to a confession of guilt?" asked Alec.

Black gave a soft grunt that was almost lost in the humming of the tires. Muir's ears twitched and his eyes in the mirror switched from Alec to Black. Alec decided he didn't like Muir.

He leaned forward, close to Muir's ear and his eyes fixed on the mirror. "He grunted, Sergeant."

The eyes in the mirror didn't alter as Alec returned to his seat.

"Mr. Sterne, don't play around with Muir," Black said very softly, "He's been with me many years and is, in many respects, a law unto himself. He is quite capable of doing things to you that an army of doctors wouldn't be able to tell you had died from anything other than natural causes."

"And he's a policeman?"

"A special kind, Mr. Sterne, and his special talents go with the turf."

"And I warrant this kind of attention?"

Black was silent for a moment. "No, you warrant me, but where I go Muir goes."

Alec sat back deep in thought. *Muir's his bodyguard? Now what kind of policeman rates his own bodyguard? Christ, the mind boggles.*

Darkness descended on the motorway, and Muir flicked on the powerful, double-banked headlights, making artificial daylight a hundred yards ahead of the speeding vehicle.

The humming of the tires and the warmth and

comfort of the seats made Alec drowsy. The lack of conversation didn't help either. Black didn't talk much and Muir not at all.

It wasn't until the vehicle stopped at a motorway filling station, near Lancaster, that Alec realized he must have fallen asleep. He looked up, momentarily disorientated. Muir was outside filling the double tanks with petrol. Black was still sat next to Alec.

"Lancaster … petrol," Black said by way of explanation.

"Oh, I'm sorry. I must have dropped off."

Black's craggy face looked down at him and nodded. "It's a statement I want, Mr. Sterne. I know you didn't do it."

"Could we possibly have some coffee?"

They sat sipping the coffee in front of a huge plate glass window, watching Muir park the car after filling the tanks.

"And how do you know I didn't do it, Inspector Black?"

Black looked calmly into Alec's eyes and then turned to look out of the window again. "We found a palm print on the front door put there after the blood had been smeared. The same palm and finger prints were found along with its colleagues on either side of the brass hearth rail, where someone had knelt to vomit."

He pulled his gaze back from the window to

look at Alec. "The same prints were on a bottle of McCallan left on the table, so … quad erat demondstrandum.

Someone called after the crime, bringing a hospitality bottle. Places bottle on table, lights lamp, surveys the scene, and because he's basically a neat person vomits into the hearth."

Alec swallowed hard at the memory. "How did you know I was there? My prints are not on file."

Black paused to sip his coffee. "We share the same good friend."

"Rod Graeme?"

Black nodded. "Without him and Dr. Grossman, you'd be in dire straits now. The publican at *The Thistle* recognized you; one of the fallbacks of being a famous face, Mr. Sterne.

Oh, by the way, he has some money for you. I doubt whether you know it, but you called a second time for another bottle of McCallan. He said you didn't know whether you were on this earth or Fuller's earth.

His quotation and no doubt apt you gave him a twenty-pound note, took the bottle, and scampered with no change."

He paused as Muir arrived to stand over the table. "Coffee, Stan?"

Muir declined, shaking his head.

Black put his cup down. "Right then, Mr.

Sterne, we'll be off."

# CHAPTER THIRTY-FIVE

The figure stood on the hill overlooking Alec's cottage surrounded by the black, rustling trees and the darkening night.

The wind danced through the swaying grass and moved through the branches, bringing groaning and sighing from the old trees. It twitched and tugged at the brown cloak of the bare-legged and sandaled figure. It gave up the struggle to move it and passed on to easier things.

Immobile, the figure watched as the car drew up outside the cottage and Ma alighted. She unlocked the cottage door and returned to help Alex from the car.

The figure on the hill raised its arm slowly, palm forward in the direction of the couple. Ma stopped as Alex stiffened. Her face was drawn and creased in pain as the stone around her neck strengthened its embrace.

The arm commenced to rise and increased Alex's discomfort, then stopped its upward journey as something made the cowled head move from the couple below to look northwards.

Moments passed before the arm came down

to stop its teasing and Ma was able to continue to help Alex into the cottage. She was unaware of the figure on the hill.

Seconds passed and then the figure turned to face north. The cowled head leaned back as though looking at the heavens and listening. Suddenly, as if summoned, the figure moved over the grass in a northerly direction.

The wind followed it and left the hilltop quiet. The leaves stopped rustling, the branches stopped creaking, and an owl, previously too afraid to appear, hooted the all clear.

# CHAPTER THIRTY-SIX

Megan retrieved the videotape from her desk drawer in the office. She looked at it thoughtfully and then punched a number on the telephone. John answered.

Megan was short and to the point. "John. Megan. Meet me in the editing suite, will you? I want to look at this tape we took at Gourock."

Megan didn't let John reply as she put the phone down and left the office, taking it for granted that he would be there.

The suite was empty and that was the way Megan wanted it. The Umatic editing equipment was still stuck in one corner, being outdated by newer digital equipment.

John was complete with a plastic coffee cup. She smiled at John and thanked him. He was a young man and a go-getter, destined to go places in the BBC.

Megan handed him the tape, and he expertly handled the switches of the complex equipment. "I'll bet you're glad they didn't throw this out, John," Megan said, nodding at the machine.

John was embarrassed, remembering his mistake and actually blushed. "Right, Megan.

Run it through first and make a copy, then edit onto the master? Or what?"

"Copy only… no edit, no nothing."

He looked at her and shrugged. "You're the boss." He took a blank tape and pressed it into the companion slot. He pressed down a few switches and gauges flickered, wheels hummed and whirred, then stopped.

It didn't take long for the twenty-minute tape to go through. He rewound the tape and looked at Megan. "Shall we have a look see?"

Megan nodded and sat on the stool next to him. He pressed a switch, and the tape began to play.

There were some exterior scenes, which put a slight grimace on John's face. That was soon replaced with a satisfied nodding as the scene switched to indoors. He had made excellent use of what available lighting he had. The colors and focus were more than acceptable on the panning shots of the walls.

There were just one or two darkish corners that could soon be put right on the machine. It was the low angle shot of the floor on the bent brass poker and hearth that made them both sit up and look at each other. The view panned up from the floor to take in the edge of the fireplace and the Welsh dresser with the darkened kitchen doorway in the corner.

John muttered, "What … the … hell?" He stopped the tape and rewound it to start the pan again.

As it reached the darkened doorway, he freeze-framed it. They looked carefully at the framed picture, and then John turned to Megan, who was still staring wide-eyed at the picture.

The shadows were dark in the corner and the focus wasn't 100 percent, but it looked as if a figure was standing there. It was watching them as they filmed. It was a figure wearing a cloak and cowl.

"That's bloody funny. There was nobody there when we took this, Megan." He looked back at the picture. "It's got to be a trick of the light. I'll lighten it a bit."

Megan rose from her stool. "No, John. Don't touch it. I want my Dad to see it. You finish your coffee. I'll be back in two minutes."

Megan left the editing suite as rapidly as she could without running. If what was on that tape was what she thought it was, then her dad needed to see it. Thank God he was working late.

John looked at the picture again as he picked up his coffee. *Yes*, he mused, *it does look like the figure of a man.* He sipped his coffee and noticed the picture tearing slightly at the edge, making the figure appear to move.

He leaned over the switches and made some adjustments. *The picture should be steady now. Yes, the tearing has stopped.* He allowed himself a small smile and a mental pat on the back.

The smile froze on his face. The figure moved. John's eyes flickered over the switches and dials. Everything was rock steady. He looked back at the freeze frame. The figure was definitely moving, moving towards the camera and out of the shadows.

John, with coffee cup half way to his mouth, was transfixed. "This is impossible," he gasped as he saw the cowled figure move to the center of Rabbie's small room.

The figure stopped. John couldn't see the face in the recesses of the dark cowl, but somehow he knew it was looking at him. John slowly stood up and started backing away from the console. His eyes were hypnotically fixed on the picture, and the figure moved again.

Its right hand came up from its side and paused again when the palm was facing John. A noise came from the picture, and John's eyes slid down to the cause.

The brass poker, bent like a giant fish hook, made a metallic sound as it stirred on the polished stone floor. Suddenly it rose, defying gravity and John's belief, to hang suspended in front of the outstretched palm.

It hung there, gently swaying for what seemed an eternity, and then John saw the hand move contemptuously. The image of the brass poker exploded through the tube with an enormous bang. It was the last thing on this earth he ever saw.

Rod and Megan hurried down the corridor to the editing suite. They heard a loud bang followed by a whoosh and a scream that was stillborn before it got to John's throat. A tremendous thud shook the mainframe of the building.

"Oh my God!" Rod started running. He hit the double doors, his impetus carrying him to the center of the room before he saw the carnage.

The tube had exploded, showering the room with deadly, razor-sharp fragments, but that wasn't what killed John. Rod and Megan looked on with horror.

A brass poker, bent and twisted like a huge fishing hook, ripped through his throat. The handle had been smashed into the new ceiling of the editing suite, some twelve feet up, with unbelievable force. John's bleeding body was suspended, swaying and twitching as the lifeblood pumped out.

***

The black Jaguar was hardly twenty miles from Glasgow when the call came through. Muir slipped in an earpiece and tapped a button. He listened and then nodded into the mirror at Black.

Black picked up the small, cell phone like extension that was recessed somewhere in the leather. "Stay on the line, Stan." Muir nodded as Black listened.

The conversation was short, and the only reply Black gave was a small grunt. He snapped the phone shut and replaced it. "You heard, Stan?" Muir nodded a reply.

Muir, a natural driver, drove with the expertise of a rally driver. He easily side-slipped slower traffic and dipped down side streets with no alteration in speed. Alec was lost as the car whipped in and out of back streets that were unfamiliar. He looked at Black.

"Our mutual friend is in a little trouble." That was it. No explanation. The granite face continued looking forward.

There was nothing else for Alec to do but sit tight. *Rod's in trouble? Jesus, what kind of trouble? And where the hell are we going?* The thoughts tumbled through Alec's head.

He soon found out, as Muir expertly navigated an acute angle right-hander and pulled up outside the front of the BBC.

Alec was amazed. He'd been here dozens of times and yet hadn't recognized one street in Muir's back street dash. He'd homed in like a heat-seeking missile.

The reception area of the Beeb was alight, and the three occupants of the car could see Rod Graeme calmly having a cup of coffee with night security. He looked up as he saw the Jaguar stop outside, and he said a few words to the watchman.

Alec looked at Rod carefully as Rod, for the watchman's benefit, welcomed them to the BBC and ushered them quickly into the administration building. He looked strained. His face lost some of its color and he was smoking.

He stopped in the quiet corridor and spoke. "Thanks for coming so quickly, Arthur." His voice was shaky, but he was getting it under control. "It's in the editing suite, on the fourth floor."

He paused to look at Alec. "My God, Alec." His voice went again, and his shoulders sagged. Bewilderment touched his entire body as his arms waved.

"Rod," Black's thick accent cut through and brought Rod back to face him. "Show us the way."

# CHAPTER THIRTY-SEVEN

It was 4 o'clock in the morning when the double doors opened, and the white, dust-coated figure elbowed his way through, noisily and with difficulty. The noise and difficulty came from trying to negotiate the swing doors whilst carrying a six-foot by three-foot hardboard sheet. It was not so much heavy as just bloody awkward.

Phil, shirt-sleeved and tired looking, peered up over his Pickwickian half spectacles. He pushed away the large Hebrew volume he was reading and stood up removing his spectacles.

The figure carrying the board came down the decked stairs and walked into the stage lights, bringing Phil back into the present. "Ah, James … I see you had some luck then?" Phil's voice was huskier than ever, and he coughed slightly to clear his throat.

"Some, Dr. Grossman … Some. How good? Well, you'll soon see." The voice was tired but obviously interested in Grossman's reaction to his nocturnal endeavors.

Phil helped him carry the board to the back of the stage area, placing it upright where the light was good. They backed away from it in order to get it in perspective and view it better.

Phil rubbed his chin, nodding. "Mmmm … Excellent, James. You really do amaze me at times."

"Thank you, Dr. Grossman."

The pair stood silently for several seconds, looking at the larger-than-life size picture. It was a picture of Alex.

"She's a very pretty lady, Doctor."

"Yes, he has excellent taste."

"HE, Doctor?"

"Ohhh … a colleague I'm working with at the moment." Phil flapped his hand nonchalantly.

"Who is she?"

Phil didn't answer immediately, but when he did, his voice was melancholy. A tinge of sadness slipped into his eyes. "I'm afraid … She is …" He paused and then continued, "The Guardian of the Stone."

A thoughtful silence descended and then Phil burst back into life. "But, James, it's not the girl I am interested in at the moment. It's this piece here."

He walked to the desk and amongst the debris, found a small piece of white blackboard chalk. He walked up to the large facsimile of Alex and drew a white square about the stone hanging in front of her shirt. James joined him.

"How big can you blow that up for me? Without losing overall sharpness," he added.

James stood looking and silently pondering as Phil carried on.

"You see these marks here and here?" He pointed out the faint scratch marks that appeared slightly white against the dark background of the stone. "Use these as your guide. I must be able to decipher that legend ... or parts of it," he added quickly as he saw the look of dismay flit across James's face.

"Keep those in focus, sharp, and I should be able to do it. Just give me some more size," he pleaded. He turned to look into James's face.

James looked back into the zealous, gray eyes. Shaking his head in disbelief, he said, "And when would you like it? ... Don't tell me ... Yesterday?"

Phil smiled at him and clapped him on the shoulder, then returned to study the picture closely.

# CHAPTER THIRTY-EIGHT

It was four am, and Rod's office was thick with the smell of cigarette smoke and coffee. Megan's face was white and her eyes were ringed with tiredness and crying. She sat silently next to Alec.

Rod was behind his desk quietly smoking and alternately taking sips of coffee. He occasionally looked at Megan and Alec.

Black, standing by the door still wearing his light overcoat in the muggy room, put his cup down as Muir entered the room. He caught Black's eye, and a gentle nod passed for a two-sentence conversation. *These two are almost telepathic*, thought Alec.

"Help yourself to some coffee, Stan," Black said.

Muir declined and instead reached into his pocket and pulled out his notebook. Black looked across to Megan and pulled a chair up to sit by the desk. "Question time, Megan." The rough Glaswegian accent softened from rough-hewn granite down to limestone.

Megan looked at Alec, who put his arm around her and gave her a little smile. She nodded, gaining strength. She took a deep breath and then told the story. She started from the taping of Rabbie Stewart's cottage with John and ended with her leaving the editing suite to bring back Rod.

Muir's pencil raced over the paper of his notebook. He never once asked her to slow down or repeat. It was obvious to Alec that he was adept at shorthand or one of its derivatives.

Black listened carefully, not stopping her but allowing her. He urged her by softening his features and nodding occasionally. He asked her to remember and tell all.

She finally finished and asked Alec for a cigarette. Black looked away from her to Muir. Again, there was the gentle nod.

"You say you left to fetch Rod."

Rod looked up at the mention of his name.

"And the picture was ... on hold?" He looked for the correct terminology.

"Freeze frame," Megan answered and then coughed as the unaccustomed smoke hit her throat.

"Ah, yes. Freeze frame ... and you were away 3 ... 4 minutes?"

Megan nodded. Black looked at her calmly and then switched his gaze to Alec.

"I got the impression, Mr. Sterne, that you recognized the weapon when we walked into

..." He waved his hand upwards.

Alec searched Black's face but found nothing. "Yes, I did. It was Rabbie Stewart's brass poker."

Muir's pencil stopped its scratching.

"Bullshit, Sterne. That's down at the office now, tagged and labeled, having been returned from forensic. I handled it myself this morning before setting off for you." There was no mistaking the animosity in Muir's voice.

Alec, far from being calm, replied calmly, "Well now, Sergeant Muir, you can add another one to your collection. An identical twin, for that was Rabbie Stewart's brass poker."

Black raised his left hand gently at Muir, whilst still looking at Alec, cutting off Muir's intended retort. "He is correct, Mr. Sterne."

"So am I, Mr. Black."

Black paused while his fingers played with his cup. Seconds passed. "Yes ... I believe you." Muir's scratching pencil momentarily paused again.

"I think forensic will bear you out." His fingers played again with his cup. "So what are we dealing with here?" It was a question softly put and meant for Alec to answer.

"A warning," Alec finally replied, "as in Biblical times."

Black raised his bushy eyebrows as Alec

continued, "A warning to Rod ... and Megan."

Rod looked up from surveying his desktop. His eyes joined Megan's to stare appalled at Alec.

"Phil Grossman says that's its Modus Operandi."

Muir snapped his notebook shut. Black waved the left hand again whilst removing Megan's tape from a pocket and placing it on the desk.

"And according to the eminent Doctor, the recipients get just the one?"

Rod and Megan's unease increased as Alec nodded affirmatively.

Black looked at the video cassette on the desk, then at Megan. "This was the tape you were looking at," he stated.

She nodded, and Black pushed the tape towards Rod with his finger end. "Has it survived the ordeal upstairs?"

Rod, thankful to be doing something, picked up the tape. He expertly flicked the spring-loaded lugs and pulled forth the magnetic tape. He held the exposed tape up at arms width, so all could see. The three feet or so of exposed tape was perfect as far as the eye could tell, apart from a small square burn hole in the center of it.

"I take it," Black said, indicating the blemish,

"that would be the place where the action was frozen?" He looked past the tape to Rod. "Could your equipment have done that?"

Rod shook his head. "No," he said categorically, "Impossible."

Black nodded. He looked over Rod's shoulder into the corner of the office where a TV and recorder stood. It was standard producer's office equipment. "Play it, Rod," he said calmly.

Megan gasped out loud. Black ignored the panic sounds of Megan and the look of dismay on Rod's face. "Rewind it and play it."

Alec felt his stomach turn over as Rod started to obey D.C.I. Black. Megan gripped his arm tightly.

The television hummed and settled down as Rod finished rewinding and pressed the play button. He didn't sit down, but joined Muir standing by the door.

Alec thought, at first, it was to enable a quick get-away should anything occur, but it was the producer in him that was taking over. Alec gave a rueful smile. Rod had the constitution of a bull.

The screen flickered into life. Alec and Megan sat mesmerized looking at the screen, not knowing what to expect but ready to duck if it need be. Alec later swore to himself that the only people breathing in that room for the long fifteen minutes were Black and Muir.

The tape finally finished and started to rewind itself. Alec found himself breathing normally again.

Black turned to look at Muir. This time the nod was a little slower and more meaningful. Black switched his gaze to Rod. "What do you think, Rod?"

"Some excellent camera work. Lighting could have been better in parts, but some really good panning shots." It was the producer talking.

Black nodded and asked, "You didn't see it?" He looked at Rod, who was bemused by the question.

Black turned his attention to Megan and Alec, raising his eyebrows. Alec and Megan shook their heads. They, too, didn't understand.

"Rod, fast forward the tape to a couple of seconds before that hole, then let it play past the hole for a couple of seconds ... then freeze it."

Rod went behind his desk and sat down. He pulled a remote control out of his desk drawer and ran the tape forward to the approximate position. He looked at Black, who nodded. Rod pressed the play button.

Megan and Alec attentively leaned forward as the tape ran through the panning shot, into a white screen, and back into the panning shot.

"Hold it there, Rod," Black commanded. The frame was frozen. "Now what do you see?"

"What I saw before," replied a puzzled Rod.

"Sweet Jesus Christ," muttered Alec. They all turned to look at him. "The poker … it's no longer on the floor."

Black nodded.

Rod swung back to the TV set. He pressed a button and rewound several frames. He restarted the tape at the top of the panning shot.

The poker was in clear vision up to the moment of the destroyed section of the tape. Immediately after, the poker was no longer visible.

# CHAPTER THIRTY-NINE

Phil was back in the small amphitheatre. He had gone home for a shower and a quick change of clothes. Considering he had no sleep at all, he looked tastefully elegant. A cream shirt and narrow dark blue tie blended well with the immaculately tailored gray suit.

He locked the doors to the amphitheatre and left instructions to the janitors not to go near. He rescheduled all lectures to be held there to other uncommitted rooms. He even managed to get a substitute to cover his own lectures.

His morning mail had been left by his secretary outside the locked doors. He absentmindedly leafed through the various envelopes as he looked at the enlargement of the stone. "Oh, well done, James ... well done," he whispered.

He paused in his fingering of the mail when he came across a small, unaddressed box. He looked down questioningly. Dropping the envelopes onto the desk, he opened the box.

The contents startled Phil. Not quite the sort of thing that one should see prior to breakfasting or after breakfast, for that matter. Phil swallowed hard, his throat hurting, as he placed the box on the desk.

He looked at the human finger lying bloody inside it. Ripped out at the knuckle, it lay gory and obscene inside its box.

Phil reached for a cigarette and went around the desk for a pull at the kosher rum. He stared at the finger under the harsh, white stage lights and slowly regained his composure.

He recalled Alec's conversation; particularly when Ma and Alex were at Galsworthy and Rabbie Stewart's badly injured hand had two fingers were missing.

"So you have found me," Phil muttered hoarsely. He took another sip of the rum. "Come along Philip. Time is running out, and this is my warning," he added grimly.

He put the bottle down and went to the back of the stage to look at the enlargement of the stone. James had made him two copies. He pasted one copy onto hardboard as per the enlargement of Alex. The other, an ordinary photograph, James suspended from a crocodile clip hanging above Phil's desk.

They blew the stone up to about an eighteen-inch square. The scratches were clearly visible, but annoyingly incomplete. Phil tried a variety of ways and languages to decipher it. Spanish was the first and obvious choice, followed by other Latin-based and European languages in order to complete the lettering, but to no avail.

He pulled on his cigarette and started to cough. He went back to his desk and took another sip of rum. The cardboard box and its evil message stared up at him.

He reached forward, covered it, and put it into the desk drawer. His coughing subsided, and he looked up to where the second photograph hung suspended from the crocodile clip.

"You are the key ... Damn you," he muttered and walked up into the seating of the amphitheatre. He stopped halfway and sat with his elbows on his knees, looking at the suspended photograph.

He took a drag on the cigarette, and the smoke caught his throat again. He coughed once, which hooked into another and another. Suddenly, Phil was into a paroxysm of violent coughing.

He dropped the cigarette and reached for a huge white handkerchief in his pocket, covering his mouth and nostrils with it. His shoulders heaved as he gasped for breath between the violent bouts.

The double doors opened behind him, and he turned as the light from the corridor flashed across the amphitheatre seating. His secretary was in the doorway.

"Are you in for calls, Dr. Grossman?" she said, looking at him carefully.

Phil shook his head behind his handkerchief, still coughing.

She nodded. "Would you like some coffee, sir?" she said concerned.

Phil nodded.

"I'll be five minutes," she said. She closed the door quickly behind her, creating a draught.

Phil turned with his elbows still on his knees. His coughing fit was subsiding.

It left him weak; his lungs felt sore, and his throat burned. He pulled the handkerchief away from his mouth to wipe his brow, but stopped the action. He saw a large violently red stain on the white cotton.

A cynical smile twitched his lips as he looked at it. "Yes, Phil ... Time is running out," he murmured.

He looked at the stage area as he put away the soiled hanky. The draught from the door had set the suspended photograph spinning gently. Phil looked at it almost hypnotically. His mind was still on the coughing fit.

He blinked his eyes to clear the excess moisture, and then he saw it. "My God ... you bloody fool, Phil," he shouted hoarsely.

He stood up, looking at the moving picture in

excitement. The strong stage lights behind the turning picture gave the impression that the picture of the tone was on both sides of the paper. The reverse side of the stone seemed to fill the room in Phil's excitement.

Phil had been working on the premise that the legend on the stone was of European origin, basing it on what he knew via the coins and the ship. European languages read from left to right.

He ran down the steep steps and to the desktop. He rummaged around and found the chalk.

Walking hurriedly to the back of the stage to the hardboard copy, he put his glasses on and paused to look more closely. With the chalk, he commenced to highlight the markings. He stepped back two paces to survey his handiwork thoughtfully.

The first letter on the right was complete. It was Hebrew, a very early form of Hebrew, but Hebrew nevertheless. He stepped in to complete what scratch marks were visible.

In some cases, it was obvious what the letter had to be. In a few cases, it was a process of elimination. It was either this, that was total gibberish, or it was this that scanned.

Twenty minutes later, sipping the coffee his secretary had brought in, he walked away from the picture to the edge of the stage area. He turned slowly to face and look at what he had completed. His eyes turned away and then looked again in disbelief.

He shook his head, but there it was. The white chalk stood out starkly against the dark background. Whilst not 100 percent complete, it was quite obvious to Phil what the word was.

Phil's lips moved silently as he read out the ancient legend … ASHMEDAI. The cup slipped from Phil's nerveless fingers to shatter on the floor at his feet.

# CHAPTER FORTY

A gentle tugging at his sleeve awakened Alec. Not the best sight in the world to waken up to was holding a steaming mug of tea. "I thought you might like a cup of tea, Mr. Sterne," Muir said quietly.

"Ah … thank you very much Sergeant. What time is it?"

Alec's watch was on his wrist, but he detected a change in Muir's attitude towards him and decided to extend the conversation.

"Coming up for eleven o'clock, sir."

*Sir? Hmmm … There has been a change.* Alec's feet hit the cell floor, and he took the mug from Muir.

He stayed the night at Glasgow Central, not as a prisoner but as a favor to D.C.I. Black. The cell door had been left open, but a cell was a cell. He would have preferred a hotel with a bathroom.

"Any news from Forensics?"

"Yes … They worked through. It's just in. That's why Mr. Black asked me to wake you."

"That's very nice of you Sergeant. It's appreciated … If you give me two seconds to slip my shoes on, I'll be with you."

Muir waited outside the cell door as Alec put on his shoes and anorak. Sleeping fully clothed wasn't conducive to feeling on top of the world when one awoke. His trousers rode up around his crotch, and he felt decidedly icky.

He followed Muir upstairs through a variety of open offices filled with men and women. Some of them were uniformed and others plain clothed. Muir and Alec didn't rate a second glance from any of them as they walked through to Black's office.

Black sat behind a desk reading a report as they entered, still clad in his light overcoat. He hadn't slept at all, and neither had Muir from the look of him.

Black looked up as they entered. He removed from his nose the most ridiculous pair of glasses Alec had ever seen. They had a metal frame, round lenses, and they were far too small for the square, granite face. *Christ, they look like war issue glasses and by the look of 'em, the 1914/18 war,* thought Alec.

"Good morning, Mr. Sterne … Sleep well?" The thickly accented voice held a tinge of tiredness to it.

"Reasonable, Mr. Black … and obviously a damn sight better than you and Stan," answered Alec. He sipped his tea and licked his fingers where he spilt them on the journey to Black's office.

He looked around the office. The back was covered in large black and white photographs of Rabbie's cottage. Shots of the floor and the brass poker that lay there were outlined in red marker.

Black stood up, stretched, and then sighed. He reached behind him and took a large, clear plastic bag off the filing cabinet. He put it on the desk in front of Alec. It contained the large, bent brass poker that Alec had last seen at Rabbie's. "Exhibit A, Mr. Sterne," Black said, looking at Alec.

He dropped a smaller bag next to it. "Exhibit B, Mr. Sterne." The bag contained droplets of molten brass that had cooled rapidly.

Black paused and then reached behind him again to produce another large, clear plastic bag.

"Exhibit C, Mr. Sterne." It contained an identical brass poker. It was identical in every detail. Black placed it side by side with the other poker.

"Exhibit D, Mr. Sterne." He placed another small plastic bag on the desk. It contained slivers of glass.

Black seated himself again, looking at the exhibits.

"Mind if I smoke, Mr. Black?" asked Alec.

"Go ahead," said Black.

Alec offered the pack, but Black and Muir shook their heads.

Silence fell on the room as Black opened a report containing several pages. Running a stubby finger down the opened page, he grunted to himself as he found the relevant passage. He reread the passage again and grunted as he finished. He closed the report and looked up.

"Alec, I don't know what to say, but ..." He waved his hand over the exhibits. "This is what we have." He paused a moment.

"This," he said, pointing to Exhibit A, "is Rabbie Stewart's original brass poker." He pointed to Exhibit B. "These are droplets of cooled molten brass that are from this poker. Forensic analysis proves that beyond all shadow of doubt.

Now the shape of the poker tells us, without having to use too much imagination that Rabbie struck someone."

Black paused and then added, "Something very hard indeed. What was it that could, on contact, melt a heavy brass poker? God alone knows. What we do know is that no human being could have survived such a blow."

He paused to take a drink of his now lukewarm tea. He looked up at Muir with the telepathic glance again.

Muir stepped out of the office and returned almost immediately with a large flask. He proceeded to warm up Black's tea with fresh tea.

"Mr. Sterne?" Sergeant Muir asked.

"Please, Sergeant," replied Alec, offering his mug.

"So that brings us to Exhibit C ... the second poker," continued Black, fishing around for his tiny spectacles. He opened the report again and read the relevant chapter without squinting this time.

"It seems that the second poker is identical, and they mean identical in every detail to the first poker. In essence, they say a clone ... An impossibility, it seems, when it comes to old brass pokers.

They go on to say that no two pieces of metal, even from the same mother ingot ... and then both used identically by different owners, which is an impossibility in itself ... Neither could have the same atom structure or molecule alignment, which these two have.

They ran a whole gamut of tests: spectrograph, microscopic analysis, you name it. They even say the molten droplets from the first poker came from the second, also ..."

Black paused and removed his tiny round spectacles, rubbing a hand over his tired face. He sighed. "That brings us to the second death, the one at the BBC. The post-mortem was carried out under my instructions with Forensics present.

The cause of death was fairly obvious to all. The only question in our minds was where did the weapon come from and from whom? Well, we'll leave the whom for the moment.

On removal of the weapon, minute particles of glass were found. Apart from on the face and clothing of the deceased, they were also found under and in the wound itself.

The particles of glass were analyzed and proved to be cathode ray tube glass, identical to the glass from the editing machine. So however wild the assumption …"

Black looked at Muir. Alec saw Muir close his eyes and nod agreement.

"The poker had to come from within the editing machine."

Alec put down his mug and looked around for an ashtray. Black pushed a saucer towards him, nodding for him to use it.

"Alec, you were brought back here for a statement, and I must admit, at first, you were under suspicion. Under suspicion, until I spoke to Dr. Grossman, and even then … well, let's say a few questions still remained."

He looked down at the plastic bags on his desktop. "This other death and its the manner, the second poker, the forensic reports, the video tape, these photos."

His hand waved at the wall behind him, "Those, and maybe because I've been around a long time, have altered that assumption. One thing is for certain, Alec. No Inspector Plod will put the cuffs on this ... thing. Good we are, Batman and Robin we ain't."

"What exactly do you want me to do, Mr. Black?" Alec quietly asked.

"Nothing, Alec ... nothing up here. No statement. We'll corner cupboard this lot and lose the paperwork. You get back to Grossman ASAP, and if you are worried about Rod and Megan, don't be. Believe you me, they couldn't be better protected."

He rose from his seat and stuck a big hand out. Alec took it.

"Stan?" Sergeant Muir took a card from his pocket and pressed it upon Alec as Black continued.

"There are two phone numbers on there. Should you need help, use them. No matter where in the world we are, those numbers will reach us immediately."

Black's hand was wrapped tight around Alec's, and Alec could feel Black's sincerity.

Alex nodded, "Thank You."

# CHAPTER FORTY-ONE

Phil left the dean's office and walked quick-paced back to his own. He just organized a week's leave of absence from the university, starting immediately.

The dean was surprised, but acquiesced. He was quite used to his favorite and world eminent lecturer leaving suddenly at short notice. Whatever this man did, it always seemed to bring the right kind of notoriety on the university.

Phil walked into his office. His secretary met him immediately. She carried out his instructions. All the books, tomes, manuscripts, everything were taken out of the amphitheatre by the janitor. They were then taken by taxi to Phil's home in Cheshire.

She typed a list of all the books and scrolls for Phil to sign them into his custody and safekeeping. He scribbled his signature and told her to top-copy the library and give a copy to each of the relevant departments.

She looked down her nose at him. She had been with him for over twenty years, and you don't tell your grandma how to suck eggs.

He gave her Alec's phone number. He told her to call him, knowing full well that once he got involved with the work on hand, he would forget.

"Give him my phone number, and tell him to call me immediately."

"Certainly, doctor."

"And no other phone calls. No one is to disturb me."

"Certainly, doctor." Her heart sank. This man was so busy. She was already dreading the putting off she was going to have to do. As if reading her thoughts, the phone rang.

"I've gone," said Phil, walking to the door and slipping on a velvet-collared overcoat. He turned at the door and threw a hand wave and a smile at his, about to be beleaguered, secretary and left.

# CHAPTER FORTY-TWO

The window bowed yet again under the pressure of the wind and rain. Once more, it distorted the reflected image of Alec and the room behind him.

His coffee was surprisingly still warm as he took a sip between drags of the ubiquitous cigarette. He pulled his eyes away from the darkened rain-lashed lane to look again at the small, brown cardboard box resting on the window bottom.

Thank God he brought it upstairs to open it and see what was lying inside. It could have blown somebody's mind, namely Alex or Ma.

Lying inside the box was a torn out finger of Rabbie Stewart. Alec could tell it was Rabbie's by the short tuft of red hairs sprouted between the joints.

He shivered again and looked back at the typewriter. It had been quiet now for half an hour or more, and Alec was getting jumpy.

"C'mon, Phil. Where are you for Christ's sake?" he muttered.

He received the phone message from Phil's secretary barely ten minutes after he arrived home and duly phoned Phil.

"Get around to my house right away, Alec," Phil's husky voice sounded even huskier on the phone.

"Phil, I can't. I've no transport."

There was a second of silence, and before Alec could explain, Rod said, "Right. I'm on my way. Wincle?"

"Yes, but ..."

"Leave an outside light on for me, so I'll know which cottage." The phone went dead.

There was little else Alec could do but wait. Waiting in that cold cottage with what was running through Alec's mind wasn't easy. A feeling of total futility and dread enveloped him since he'd been home. He had some shocks in the previous weeks, but absolutely nothing compared to the shock he received when he arrived home.

He checked his watch again for about the fortieth time as he reached across to stub out his cigarette. As he did so, the headlamps of a car appeared across the valley. He held his breath as a feeling of panic unaccountably swept through him.

It had to be Phil. Alec just had to get out of that house, if only for a few hours. The headlamps slowed down near *The Ship*, highlighting the raindrops on the outside of

Alec's window.

*Christ, one of Frank's customers,* Alec disappointedly thought. But as he looked, the car picked up speed and came down the hill. When it passed the telephone kiosk by the bridge, Alec could see it was a Rolls Royce.

"Phil! It's got to be," Alec said to himself as the car rolled smoothly over the narrow bridge. It came up the lane to the cottage, finally slowing and then turning silently onto the paved parking area.

Alec stood up and went quickly downstairs to greet him. Phil waved as he left the car to run for the door, rain gusting over him.

"Phil, thank God ... I was beginning to get worried."

He closed the door behind him, frustrating the rain from its intention of flooding Alec's small hallway.

"Well it does take some finding, this place." His hoarse voice was a most welcome sound in Alec's ears. "It's a good job you put the outside light on," he added smiling.

They were standing in the small hallway, and Phil was about to slip out of his overcoat when Alec stopped him.

"Keep it on Phil. You'll need it."

The gray eyes pinpointed down to twin, gray beams again as they looked at Alec. Phil nodded understandingly.

"Before we go to my room, Phil … I'd like to introduce you to someone."

He opened the lounge door wide, and the light from the hallway shafted across the darkened room. A figure in the chair sat hunched and motionless, still looking out of the window.

A mug of coffee Alec had left there earlier lay untouched and was now cold. A cardigan Alec had pulled around her to keep her warm had fallen away from the thin, emaciated shoulders. The gnarled, old fingers were clenched knuckle white.

The light from the hallway cut through the thin, white hair, showing the scalp. It was pink in parts and brown in others. The brown matched the color of the wrinkled skin at the nape of her neck.

Phil looked at Alec, querying.

"I'll just put a lamp on, Phil," Alec said softly. He crossed the room to kneel down and plug it in. The warm glow bathed the room in its soft light, just as Alec heard Phil speak.

"Good evening, Mrs. Sterne. I'm Phil Grossman, a friend of your son's."

Phil was by the chair, leaning over the thinning white hair and smiling down. His face was warm and pleasant.

Alec's voice caught in his throat, and Phil looked up at the sound. Alec moved over to join them, slowly shaking his head at Phil. He knelt by the old dear, taking the gnarled and twisted hand between his.

He coughed to try to clear his throat and blinked away the moisture in his eyes. "This …" He coughed again. "This isn't my mother, Phil … This is … Alex."

There was no denying the shock on Phil's face. He lost his composure for a second. He stepped back as though he'd been punched. A subliminal impression of the larger than life photograph of lovely Alex shot before him. He looked down again at the reality of the present and was visibly moved.

"Oh my God." He mouthed the words; the actual sounds dying in his strangled vocal chords. "Alex?" he mouthed again to Alec.

Alec nodded and pointed to the stone visibly resting on the emaciated breasts. Tears formed and fell unashamedly down his face.

Phil looked down from his short height at the couple, and a deep sadness gripped him. His small, soft hand stretched out to rest on Alec's bowed head.

That cold, silent room was like the waiting room by River Styx awaiting the dreaded boatman.

There was a movement from Alex. Her gnarled and twisted right hand slowly moved. Phil hypnotically watched as she slowly and painfully raised it to place it on top of Phil's hand. The effort was great, but no greater than her next movement.

She summoned her strength to move her head and look at Phil. Her eyes had lost all color and were deeply set in the sallow, wrinkled face.

What was lost in physical color was more than made up for by what Phil read there. There was tenderness, an understanding beyond all comprehension. Phil nodded gently at the unspoken question he read there, and the nod was accepted.

She allowed her hand to slip away and caress Alec's cheek. Alec raised his bowed head to look at Alex through tear-filled eyes. The tears once again ran unashamedly down his face, and Alex's gnarled fingers slowly attempted to wipe them away. Infinitesimally, her head moved from side to side, and her thin, creased lips formed the word 'no.'

Alec understood and nodding gently, wiped away the tears from his face.

"Remember … the … water … Alec." The syllables were formed and expelled in almost a whisper by emptying her lungs.

It was painful to listen to, but Alec

357

understood and smiled at her.

The stream and the little Niagara that she found at their campsite, just weeks before, flashed through his mind. He started to fill up again.

"Alec," Phil's hoarse whisper stopped him.

Alec looked at him, and Phil nodded his head towards the door. Alec returned the nod, understanding.

He rose and looked down at the wizened figure of Alex again. He gently pulled her cardigan around her shoulders, and then leaned forward to lovingly and gently kiss her on the lips.

Alec made coffee, and they went upstairs.

"Where's your mother, Alec?"

Alec recovered his composure and lit a cigarette whilst drinking his coffee. From somewhere deep inside him, a cold anger grew. He had cold anger and determination.

Phil could feel the difference taking place in Alec. He could almost touch it and catalog it. He'd need it!

"Her sister, my aunt ... she's been taken to the hospital. Ma left me a note. She should be back later tonight."

Phil realized the absolute shock Alec must have from seeing Alex like that. There was no one to warn him. The experience was bad enough for Phil. His only prior knowledge of Alex was a photograph taken just weeks before of a lovely and vibrant girl.

Alec reached for the small box on the window bottom and threw it for Phil to catch. "Have a look at that," Alec said grimly.

"I don't need to, Alec," Phil replied.

Alec registered surprise and then realization. "Oh ... Don't tell me, Phil. You got the other one?"

Phil nodded.

"The bastard." He took the box from Phil and replaced it on the window bottom.

"Not really, Alec. It's a warning ... The usual way in biblical times. It used to be an animal that belonged to the offender that they quartered and placed in the four corners of the territory. It graduated to the offender himself being butchered and hung as an example to others of the same ilk.

It was the same in this country. Right up to a couple of centuries ago ... You must know the phrase: Hung, drawn, and quartered?"

Alec nodded.

"Same thing," finished Phil in his matter-of-fact tone.

"Talking of warnings," Alec said and went on to quickly fill in the details of what went on in Scotland.

Phil listened quietly and attentively, nodding occasionally as though mental pieces of a jigsaw were slotting into place. "Thank God for open-minded policemen," he said when Alec finished. He drank the remainder of his coffee and put the mug down.

"Alec," his hoarse voice held a note of somberness, "We haven't much time and I hate to say this, Alec … but Alex … is nearing the end." He coughed the sad words, as softly and as gently as his unnatural voice would allow. "When she goes … he has the stone!"

Knowing the effect his words would have on Alec, Phil wandered over to Alec's typewriter searching for a psychological peg. He found it.

"What's this?" he said, picking up a sheet of paper.

Alec crossed to look over his shoulder and then tried to explain to Phil the machine's frantic behavior.

Phil looked at it carefully with the eye of an expert used to viewing apparent gibberish. "This isn't gibberish, Alec. Look. It's two words typed over and over again with no spacing … Sometimes it's with no beginning, sometimes with no ending, but the two same words nevertheless. Two words you wouldn't understand as they are writ. They're in Aramaic, and don't even begin to ask me how an English typewriter can possibly write in a dead language."

Silence descended again.

"And the words?" asked Alec.

"Rabbi, beware," Phil softly replied.

"What the hell does it mean?" a totally mystified Alec asked. He looked at Phil, and Phil gave him a grim half smile.

"C'mon … make Alex as comfortable as you can. We have to go."

Alec brought down a duvet to wrap around her, but Phil stopped him. He pointed out that Alex had probably survived as long as she had because of the cold. His own aura was working against him. The simple matter of breathing was an effort for Alex, but in the cold atmosphere she required less oxygen. Alec reluctantly agreed with Phil's findings and left the room to turn off the kitchen lights.

Phil let him go and then crossed to Alex, crouching on his knees in front of her. He put his warm, soft hand on her cold, fleshless arm.

"Hang on, Alex," he urged hoarsely, "hang on my girl for the sake of Alec … for the sake of mankind."

She didn't appear to move, but as Phil rose to join Alec, he knew in his heart that she heard and understood.

# CHAPTER FORTY-THREE

The Rolls, silent and sure-footed on the wet lanes, sped them in complete luxury to Phil's home. Alec settled back and looked across at Phil. His small frame was encompassed in the rich leather and at natural ease behind the polished wheel.

"You don't sell yourself short when it comes to the better things in life, do you, Phil?" he asked, reaching for his cigarettes.

"Alec," Phil replied, looking briefly across at him, "I'm a rich man … thanks to my father …" He paused and looked across again, "And one thing I don't allow in my car, Alec, is cigarettes. I don't smoke them in my car … you don't smoke them." He pushed a button on the dash and smiled.

Alec's chagrin turned to amazement as he looked at the little tray of cigars that just popped out.

"Now you know I smoke heavily, Alec … but cigarettes in a Rolls? Heaven forbid!"

They sat back with lit cigars in the quietness full of thought.

Phil broke the silence. "My father was a

kosher butcher, Alec, and a damn good one ...
Came over to this country with but two words of
English and with one and sixpence in his
pocket."

He paused to turn on the car's air
conditioning to take out the cigar smoke. "He
died rich, but disappointed." He looked across at
Alec, "Disappointed because he wanted his only
Son to be a Rabbi."

Alec looked back at Phil as they waited at the
traffic lights. "The typewriter?"

Phil nodded. "Nothing is a secret, it seems, to
Ashmedai."

"Ashmedai?"

"Yes, Alec, Ashmedai. I deciphered the
scratches on the stone."

"What does it mean?"

The lights changed, and Phil toed the
accelerator. He waited until he cleared the
junction before answering.

"It's Hebrew, Alec. Hebrew meaning *The
Destroyer*, or another interpretation is *The
Bringer of Destruction*." Phil's voice was cold
and grave.

Alec shivered, "Jesus H. Christ, Phil!"

Silence fell again, and it wasn't disturbed
until they pulled into the grounds of Phil's old
country mansion set in the Cheshire Plain.

The house was large and to Alec, had an

Elizabethan air about it. The outside coach lamps threw their light across beautifully manicured lawns and bushes, showing a tasteful and well-maintained opulence.

The Rolls crunched to a halt outside the Doric-columned main entrance. It was obviously a much later addition to the original house but wholly within keeping.

They quickly alighted, and Phil ushered Alec through the doorway. *The door contains enough oak to make half a dozen doors for the average home*, Alec thought to himself.

He followed Phil across a large checkered marble hallway, through a low Gothic-arched doorway, and thence into Phil's holy of holies.

Alec stood and reverently surveyed the room as Phil hurried on, removing his overcoat.

It was one of the most beautiful rooms Alec had ever seen. He was dumbstruck. It exuded a warmth and character that seemed to embrace and envelop. One could almost touch it.

Running down the full length of the room on Alec's left and right were large, very high and rectangular deep rich mahogany bookshelves. They were filled to entirety with a wonderful collection of tomes of myriad colored backings.

To the right of Alec was a mahogany spiral staircase leading up to a gallery that ran around three sides of the room. Even more burnished bookshelves, reaching up to the ceiling, resided there.

Facing Alec at the far end of the room, the wall was taken up with a stained-glass window. It was huge in overall size, but actually made up of several Gothic-arched rectangles divided by delicate stone columns. It was breathtaking.

The floor in front of the window was higher than the rest of the floor; in fact, it was almost a small stage, in the center of which was a lectern.

In the center of the main floor area was a bizarre sight that brought a smile to Alec's face.

Amongst all the centuries-old polished wood, books, and glass lay a full-sized snooker table. It was bizarre, but apparently there for a purpose other than for playing on. It was covered with a dust sheet and atop was a huge piece of heavy plate glass covering the whole table. Open books, pieces of scroll, and photographic color plates littered the entire surface.

Alec nodded to himself as he looked, remembering Phil surrounded by books and paraphernalia on the stage in the little amphitheatre. It was ideal for the purpose to which Phil was putting it.

Phil turned. "Let me take your coat, Alec." He saw the look on Alec's face, "Ahh ... I see you like my library."

Alec nodded, still trying to absorb the sight.

"It's … well, it's beyond words, Phil. It's something else."

"Yes. It is ... functional," Phil replied, mischievously smiling as he took Alec's coat.

Alec approached the edge of the snooker table and turned to survey the wall behind him. He caught his breath. The sound made Phil turn around. He saw at what Alec was looking.

The janitor from the university had brought in the larger than life portrait of a radiant Alex.

"Oh, God. I'm so sorry, Alec … I'll move it."

"No … no, Phil." The muscles of his jaw tightened into two white mounds on his face. He turned to Phil. "Where do we start?" he asked firmly.

Phil nodded. "Well, Alec, where to start is a problem. So what I intend doing is just talk … You listen. I'll be talking across the full spectrum."

His hands waved over the books and artifacts lying on the snooker table. "I'll be throwing up some ideas, some facts, some premises, some possibilities, some … outrageously unthinkable, but keep an open mind," he emphasized huskily, "Some based on a modicum of fact and allied with a little imagination have helped put the walls up and the roof on."

He crossed to the lectern on which an open Torah was placed. "This, Alec, is the Torah ... or

Pantateuch. Along with the Talmud, the foundation of Judaism."

Alec stood alongside Phil and watched his smooth, small hands lovingly finger the old, hand-tooled leather. He continued, "It is made up of five books: Bereshith, Shemoth, Va-Yikra, Bemidbar, and the Debarim. Names of which you wouldn't recognize, but are, in actual fact, the first five books of the Old Testament: Genesis, Exodus, Leviticus, Numbers, and Deuteronomy. Those names, of course, you do recognize."

Alec nodded and Phil continued, "It is written, as you can see, in a language you don't understand. This particular Torah is in early Hebrew and part Cuneiform. It is very old and was given to me by a dear colleague in Israel."

He paused and gave a wry smile. "If his department in Israel knew what he had done, no doubt, he would be severely chastised ... but I have no pangs of guilt about it. I have put many archaeological treasures into Israel's museums from this particular dig, where this came from. I feel amply rewarded with something like this ... something very dear to my heart."

He paused for a moment as he caressed the ancient leather. Then he took Alec's arm, stepped down from the dais, and walked to the large table. He motioned for Alec to sit on a stool, whilst he sat in what Alec took to be a cross between a large baby chair and a cut down tennis umpire's chair.

"Now around us are quite a few examples of the languages in use at … ah, let's say 3000 B.C. … an early form of Hebrew, as you have just seen, Aramaic, and Greek."

Phil pinched the bridge of his nose between the eyes. "Nearer to us, in time that is, we have the Latin, Anglo Saxon, and of course, the English.

So, if we took, say … a green apple in early Hebrew. By the time it was translated into Hebrew proper, then Aramaic, Greek, Latin, Anglo Saxon, through to English … there is every possibility of our green apple turning into a Victoria plum! See what we're up against?"

Alec smiled at Phil as Phil rose.

"How about some coffee, Alec?"

"Love some."

Alec watched Phil as he filled a couple of mugs. He found himself in total wonderment of the man. Learned, gentle, and yes, loving. Had he not just seen how he was with Alex? There were unbelievable depths to this man, and his father was disappointed?

*I would only be too proud to call this man my father*, Alec thought as Phil returned with the coffee.

"I could feel your eyes on me the whole time Alec … You okay?"

"Absolutely."

"Good." He settled back in his chair. "So you do understand what I'm getting at and some of the problems that face us?"

Alec nodded.

"In short, there are portions of the Christian Bible and the Torah that are arguable … especially when one knows that before being actually scribed, that for a thousand years or more, the leaders recited them by rote to their children for them, in turn, to memorize and pass on to their children … hence the word Rabbi, meaning teacher.

At first glance, a good method, for them the only method, but here in England we have a saying: A good story loses nothing in its telling.

In short, that green apple could well become a bushel! Now comes the part where you say 'What the hell has all this got to do with the price of gefilte fish?' So I will preempt you.

What we have is a name … a name unused for thousands of years. Biblical! What we have are actions, warnings, etc. Biblical! 'Tis there we must look, Alec."

"So that's what Rabbi means? Teacher? Well, your father wouldn't have been disappointed, Phil, for that's what you are!"

Phil smiled. "Not quite. I wanted a wider view of things, no constraints and not to specialize in just one thing. The title, Rabbi, was given to the compilers of the Talmud. The Talmud is a compilation of Jewish laws, history, ethics, and legal rulings," he quickly explained, "And so it has come down that the title, Rabbi, is held by religious leaders who are qualified to decide Jewish legal questions."

He leaned across the table as he finished speaking and picked up a large photograph. "By the way, that's the stone."

Alec looked at the stone with the completed legend in Hebrew running across the bottom. "This is similar to the writing in your Torah, Phil."

"You have a quick eye, Alec. Yes, true, early Hebrew, so that gives us an approximate date to work on, although ..." Phil's voice became quite grim. "I have a feeling that whoever inscribed the stone could just as easily have written it in English. That language wouldn't be born for another 5,000 years. No, listen to me, Alec," Phil said, cutting across Alec's amazement and attempted reply.

"The question is from whence and why? There has to be a why ... and I think I know!" He paused to pull a cigarette and light up.

"Imagine a world 5,000 years ago. A

population ... oh ... much smaller than it is today. A city had possibly 20,000 inhabitants, if it was lucky; a small town by today's standards. This had to be, so agriculturally they could sustain themselves.

What we would call a track would be a motorway to them. The nearest thing to farm mechanization and fertilizer would be a bullock. So, for a start, I think we can take with a pinch of salt, the size of the Exodus, as the Old Testament tells us.

600,000 people on foot, walking into the desert with only what food and water they could carry? No, they would need 300 tons of food a day, and that's without the weight of water. The Tribes of Israel just had to be smaller than what the Bible would have us believe, and this bares me out."

He suddenly pushed his unusual chair sideways down the edge of the table. Its wheels carried him quickly to the end of the table and back again in less time than it would have taken Alec to rise from his seated position. Holding the open book he retrieved, Phil said, "Listen," and he quoted,

*"For thou art an Holy People unto the Lord thy Go:;*
*The Lord thy God hath chosen thee to be*

*a special people unto himself, above ALL people that are on the face of the earth.*

*The Lord did not set his love upon you, nor choose you, because ye were more in number than any people; for ye were the fewest of all people."*

He looked up at Alec. "Two special passages to note: f*or ye were the fewest of all people...* Now, if 600,000 Israelites left Egypt and were forty years in their meanderings ... allowing for natural wastage, and what mankind seems to do best ... when those words were spoken, they would have numbered well over a million! So, if they were the *fewest of all people*, the world had one heck of a population problem.

Remember what I said about arguable passages? Now bear with me, Alec, if I appear to be digressing. Believe me, I'm not."

Alec nodded, totally engrossed.

Phil continued, "If, as I believe and more than a few of my learned colleagues believe, the population of the world at this particular time was quite sparse. It makes the next passage to note more significant. *The Lord thy God hath chosen thee to be a special people ... above ALL people ...* Instant envy must have been aroused amongst the uncircumcised and that sets the scene for an adversary.

Anyone that tries to bring about perfection, whether it be in his front garden or society, will bring out envy in someone." He paused to cough gently into his hand. "Catching on Alec?"

"Yeeees ... Sounds a bit far-fetched, but I'm all ears."

Phil smiled. "By the way, Hebrew for adversary is Satan." Phil coughed again and reached for his handkerchief. "Let's have some coffee, Alec."

They both crossed to Phil's perk that had been simmering away and helped themselves. Then they returned to their seats by the large table.

Phil collected his thoughts, wondering why he hadn't yet seen that almost manic gleam of realization in Alec's eye. Phil loved to see that in a student; in fact, he lived for it.

"This ..." he started slowly and thoughtfully, "no doubt, gives you the impression that we are a persecuted race ... not just by the human race, but also by a superior power."

The quizzical look on Alec's face made Phil stop.

"Alec, the whole universe, which includes this world of ours, is held in balance. Where there is drought, next door will have a deluge. Where there is sun, there will be snow. Where there is love, there will be hatred. Where there is good, there will be evil.

Nature, and through nature, evolution tames us all for the sake of balance. So, if I happen to name one thing, you can bet your sweet life, it will have a balancing, shadow self. Which one we are dealing with … I know not yet!"

Alec nodded slowly as if catching on.

Phil continued, "So, okay. What the heck has this got to do with your predicament? Well, believe me, Alec, I didn't like the line down which my research took me, but there are too many coincidences. Anyway, let us get away from this and concentrate on the whence."

He pulled the Old Testament towards him again. "Remember to keep your mind open at all times, especially of aberrations in this …" He prodded the open book. "due to memory and translation, right. As our American friends would say: let's run it up the flagpole and see what happens."

Alec waited, but couldn't help smiling at Phil as he sought the relevant passage.

"This is from the Bereshith," he looked up smiling, "Sorry, Genesis.

*And the Lord said unto him, Therefore whosoever slayeth Cain, vengeance shall be taken on him sevenfold.*

*And the Lord set a mark upon Cain, lest*

*any finding him should kill him."*

Phil looked up at Alec over his Pickwickian glasses. "Here we are dealing with the first crime in a perfect world, and which Lord are we seeing here? The Lord God Almighty or the lord of the underworld?

The word Lord comes from the Hebrew Yahweh, which in turn comes from the verb, Hawah, which means to be, to exist.

We already know evil existed in earlier conversations we've had. Is this the lord of the underworld looking after his own, a murderer … 'Don't touch this boy. He's doing my work.' … *set a mark upon Cain?"* Phil was musing out loud.

"The stone?" asked Alec. Phil shrugged his shoulders.

"But, Cain? Ohh, c'mon, Phil."

"In a perfect world, why let a murderer live to upset the balance? It is a possibility," Phil said calmly, "I told you to keep an open mind.

There is another thing, whereas everybody around Cain was given an age at his death. There is no mention, whatsoever, of Cain's dying. Now is that because he was expunged from all records or the fact he didn't die?"

Phil took a sip of his coffee and pushed away the Book of Genesis. He slid his mobile chair swiftly down the table again, beckoning Alec to follow. He reached out and picked up a leather scroll.

"This is the Megillah, the scroll of Esther, Alec. A very interesting story regarding a pretty and very brave Jewish girl, who became the wife of a very powerful King of Persia, Ahasuerus … around, oh, about 500 B.C.

Now the King's Chief Minister, a man called Haman, used his guile on the King in order to get him to issue a proclamation to rid his Kingdom of Jews.

Now all this because Esther's uncle, Mordecai, refused to bow to him. By rid, Alec, I mean kill. The King, not knowing, of course, that his favorite wife was Jewish, agreed.

To cut a long story short, all turns out well in the end thanks to Esther. The reason I'm filling in the background on this historical event is because of this particular passage."

He undid the scroll and read.

*"… and Esther said, the adversary and enemy is this wicked Haman."*

Phil looked up at Alec over his glasses. "Adversary, Alec. An unusual choice of words, especially if we translate it back."

"Satan?"

Phil nodded, putting down the scroll and

pulling a large colored photograph towards him. "This is a plate taken of a recent find at a dig in Iran."

Alec looked at the photograph of a central figure surrounded by others in bas-relief.

"There is good reason to believe that this find is of King Ahaseurus and his court." He stabbed the picture with a manicured finger. "Look carefully at this figure."

Alec leaned in closer to the picture. Time took its toll on the material in which the figures were etched, as to be expected. It was chipped and worn, but the group as a whole, was easily discernable.

They were dressed in the clothes of the period, some carrying symbols of Office. The figure to which Phil pointed wore a cloak with hood raised. The others, apart from the centrally seated figure, were all bareheaded.

Phil handed him a large magnifying glass. "Look closer, Alec."

Alec did so. The face, partly hidden by the hood, was worn by time, and no facial feature was left in good enough condition to distinguish. An adornment that hung and rested on the forehead was clear. It was triangular in shape.

"My God. Phil, it looks like the stone!" Alec breathed.

"Yes, and by the symbol of Office that he's

carrying, that is Haman."

Phil moved even further down the table with Alec close behind. He pulled a large, modern book towards him and commenced leafing through the thick plate photographs.

"Let us jump 2,000 years to around the date on Rabbie's coins. Look at this. It's a plate from the British Museum, a plate of Queen Isabella the Catholic of Spain, circa 1480 or thereabouts."

Alec was prepared. He took a cursory glance at the disdainful central figure, and then he saw the figure in the background again, but this time he was in color. The deep brown robe, almost black with the age of the oils used, fell to bare, sandaled feet. The hood was erect and once again, almost totally hiding the face. The artist had used a stone pendant, lying on the forehead of the figure, as a highlight to offset the darkness of the cowls interior.

Alec looked at Phil, bemused. "Ohhh, there's more to come, Alec," Phil said, with a grim smile, "but let us deal with Isabella first.

Her one most notorious deed was to banish all Jews from Spain within twenty-four hours … and on pain of death! Needless to say, thousands died, and who was doing the advising?"

Phil's finger stabbed down again to rest on the cowled figure.

"Onwards, Alec … or should I say, backwards. 1,400 years back. This time to 72 AD. Massada, to be precise. An infamous moment that will stand out in Jewish history for all time. Jews, religious zealots under the leadership of one Eleazar, lived on top of a precipitous pinnacle. It was a small village, not large by any means. They made various forays against the Roman army that occupied the country, but they could be best described as throwing strawberries at a rhinoceros; easy to shrug off. So what was it that made this incredibly powerful army of Rome decide to wipe out little Massada? And on whose advice?"

Alec waited patiently. He knew an answer was forthcoming.

"They were certainly no threat to the great Roman army, and yet they surrounded Massada with a complete circumvallation, employing two great camps containing half a legion apiece … plus six smaller camps for all the auxiliaries. For two whole years, Alec, they surrounded Massada, and during those two years, they built a road up to the pinnacle. It was an absolute incredible feat of engineering."

Whilst he was talking, Phil, using various objects on the table, created a model with a glass as the pinnacle and a twelve-inch rule perched from the top down to the table. Phil leaned back in his chair.

"Someone, Alec, was determined to wipe out those few Jews. On the night that the Romans actually finished the rampart and were preparing to enter the village at dawn, the entire community of Massada committed suicide," Phil's saddened voice trailed off.

"Every man, woman, and child," he continued, "a Pyrrhic victory for the Roman general, Flavius Silva."

Phil pulled yet another book towards him, opening the dog-eared pages to a marker. "This is a description of Flavius Silva at his so-called moment of triumph. It's by a Jewish historian called Josephus. A man, I might add, not renown for his accuracy," Phil added cynically, "but nevertheless, something to draw on …

*and his anger turned to a great sadness*
*as he beheld what had befallen the children*
*and the women of the village. What foul*
*advice*
*have I heeded, he asked of his Army.*
*Bring me Asmodus, and the Captains of his*
*Army brought before him the robed and*
*frontletted Advisor."*

Phil pushed the book away and looked up over his glasses. "Note the name, Alec … and the description *robed and frontletted*. A frontlet, by the way, is worn on the forehead. Not the best and most accurate description, Alec, but a little imagination? Coincidence?"

Phil's gray eyes were steady on Alec. Alec nodded and set down his empty cup. "More than a coincidence, Phil."

Phil coughed to clear his throat. It hurt, and if anything, his voice was becoming huskier. He coughed again and felt a spasm starting in the pit of his stomach. He waited, breathed deeply, and swallowed. His saliva was thick and tasted of iron.

He reached for his handkerchief. Alec waited, silently concerned for Phil and noticing Phil's babyish complexion was whitening.

"You okay Phil?" he asked gently.

Phil nodded and then exploded into his handy in a fit of coughing. Alec reached across and patted him on the back. "Easy Phil ... easy. You're talking too much. I'll get you some more coffee." He left Phil exploding into his hanky and went quickly to the perk to refill the two mugs.

Phil's coughing subsided as Alec returned. Phil quickly folded his hanky to put it away, but not before Alec saw the bright red stain spreading across the snow white material. "Jesus Christ, Phil."

Phil waved his hand and shook his head. "It's nothing, Alec," he lied. Smiling, he thanked Alec for the coffee. "Onward, Alec," he said jovially, dismissing the incident and pulling his chair up to the table. He stopped and then looked down at a James I English Bible. Alec stood a second, looking at Phil with concern, before he joined him.

"This, Alec, is your very own English Bible - the best example for my money. Its date is about 1611, ordered by James I, hence its name. It was actually a revised edition of the Bishop's Bible ordered by Elizabeth I in 1568, or thereabouts. Of course," he said, "you know that," looking up at Alec, his gray eyes twinkling.

Alec couldn't help but laugh.

"Right. Now this is a passage from Revelations. It ties in with another piece of Jewish history, which I will tell you about immediately after this."

He looked down at the open page and then began to quote,

*"and I saw an Angel come down from Heaven*
*... and He laid hold of that old Serpent which is Satan,*
*and bound him a thousand years and cast*

*him into*
*the bottomless pit, and shut him up and set a*
*Seal upon*
*him, that he should deceive the Nations no*
*more, till the*
*Thousand years be fulfilled, and after that he*
*must be loosed a little season."*

Phil looked up again over his half glasses at Alec. "Set a seal upon him? The stone, Alec? Bottomless pit? The sea itself has been described many times as a bottomless pit. The Nations? The Twelve Tribes of Israel."

Phil pushed the Bible away and turned to face Alec. "Massada happened about 72 AD. This passage was written about 96 AD. Now assuming that this is factual, adding a thousand years brings us to as damn near as it is to swearing to 1190 AD."

He paused to fish in his pockets for a cigarette and lit up. He waved away Alec's muted protests at his self-interest.

"In York," he continued, "in 1190 AD, another Massada ... a greater Massada occurred. It was a mass suicide by the Jewish population of York. They had gone into the royal castle for protection under the auspices of the newly elected Sheriff of York."

He waved a hand over a scattered pile of

color plates. "Do I need to show you a facsimile of the Sheriff of York?

Alec shook his head.

"No, I thought not," Phil said grimly, "But what kind of pressure is brought to bear that makes whole families commit suicide by the dozens, Alec? Obviously something we haven't met up with yet."

A silence fell on the room, as though a minute's silence for the remembered dead. Alec heard a distant chime coming from within the depths of the house. Its melodic sounds slowly shook them from their reverie.

"Phil, you mentioned the sea as a bottomless pit. Why?"

Phil brushed away some cigarette ash that fell onto his jacket. The pause gave him time to line up his thoughts.

"The stone, we know, has a peculiar affinity with water. Your own experience in the bathroom with Alex has told us that. We also know that it should be worn like the tefillin or phylactery, on the forehead.

It must be seen and not worn around the neck where a piece of clothing could obscure it. After all, it's a mark placed by an ethereal hand. For a specific reason, it cannot be removed when worn around the neck as per your testimony.

Whether Ashmedai pulled the stone down

around his own neck on that sinking vessel in order not to be separated from it we will never know. Should he have remained there for a thousand years instead of being disturbed after 400 years? Once again, we will never know. But cast your mind back to Cain..."

Alec nodded as his actor's memory flicked the pages of Phil's script.

"The Lord and His right arm have visited the earth many times, the Bible tells us. He has rid the world of evil in many ways, violent and quick ways. *Vengeance is Mine sayeth the Lord.*

When He strikes, there is no jumping out of the way. So when it comes to the time of Noah, why did He use a method that was slow? The Flood was very slow. It seems to me that the Almighty was after more than just wiping out the evil that lay upon the earth. He was after the epitome of evil, Ashmedai; flooding the earth would accomplish that. The passage that I read to you from the Bereshith?"

"And the Lord set a mark upon Cain?"

"Yes, excellent memory, Alec. Well that would be about 4005 BC or thereabouts. The Flood was just a few years after in about 4000 BC."

Alec rubbed his hand across his face despairingly. "Christ, Phil. If the Almighty can't kill this thing, what bloody chance have we got?"

Phil shook his head.

"Kill it? No. Contain it? Yes. It can be contained. We have positive proof of that. But on no account must Ashmedai and his phylactery be conjoined, Alec … on no account. If they are, God help the millions of Jews that inhabit this Earth … and God help mankind without them.

"Tell me Phil," Alec asked quietly, "why it is that he hasn't harmed me? He's wasted no time with others."

"Good question, Alec. I thought about that until you told me what you and Alex had done. The answer is simple. You fed him! You fed him when he needed it most, and not only that … you gave him meat.

Ashmedai comes from a time when people lived on dates, figs, cheese, and bread. Meat was a special occasion commodity eaten maybe once a year. To kill an animal in order to give a guest meat to eat showed him great respect. In a word, you honored him!"

Alec shook his head in amazement and looked away from Phil to look at the large photograph of Alex. He took in the smiling face and the lithe figure. Once again he started to feel cold anger flushing through him.

"Contain it …Contain it," he muttered,

"how the hell -," Alec stopped and then turned to Phil more than a little excited. "Phil, can you recall what Alex said to me?"

Phil looked puzzled and leaned back. "Yeees … I think so. She asked you something like, 'remember the water?'"

"No, Phil, she didn't ask me. She told me to remember the water. She was telling me something … trying to help. The answer has to be water."

Phil nodded, he looked tired.

"Right. We will have a coffee, and we will talk further about it."

Alec felt lighter as he headed for the perk. *It could well be the answer*, he thought, *but how to carry it out? Jesus.* He reached the perk, and it was empty.

"Phil," he said and waved the empty glass bowl.

Phil looked up and smiled. "Through the small door, Alec, you'll find a tap in the conservatory."

Alec found the almost invisible door in the wood paneling and passed through into a long, glass-covered conservatory. The smell of decaying plants and damp humus filled his nostrils as he looked down the room. Some of the panes of glass had splashes of whitewash on them in an effort to keep out some of the sun.

The room still had a humid, dead smell about it in total contrast to Phil's lovely library.

He found the tap and started to fill the perk's glass bowl. He looked down through the two tiny windows over the sink overlooking Phil's library. He smiled and shook his head gently as he saw Phil leave his chair and cross to the lectern to read his Torah.

Alec turned off the tap once the bowl filled to the required level and looked down at Phil again. He started to turn to leave the conservatory, but froze, mid stride as he saw the figure.

Panic welled through him, and his chest muscles refused to move his lungs. Hypnotized, he stared as the brown-cloaked and hooded figure stood motionless at the opposite end of the large library facing the still reading Phil.

Alec forced his legs to move down the three steps to the open door leading to the library. The figure, sideways on, was immediately opposite Alec. It was the sound of Alec's unsure footsteps that brought up Phil's head. The words he was about to speak were cut dead in his throat when he saw the figure. His head turned slowly to face fully Ashmedai.

Silence fell upon the room, and Alec's breathing didn't improve. Phil turned ashen. His small hands were gripping the Torah. He was bracing himself for what he knew was about to come.

The seconds passed each one longer than the previous one. Alec had difficulty in controlling his bladder, and his hand holding the glass bowl started to shake. Water slopped onto the polished floor making a hollow, slapping sound. It startled Alec into taking a step forward.

Immediately, he seemed to be held by some force as Ashmedai's left hand moved its fingers in Alec's direction. It spoke, and the voice that came from within the depths of that dark cowl raised the short hairs on Alec's neck.

"ALEC NORTH."

*North? God, only my mother knows my real name*, Alec thought frantically as the fiendish voice went on.

"THOU DIDST SUCCOUR ME IN MY HOUR OF NEED. KEEP THY DISTANCE."

A violent rage swept through Alec. "Succoured you? Succored you!" he screamed at Ashmedai, "I gave you a plate of fucking stew, you scum ...yo-"

Then fingers flicked, the only movement from the still figure facing the ashen Phil. Alec shot backwards to be hit and held against the bookshelves. The force stunned him to almost blackout. Alec was held stunned and immobile and forced to watch the cat and mouse game

Ashmedai played with Phil.

"THOU HAST DONE WELL RABBI …
FOR RABBI THOU ART." The words came
slowly in an unearthly timbre that raised the
hackles and ran up and down the spine. The
even spacing of the words was like a drumbeat
inside the head.

Ashmedai raised his right hand slowly. He
moved the brown hand with the palm facing
towards Phil. Phil immediately sucked in his
breath as the power of Ashmedai grasped him,
held him, and lifted him some three feet off the
dais. He still held the leather Torah tight.

Alec tried to scream, but he couldn't.
Tears filled his eyes as he saw the pain written
on Phil's face.

Ashmedai spoke again with mocking
pleasure filling the stolen words. "TOLD NOT
MY FATHER SAYING? THEY THAT
CHASTISETH MY ON … CHASTISETH ME,
AND WHOSOEVER CHASTISETH ME …
SHALL SEE MY KINGDOM."

The hand flexed slightly, and Phil grunted
as he was lifted again. Blood appeared from the
corner of his mouth. He was fighting the pain,
but his gray eyes were starting to glaze.

"THOU DOST NOT ANSWER RABBI.
HAST THE CRAB TAKEN THY THROAT?"

More blood ran down Phil's chin to drip

onto the tightly clutched Torah. Alec heard the mind-bending creaking and then the dry twig snapping as Phil's ribs gave way.

Alec fell to his knees, and the bile in his stomach rose with the sounds of Phil's bones breaking. Alec crawled to the library door as Ashmedai's total attention was focused on Phil.

He staggered upright at the door and turned before he fled.

Phil's tiny figure, some ten feet above the ground, was a bloody, pain-wracked doll. Even so, Alec heard the husky voice happily whisper from the doorway. "Israel …Oh, Israel … The Lord -" He got no further.

The holding hand flicked contemptuously, and Phil's broken, dying body hurtled back to smash through the stained glass window.

\*\*\*

Alec fled across the hall to the large front door with adrenalin and fear pushing him. Throwing open the half-ton oak door as though it was tissue paper, he started to run down the shale driveway.

He passed the parked Rolls and on towards the entrance. He suddenly skidded to a halt amidst a shower of shale as a single thought managed to creep through his mangled brain.

He ran back to the car and opened the door. The keys hung from the ignition. He jumped in and turned the key. He shoved the automatic shifter into drive, and the great car shot forward throwing shale in all directions.

Alec searched around the darkened dash panel for lights. After a few panicky moments, he found them. He drove fast and automatically as though on auto pilot. He covered almost ten miles before he realized tears were still rolling down his face.

Fear was sitting on his shoulder, and like the sailor and the albatross, he couldn't escape it. His left hand was pounding his thigh as he drove. *Rabbie, the cameraman, and now Phil. Is Alex next?*

He dried his face with his sleeve. Suddenly, he could feel a coldness and hardness pumping through him. His jaw clamped tight as anger ran from his brain down to his limbs. He knew what he had to do, and the realization pulled his mangled brain back to something close normal.

He started to focus, and in doing so, he calmed. After another mile, his brain was like a razor. He checked over the instruments of the Rolls. Everything was okay, but the tank was only half full. That was not enough; he needed a full tank. He slowed his speed and began looking for a garage. He checked his watch which read 12:40. It'll have to be an all night station.

"Christ. Isn't it always the way?" he muttered as he attempted to throw the Rolls around a fast bend. The Rolls was having none of it and stuck like glue to the right line. Alec was then in the glare of an all night filling station as though the Rolls knew exactly what he needed. Alec's admiration for the car increased a hundredfold.

After filling up with both petrol and caffeine, Alec settled back into the leather to enjoy the sheer luxury of the Rolls. The workmanship cocooned him and brought him back to earth from his nightmare.

The Rolls hissed down the country lanes, and before long, he was pulling up outside the cottage. He was ready to turn in when he saw Ma run out heading for the VW. He flashed the lights and stopped her.

The look on her distraught face told him all. She didn't need to tell him that Alex just died. He held Ma as she sobbed on his chest. A deep feeling of sadness drifted through him. He went into the cottage while cradling Ma. He gently told her to make some coffee, and he'd sort things out. He left her in the kitchen to slip silently into the lounge.

He stood looking at the tiny, frail, gray-haired figure slumped in the corner of the chair.

He shook his head gently. They had a few, wonderful, happy days together that were all too short and all too brief. Alex's life had not been a happy one. What little happiness she had was snatched from her through Alec. The irony wasn't lost on Alec. *The Lord giveth and the Lord taketh away.*

He walked across the room and switched the lamp on. He paused and then moved over to Alex. He dropped to his knees beside her body. Her head lay back, and her closed eyes were no longer looking out of the window. Serenity touched the deeply-lined, ravaged face.

Alec felt like crying again. He was so deeply touched, but he didn't have a tear left in him. He leaned forward and gently kissed the cold lips that once brought so much desire and love. He looked down to her breast where the symbol of evil lay. Alec felt his nostrils flare as the anger took him again.

As gently as he could, he lifted the leather thong over Alex's head. The pendant came easily to rest inanimate in the palm of his hand. His hand tightened on the stone until his knuckles showed white and the stone's edges dug into his palm. He stood up and after one final look at Alex, left the room. He closed the door silently behind him.

# CHAPTER FORTY-FOUR

The Rolls swept onto the M6 Motorway, taking the tight service road bend as though it was on rails. Most cars at eighty mph would have slid a yard or two offline, but not the Rolls.

Alec slipped over to the fast lane and toed the accelerator to 100 mph. The car was quiet, so he could hear himself think.

He had told Ma to go back to her house and leave poor Alex and everything. She understood, God bless her, and left. He had found the card and punched the first of the two sets of numbers printed on it into the telephone.

The phone rang at the other end and then hummed as though rerouting the call. After several seconds, it rang again and this time to be answered almost immediately.

"Muir," was the crisp answer.

Alec answered and asked Stan for D.C.I. Black. Seconds passed and then Black answered. Alec very quickly told him, and no doubt Sergeant Muir, about Phil and Alex.

When Alec finished, Black spoke, "Dr. Grossman's address, Alec?"

"Christ, Mr. Black. I know where, but not the

address."

"Not to worry. Stan's working on it now. Now your address?"

Alec told him. He could hear Muir's pencil scribbling in the background.

"What do you intend doing now, Alec?"

"Setting off for Scotland, hell for leather, and this bastard's going to be with me all … the … fucking … way," Alec said grimly.

"What car will you be driving?"

"The same one I escaped in. Phil's Rolls."

"Registration number?"

"D.P.G. 100 … It's maroon."

"Color is immaterial, Alec, at this time of night … and also the speed at which you will be traveling."

"That's true, Mr. Black."

"Destination?"

"That's for you to tell me." Before Black could question, Alec went on, "In Rabbie's Welsh dresser there were some notes and locations where he went diving … I want them."

"Right."

"I know it's somewhere near the Moray Firth How will I get them?"

"You just keep driving, Alec. We'll deliver them, and Stan and I will attend to everything down at your end," he added gently.

"Thank you, Mr. Black."

"God go with you, Alec Sterne," and the phone went dead.

The car hummed along, and Alec took his cigarettes out of his pocket. He put one in his mouth and then remembered what Phil had said. He took the cigarette out and searched the dash for the little button Phil had pressed.

He found it and took a cigar from the small veneered tray. He lit up and sat back in the seat, remembering that slightly embarrassed, self-satisfied look on Phil's face. He smiled at the memory.

The traffic was thin on the motorway but not thin enough that it didn't warrant a police traffic car sitting in silent vigil by the roadside. It was, no doubt, hoping and praying for an 'Alec' to come whooshing by to relieve the boredom. His prayers were answered.

Alec flashed passed him and looked into his rearview mirror. He saw the police car fire its lights up and scream out onto the motorway in pursuit.

Alec shook his head. "I hope you've been busy on that phone, Mr. Black," he muttered.

The police car, making heavy going of it, started to gain. The headlights grew bigger, and its flashing blues and reds spun into the interior of the Rolls. Then suddenly, the headlamps flashed, the blues and reds switched off, and the police car swung to the side.

"Well done, D.C.I. Black," Alec muttered.

He wouldn't have stopped anyway. He still had plenty of pedal left under his right foot, if needed. Luckily, it wasn't.

Another hour and a cigar saw him approaching the outskirts of Glasgow on the M74, and the petrol gauge requiring some attention. The rear lights of two cars in the distance brought his attention back to the road. They were running level with each other. One was on the inside lane of the three-lane highway, and the other was in the outside lane, which left the center lane free.

Alec's speed was quickly bringing him close to them. He changed to the center lane, to hell with slowing down. It wasn't until he changed lanes that he noticed the third car, lying in arrow formation with the other two. It was taking up the center lane, totally preventing him from bursting through.

"Damn," he muttered.

By this time, he was between the two outer cars and almost up the backside of the car in the middle lane. He looked at his speedometer. It registered exactly 100 mph.

The two cars jockeying him increased their speed, as had the car immediately in front of him. He looked across to the car on his right. It had no markings and was black in color.

"Now there's an oxymoron for you, Alec," he said quietly.

As if on cue, all three cars lit up their hidden blues, and the penny dropped for Alec. *Black Jaguar. Of course, it has to be D.C.I. Black with Muir and colleagues.*

A motorway filling station loomed up, and the four cars checked their speed and entered. Alec followed the black Jaguar on to the pumps and jumped out to replenish the Rolls.

A voice called out, "Leave that, Alec." It was Black. Muir came forward and took over the job of filling the Rolls while Alec joined Black. They shook hands, and Black offered Alec some coffee from a flask.

"Thanks, Mr. Black."

"You are more than welcome, Alec. Stan and I would like to extend our sincere condolences to you. We are both deeply sorry for what has happened ... deeply sorry."

Alec looked at the granite face and listened to the kind words. He looked across at Sergeant Muir, who was in earshot of the conversation, and received a gentle nod.

"I thank you both for your kind words and your help, but no more kind words, Mr. Black. I am about to fall apart, but I have to get this bastard first ... before I can afford that luxury."

Black nodded and produced a sheaf of papers from under his arm. "These are the papers you required. We've had a look through."

He came to Alec's shoulder. "You're heading for a fishing village called Rossie. Here."

He handed a typed sheet of paper to Alec. "This will make it easy. Follow those directions to the letter."

*Don't say it, Mr. Black ... Don't say those dreaded last words you can't go wrong,* the thought rushed through Alec's head.

Black continued, "To the letter and at the bottom." He stabbed his finger. "Approximate distance from shore, if you are going to do what I think you're going to do."

Alec looked at the granite-hewn face and then nodded grimly. "I am … or at least, I'm going to try … or die trying."

Black nodded and put his arm around Alec, squeezing him. Shades of Rod Graeme, but Alec appreciated it.

Muir arrived and that look passed between them again. Black nodded.

Alec returned the flask cup and shook Black's outstretched hand. Muir extended his. "Best of luck, Mr. Sterne." Alec shook it, gaining strength from this strong, young man.

He nodded and returned to the Rolls. He paused at the door and turned, but Black read his mind about the payment for petrol. His arm waved Alec up the motorway.

Alec attempted a tight grin, entered the Rolls, and started the engine.

# CHAPTER FORTY-FIVE

Rossie appeared out of the darkness, seemingly from nowhere. Its handful of white-washed cottages and pub looked slab gray in the darkness. It was perched on the shoreline and invisible from the road.

Alec slid the Rolls silently over the cobbled street, for Rossie was as dead as the grave. Mind you, what place wasn't at 4:30 in the morning? It was too early for the boats to leave for their fishing.

Alec pulled the Rolls onto the pub's tiny car park, so quietly he didn't even arouse a dog asleep nearby. He slipped a thick sweater on, in place of the anorak he had been forced to leave at Phil's, to keep off the early morning chill.

With the torch from the car and a length of nylon twine he brought from home, he set off for the pebbled beach. As he walked, his hand pressed against his trouser pocket, against the lump resting there that was the stone. The adrenalin was flowing again; panic and fright was an eyelash away.

He kept yawning. He knew what that meant.

It wasn't tiredness; it was his body requesting more oxygen. He breathed deeply of the clean, salty air. With the aid of his torch, he made his way across the difficult surface to the boats beached there by the locals.

There were about nine boats in all as he inspected them. Some were too big for him to handle, and some, as he checked the bottom, were not right for his purpose. But, sure enough, he found the one.

Ten minutes of fiddling by the light of the torch in the bottom of the boat had him ready. He made up a set of oars by going around to all the boats. After heaving and sweating, he managed to get the boat in the water.

He rowed as steady as he could, unaccustomed to the exercise. He used the lights that started to blink on in the village bedrooms, and he made his way to the location Mr. Black had typed for him.

The sea was flat calm, and a mist started to bank up about two miles away, like a soft gray rolling wall. The dawn light still hadn't fully broken through, and the black velvet night sky was streaked with a dirty gray.

The sea was like thick, black molasses, dripping off the ends of the oars as Alec labored with their awkward balance. He looked up to check the distance and was surprised to see how far he was out. He looked to his right, and there he could just make out the plateau where he and Alex had camped. The little waterfall helped him to pinpoint the spot.

He pulled the oars in, when he judged he was right. He was. Some 200 feet below him lay the ill-fated *San Domingo*.

It was quiet. The mist rolled in around him. Like cotton wool, it muffled the sounds of the sea and hid the twinkling lights of the village. *All alone by the telephone … There's that damn song again.*

He rested in the boat, head bowed, and arms around him to keep the chill out. It had got cold. *God … it got cold.* Alec shivered, and he felt that awful gut-wrenching feeling as he realized why the temperature dropped.

A sound made him turn his head. Again, he heard it, and his stomach turned over. *Slap. Slap. Slap.* The slow slapping sound was coming towards him.

"Oh Jesus … sweet Jesus, help me now," he whispered as he checked the bottom of the boat. *Slap. Slap. Slap.* It was closer. Alec was near to panic; he was a hair's breadth from passing out. *Slap. Slap. Slap.*

"Oh, sweet Jesus … sweet Jesus."

*Slap. Slap.* The figure came through the mist, some ten yards from the boat. The sandals were slapping on the water as he walked slowly towards Alec.

Alec's mouth fell open in fright and disbelief. "Oh ... my ... God."

Ashmedai stepped into the boat, and what passed for laughter emanated from the hood as it looked down at Alec. Alec could not see beyond the darkened recesses of the cowl. He could only see the evil, red glow in the dark eyes as they stared at him. The laughter raised the hairs on Alec's neck and seemed to increase the palsy-like shaking of his hands and body.

Silent seconds followed as Ashmedai continued looking down at Alec. Then he spoke to Alec. "Didst think thou couldst hide from me?" The evil voice intonated slowly. The total arrogance was overwhelming.

Silent seconds passed again as he, no doubt, waited for a reply from Alec. Alec was hard pushed to breathe, and he knew his vocal chords couldn't react. He waited, scared shitless.

"Thou wouldst take my birthright?" The evil voice playfully questioned, like a tiger with a tethered goat.

Alec stayed silent, because he could feel himself regaining control of his body. The probable cause was great anger.

"Thou wilt rise," the voice commanded. Alec stood up. He didn't know how, but stand, he did.

The boat didn't rock; it was as though set in concrete.

They stood there, seconds passing, looking into each other's eyes. "Forsake thou the riches of the earth, Alec, north for a Jew?" The voice held an unreal quality, mockingly disbelieving.

Alec held his silence, knowing full well it was within Ashmedai's power to reward him but for a plate of stew. He must have unwittingly shaken his head for Ashmedai spoke again.

This time the voice was harsh. "Disbeliever, my birthright."

Alec put his hand in his pocket, and let the stone dangle by the thong from his fingers. His hands were still shaking, but getting stronger. The eyes didn't moved from Alec's face, but their red glow deepened. Alec moved his right foot fractionally to equalize his weight and felt the tug of the nylon cord around his ankle.

"Thou wilt anoint me with my birthright, disbeliever." The voice again was mocking and commanding.

Alec moved the stone to hold the leather thong with two hands as the hood dropped away, uncovering the head of Ashmedai.

Alec gasped. This wasn't the face of the old man he remembered. To be sure, the eyes and the nose were the same, but not the face.

The face was incredibly handsome; the face

of a young man. It was a face of youth regained. A terrible thought struck him as he thought it was a face of youth stolen. Anger welled within him as he thought of Alex, but he held it in check. He became as cold as the aura of the figure in front of him.

Ashmedai lowered his head. It was an arrogant command, and a command that Alec gladly obeyed.

He stepped forward. The nylon cord tightened painfully around his ankle and then subsided. The bung from the bottom of the boat soundlessly eased out lubricated by the wet seaweed Alec had placed around it earlier.

Alec's hands hovered over Ashmedai's head and reverently placed the stone on his unlined forehead. Alec's thumbs lay inside the thong, and he allowed the stone to nestle for a moment. Just as Ashmedai began to raise his head, Alec looked him square in the face.

"You ... arrogant ... fuck." His thumbs thrust down on the thong until it was around his throat.

Alec took a step back. The water was lapping near his calves. He looked straight into the blazing eyes full of evil fury. He calmly said, "For a Jew ... Ashmedai ... for a Jew and for a lovely girl."

Alec spoke no more as Ashmedai raised his arm. Pressure cracked Alec's ribs and made breathing impossible. He floated some ten feet above the boat. He felt, rather than heard, that terrible, dry twig-snapping and blood ran down his chin.

The pain was unbearable, but from somewhere Alec managed a grin. He looked down from his height with a bloodstained, pain-twisted grin, following the direction of Ashmedai's eyes. The boat was close to sinking. Water lapped around his legs just below the knees.

The red eyes lifted to focus on Alec's bloody, grinning face. The hand flicked, and Alec hurtled back to shore at an incredible speed.

The last thing Alec heard was a high-pitched demonic scream.

It was a scream that would last a thousand years.

Finis

8345272R0

Made in the USA
Charleston, SC
31 May 2011